For Ted, Rhiannon and Gareth

with love, always

Dottie Flowers and the European Caper

Acknowledgements

Special thanks to my Fiction Highway Guild colleagues, Liz Bryant, Jan Collis, Karen Kachra, Donna Kirk, Jennifer Mook-Sang, Kimberly Scutt, Linda Shales, and Barbara Winter for their insightful critiques and constructive suggestions; and to my readers, Michele Fisher, Ted Gale and Barbara Winter for their shrewd observations and thoughtful feedback.

Heartfelt gratitude to friends and family for their ongoing support, especially my husband Ted, whose faith in me never falters.

Chapter 1

Dottie and Mabel strained to listen as the announcement blared over the Marseille Provence Airport's PA system. "It's in French," Mabel grumbled. "How on earth do they expect us to know what they're saying?"

"We're in France, Mabel," Dottie said. "What do you expect—Chinese?"

"Of course not," Mabel laughed. "After our late departure from Paris, I just want to get in the rental car and drive to St. Siffret."

A second announcement, this time in English, informed passengers that the release of luggage from the Paris flight had been delayed. "It could be a while," Dottie said. "We might as well sit down, if there's space."

Once they found seats, Dottie opened her new P. D. James novel. After a futile attempt to read the first few pages, she closed the book. The words of Dr. Parker, her family doctor, kept flashing through her head. "Your blood pressure's up again. You need to slow down a bit, Dottie. Put your feet up; take a vacation."

Running a successful real estate company took perseverance and lots of energy. She didn't have time to slow down! Still, her doctor's warning had scared her a bit. When Tom Snead had offered to treat her and Mabel to a month in Europe, Dottie pushed away her misgivings about him and decided to accept. Now, she was having second thoughts.

Mabel peered at Dottie over her purple-winged glasses. "What's wrong?"

"I'm bothered about agreeing to Tom Snead's offer."

"We've gone over all this, Dottie," Mabel said. "He conned us last summer; we know that. But he apologized, and things turned out all right in the end."

"That's true," Dottie admitted.

"Tom's house in St. Siffret looks very appealing from the photos he sent us," Mabel said. "And now that we're in Provence, we should make the most of it."

Dottie agreed. "And don't forget our two weeks in Tuscany. I'm looking forward to seeing Florence and Sienna."

"I can't wait to sample some authentic pasta dishes. And Italian desserts!" Mabel paused. "Do you mind if I leave you here for a while? I need to stretch my legs."

"Go ahead." She smiled at Mabel. "And thanks."

"What for?"

"For listening."

"What are friends for? I'll see you shortly."

"There's no need to hurry. I'm going to read my book." She lifted the rhinestone-framed glasses that hung around her neck and placed them on her nose.

Apart from sightseeing, Dottie welcomed the chance to meet new people. Melissa, a colleague of hers, had met her future husband on a Mediterranean cruise. *You never know who might turn up on a vacation like this*, she mused. Divorced for several years, and with her children raising their families, Dottie missed having someone special in her life.

Dottie had just finished Chapter 1 when a third message boomed over the PA system. With apologies for the delay, the announcer invited passengers from the Paris flight to pick up their luggage. Dottie headed to the assigned carousel. Before long, she spotted her red suitcase and grabbed it just as it reached her. She lifted it onto the luggage cart. Mabel's suitcase was nowhere in sight. Neither was Mabel. Where had she gone?

Dottie craned her neck to see over the crowds. Finally, she saw her friend in conversation with a white-haired man in a beret. Dottie waved, but all she succeeded in doing was attracting the attention of a young man who thought she was waving at him. Dottie fumed.

Mabel should be looking out for her suitcase, not chatting up some Frenchman!

A battered-looking black suitcase with a red label rolled onto the carousel. At last! Dottie tried to grasp the handle, but somehow the case slipped out of her hand and fell on her big toe. She sucked in her breath. Once the pain subsided, Dottie flung the suitcase onto the luggage cart and headed over to Mabel. "If she's forgotten the car rental receipt," she muttered under her breath, "I'm getting the next flight back to Toronto."

Mabel was all smiles. "Oh, there you are, Dottie. Let me introduce you to Monsieur Bouchard."

He was older than Dottie had first thought, probably in his mid-seventies. Holding a leather attaché case in his hands, Monsieur Bouchard acknowledged the introduction with a half-bow. "It is a pleasure to meet you, Madame Flowers."

"You will never believe this," Mabel enthused. "Monsieur Bouchard lives in St. Siffret, on the street next to ours!"

Dottie was about to respond when she realized that Monsieur Bouchard's attention had wandered. His eyes were fixed on a young couple as they walked hand-in-hand toward the exit. The woman wore designer sandals and a skimpy black dress that revealed smooth tanned legs. Dottie sighed. No spider veins there. Her chestnut hair was cut in a geometric style, short and straight, with bangs. The man's dark hair was collar-length and slightly wavy. He wore black, also, his shirt open at the neck.

The couple exited the terminal and disappeared from view. His face taut, Monsieur Bouchard stared after them. Dottie frowned. "Are you all right, Monsieur Bouchard?"

He blinked rapidly, and then looked at Dottie. "Of course." He cleared his throat and smiled at the two women. "You have a three-hour drive ahead of you. I look forward to seeing you in St. Siffret." With another half-bow, he hurried away.

Mabel smiled at Dottie. "Isn't he charming?"

"Yes, but did you see his reaction when he spotted that young couple? Something about them bothered him."

"What young couple?"

Dottie sighed with exasperation. "Never mind. Let's concentrate on the car rental." She cleared her throat. "Do you have the receipt, Mabel?"

"I thought you had it."

Dottie could hardly believe her ears. "You're in charge of the car rental. In fact, it's the only thing you're in charge of!"

Mabel opened her large floral carry-on bag and rooted inside. She searched through each zippered pocket and eventually produced a scrunched piece of paper. "Here it is."

Dottie snatched it from Mabel's fingers. She smoothed the receipt and peered at the car rental name. "I've never heard of this company."

"Arnold recommended it."

Dottie thought about her friend, Arnold. An endearing English gentleman, he knew plenty about horses, but until he'd married Mabel's niece, he'd never been to Europe. What would he know about European car rental companies?

After a brief search, they found the rental desk and got in line. Dottie noticed a security guard strutting around the car park, a vicious-looking Rottweiler by his side. The veins in the dog's neck stuck out as he strained to escape.

"I'm glad that man's holding the leash tightly," Dottie whispered. "You know how I feel about dogs."

"What do you think he's looking for?"

Dottie looked around. The car park seemed so peaceful in the afternoon sun. She chewed her lip. "Drugs, I guess."

The clerk handed the couple in front of them a set of keys. Once they'd left, Dottie stepped to the desk. Looking bored, the clerk asked, *"Comment puis-je vous aider?"*

Dottie gave him the rental receipt. He scrutinized it, then keyed in something on his computer. "I am afraid, *madame*, that we don't have the automatic vehicle."

"We ordered an automatic in Canada."

The young man tapped on his keyboard again. Five minutes later, he announced, "I have found you the automatic."

"Good! Could you show us where it's parked?"

"It is not here yet."

"What do you mean, 'not here'?"

"It will be here in two hours. It has to be brought from the other side of Marseille."

Mabel spoke for the first time. "We'll take a standard shift car."

The young man looked relieved. "Very good, *madame*. Just sign here."

He pushed a form in front of her.

Sheila Gale

Dottie grabbed the form. "Mabel, what are you doing? You can't drive a standard!"

"Of course, I can. I learned to drive in England before I immigrated to Canada. Everyone drove standards in those days."

"That was forty years ago!"

Mabel patted Dottie on the hand. "Don't worry, dear. It won't take me long to get the hang of it again."

"I won't be able to drive!" Dottie spluttered. "I thought we were going to share."

"Never mind, you can sit back and enjoy the scenery."

Dottie tried to imagine a whole month of Mabel's driving. Could her nerves handle it? "All right. On one condition—that you obey the road signs and don't drive over the limit."

"Of course," Mabel said. A few minutes later, the young man escorted them to a tiny blue Fiat and handed Mabel the car keys. With a faint smile, he wished them *bon voyage*.

After they piled their luggage into the car, Dottie looked at the map. "The route to St. Siffret seems straightforward."

Mabel didn't reply as she fiddled with the gearshift. "I think I'll drive around a bit, just to familiarize myself with the car." For the next twenty minutes, they lurched around the parking lot. The car stalled several times as Mabel struggled to get the hang of the gears. Finally, she turned to Dottie with a grin. "I knew all those driving lessons with a standard shift would come in handy." She opened the Fiat's small sunroof. "Let's get on our way."

The traffic was light, but Mabel kept to the speed limit, more or less. At one point, a frustrated motorist honked his horn as he tried to overtake their car, but instead of speeding up, she slowed down a little and waved him on.

"I'm impressed," Dottie said. "You showed great restraint."

"I'm not used to the roads and not entirely comfortable with the gears. Once I've been driving for a day or two, I'll give the likes of him a run for his money."

Dottie shuddered. "Thanks for the warning."

Clusters of wild flowers and red poppies painted the roadside as they sped along in bright sunshine. After a while, the road began to climb, and the wildflowers gave way to bleached-white rocks and grassy banks. Soon, they were high up. The road wound its way to a viaduct. From the top of the viaduct, Dottie saw the river far below them, with air mattresses and rubber dinghies bobbing in the current. Children splashed in the water, and picnic baskets and tablecloths were scattered along the riverbank.

They arrived in the small market town of Uzès around three p.m., just as shopkeepers opened for afternoon trade. In a schoolyard near the stores, men played a game of boules, watched intently by a small group of spectators. As they drove past the men, Dottie noticed a corner shop with *L'epicerie* in bold letters above the door. The grocer busily rearranged fruit and vegetable boxes in front of his store.

"I'd like to go in and see what else they sell," Dottie said. Fortunately, there was a small car park across the road, Mabel pulled into the last space.

Inside the store, Dottie breathed in the delicious aroma of coffee beans, mingled with fresh baked bread. Tempted to linger, she checked her watch. "We just need some basics, Mabel. We can shop at a *carrefour* tomorrow."

"What's a carrefour?"

"A supermarket."

"I'm glad you can speak French."

"I wish! I hope I know enough to get by."

They filled the wire basket with croissants, brie, orange juice, cream, and coffee. For dinner, they picked up a quiche, salad ingredients, fresh strawberries, and a bottle of of local red wine. Dottie tapped the basket nervously as she got in line at the cashier's desk. The grocer, a red-faced man with a canvas apron wrapped around his large belly, chatted with his customers as he rang up their groceries.

Everyone seemed to talk very fast. Dottie couldn't understand a word of what was said, even though she'd taken French lessons in preparation for the trip and memorized some key phrases. Finally, it was her turn. She took a deep breath. *"Bonjour, monsieur. Comment allez-vous?"*

With a pained expression on his face, he replied, *"J'ai un mal de tête, et un mal de gorge. J'ai besoin de quelque chose contre un rhume."*

Dottie's face grew warm. What was he saying? He didn't wait for a reply but began to ring up the food items on his cash register.

"Combien, s'il vous plait?"

"Vingt-deux euros."

Dottie did a quick mental check—*vingt-deux* was twenty-two. She handed him two twenty-euro bills.

As he gave her the change, the man's face broke into a wide grin. "Thank you, ladies. I hope you enjoy your holiday."

Dottie shoved the change into her jacket pocket and grabbed the groceries. "You'd think he would've stopped me from making a complete ass of myself!" she muttered as the two women walked out of the store.

"You should have seen your face, Dottie!" Mabel tried hard not to laugh. "I wish I had my camera handy."

Suddenly, they heard squealing brakes. A small white car roared out of the car park, churning a cloud of dust.

It veered close to the sidewalk, missing Mabel by inches. "Idiot!" shouted Dottie. With the heavy volume of traffic, the car was forced to slow right down. It was a Fiat, the same make as theirs. Dottie mentally noted the license plate number. She looked at Mabel. "Are you all right? That was a close call."

Mabel's face had paled. "I must admit I feel a bit shaky."

They hurried across the road to their car. "Oh, dear! Look at that!" Mabel cried. She ran her hand over a dent in the bumper. "It's the driver of that white car; I'm sure of it. That's why he was in such a hurry." Mabel looked around. "There doesn't seem to be any other damage."

"We'll have to let the rental company know."

"Tom doesn't have a phone in his house in St. Siffret, remember."

Dottie suddenly regretted her decision not to get her cell phone authorized for use in Europe. She didn't relish the idea of trying to call the rental company from a pay-phone, but they didn't have any choice. "Let's get these groceries into the car. The sooner we get to St. Siffret, the better." Within a few minutes, they were ready to leave.

As she was about to get in the car, Dottie noticed a half-empty packet of Players cigarettes on the ground, close to the passenger door. A cigarette smoldered nearby. Next to the packet was a small piece of bent wire. Had the driver of the white Fiat tried to break into the car and panicked when they'd walked out of the grocery store?

Chapter 2

The air had grown cooler, a welcome relief from the oppressive humidity in the town, but gray clouds threatened rain. Mabel drove cautiously up St. Siffret's narrow cobblestoned street past homes built into the rock. Behind wrought-iron gates lay tiny walled gardens, where clay pots of red geraniums flourished, and blue and white lobelia tumbled out of hanging baskets.

Passing under an archway, they found themselves in a large courtyard. Dottie recognized the clock tower on the left from Tom's photos. To the right of the tower stood a narrow limestone house, its small front garden filled with poppies.

"Here we are, Mabel."

Mabel pulled up in front of the house. "The photos don't do it justice. It's delightful."

They managed to get their luggage inside just before it started to rain. The front door opened on a dining room with a stone fireplace. A bottle of Merlot sat in the middle of a large wooden table, with a handwritten note attached to it. Mabel removed the note from the bottle. Dottie read the message over Mabel's shoulder. *Welcome to Maison Francais, dear Dottie and Mabel. Tom. P.S. If you need anything, you can ask Marcel next door. He checks my house when I am away.*

"How thoughtful!" Mabel commented. She put the note down on the table. "I still feel a bit shaken up after that vehicle nearly ran me over."

Dottie Flowers and the European Caper

"I'm convinced the driver was trying to break into our car," Dottie said. "That piece of bent wire I found by the passenger door looked very suspicious."

"And don't forget the smoldering cigarette."

"When the driver spotted us, he must have panicked and driven off in such a rush that he hit our car."

"Fancy starting a vacation with a big dent in the bumper." Mabel remarked. "Even though you got his license plate number, I doubt we'll see him again."

"We'll find a pay-phone in the morning and call the rental people."

Mabel yawned. "If we'd taken one of those all-inclusive coach tours, like a lot of seniors do, we wouldn't have to worry about things like that. I'm too old for all this excitement."

"Mabel Scattergood, you know you'd hate a bus full of seniors!"

Mabel laughed. "I think you're right."

"It's been a long day. Let's unpack our bags, have a quick meal with a glass of wine, and go to bed." Dottie paused. "I know you prefer white wine. We should have picked some up at the grocery store."

"It doesn't matter. For a change, I sometimes have a glass of red wine with my dinner."

They carried their luggage upstairs to the second floor and switched on the bedroom lights. The first bedroom overlooked the square. A bookcase crammed with paperbacks and hardbacks sat beneath the window. The walls were painted a rich yellow ochre, complementing the dark hardwood floor and deep blue bedspread. The second room was decorated with floral wallpaper and a matching bedspread. Even the cushions on the rattan chair matched. Dottie couldn't imagine sleeping in a room surrounded by red poppies, purple irises, and yellow sunflowers.

"Oh, how lovely!" Mabel exclaimed.

"You take this room," Dottie insisted.

"Are you sure? It's quite a bit bigger than the other one."

"That doesn't matter. I like the view over the square." Before Mabel had a chance to argue, Dottie hauled her bags into the other room.

She'd just finished unpacking when Mabel yelled, "Dottie, you'd better get in here!"

Dottie rushed into Mabel's room and saw the open bag lying on the bed. Inside lay blue-striped pajamas and a man's shaving kit.

Mabel stared at the contents. "Now, what do we do?"

Dottie frowned. "I took what looked like your bag off the carousel, but I didn't check the label."

"It's not your fault. I should have been watching out for my suitcase instead of talking to that charming Frenchman."

"Why did you open the suitcase, knowing it wasn't yours?"

"I thought it was mine. I would have realized it wasn't if I'd remembered to bring my luggage key."

"So how did you open it?"

"I found an old nail file in the bathroom's medicine cabinet. After a bit of jiggling, the lock sprang. It was a trick I'd learned from my hubby Alf," Mabel said. "Fortunately, I brought a spare toothbrush and a pair of undies in my carry-on bag. Who knows when I'll see my suitcase again."

"We'll have to phone the airport."

Mabel plunked down on the bed. The case, which balanced precariously on the edge, fell on the floor with a thud. The striped pajamas, boxer underwear, and several pairs of socks scattered in all directions.

Dottie sighed. "We'd better repack it. Come on."

They lifted it onto the bed. "That felt heavy, considering it's empty," Mabel remarked.

"You're right." Dottie noticed that the bottom of the case seemed to be separate from the sides, as though it had been inserted later. After a bit of a struggle, she managed to lift the section out. Underneath, about a dozen plastic bags containing white powder were jammed together in two rows.

Mabel blew out a long breath. "Good heavens!"

"Never mind the airport," Dottie said. I think these bags contain drugs." She picked one up. She unzipped it, dipped her finger in the powder, and tasted it. "I've no idea what drugs taste like, but it's definitely not icing sugar. It's got a bitter taste."

"We'd better let the police know right away, Dottie. Maybe this Marcel next door will let us use his phone."

"I don't think we should get anyone else involved," Dottie said. "We need to find a pay phone." She blew out a long breath. "Here we are, about to search for a phone in a strange place where everyone speaks French."

"And it's dark already. Come on, we'd better get started." Mabel opened the door and peered out. "At least, it's stopped raining."

As they stepped outside, Dottie looked back at the house. She had the uncomfortable feeling that drugs in a suitcase were only the beginning of their troubles.

Chapter 3

Dottie and Mabel walked down the short garden path just as the clock on the tower struck ten. When the chimes ceased, an eerie silence fell over the square. Once Dottie's eyes adjusted to the darkness, she saw the cross in the center and the stone seat at its base.

The angry howls of a catfight sent her jittery nerves into overdrive. "I don't know about you, Mabel, but this is very spooky. You'd think they'd have some streetlamps around here."

Mabel's breath came out in a whoosh. "You're telling me."

Dottie pointed across the square. "Let's try that street. Maybe we'll find someone to ask about the nearest phone booth."

"The sooner we let the police know, the better."

They started down the street. Wet cobblestones sparkled in the glow from brightly lit windows, but it wasn't easy walking. Dottie's sandals slipped on the uneven surface. "These weren't designed for cobblestones. I should have changed into walking shoes and brought my flashlight."

"We'll manage; I think I see light ahead."

The faint strains of a band playing Frank Sinatra's signature tune, *My Way*, echoed through the narrow street. As they wound their way down a steep hill, the music grew louder. They found themselves in a large square with an outdoor café, crowded with noisy patrons and waiters dashing about with trays of food and drink. The women wore dresses and high-heeled shoes. Most of the men were dressed in slacks and sports jackets.

A vapor of acrid smoke hovered in the air. Mabel crinkled her nose. "What's that smell?"

"Gauloise cigarettes." It took Dottie back to university days in Montreal, when she and her friends smoked the French cigarettes and ordered Turkish coffee.

The band finished their Sinatra rendition to an enthusiastic round of applause and began to play a livelier piece, which Dottie didn't recognize. "I'll ask someone at the café about a public phone."

Pulling a phrase book from her jacket, she turned to the section on telephones and repeated the question several times to herself until she'd memorized it. Satisfied, she closed the book.

"*Bienvenue, mesdames!*" A short round man dressed in a tuxedo stood in front of them. He beckoned them to a table covered in a white cloth.

Dottie glanced at her white slacks and navy-blue cotton jacket and Mabel's lime green capris and flowered top. "We're definitely not dressed for a party."

"True, but we're not the only people dressed casually," Mabel said. "We might as well have a drink. How do you ask for a glass of white wine?"

Before Dottie had a chance to reply, a waiter rushed to their table. He placed two glasses containing a pale liquid and a plate of appetizers in front of them and dashed off. "That's weird. We haven't ordered anything."

"What's this?" Mabel sniffed the contents of her glass. "It smells like aniseed."

Dottie took a small sip. "It's good. I think it's called Pernod." She examined the pâté, artichokes, miniature quiches, and *escargot*.

Mabel made a face when she saw the snails. "It's difficult to imagine that people actually eat these things."

A few minutes later the waiter returned and asked if they'd like another drink. Here was Dottie's chance. Clearing her throat, she pretended to hold a phone to her ear. "*Où est la cabine téléphonique, s'il vous plait?*" The waiter frowned. "Telephone booth," Dottie plowed on. "You know, tel-e-phone!" She retrieved the piece of paper with the address of Tom's house and handed it to him. "*Il n'y a pas un téléphone. Er—Maison Francais il n'y a pas un téléphone.*"

He shrugged his shoulders and walked away. "Well, so much for my French," Dottie muttered. "I wonder if there's someone here who speaks English."

Glancing around the café, she noticed two men sitting at a nearby table engaged in an animated conversation. The younger man ran his fingers through a mop of red hair as he spoke. His companion leaned back in the chair, hands laced behind his head. White hair, worn collar-length, complemented a tanned, weather-beaten face. That, with an open-necked checked shirt, faded blue jeans, and leather sandals, convinced Dottie he must be an artist of some kind. Something about him seemed familiar. Had she met him before?

A cheerful female voice interrupted Dottie's confused thoughts. "'ello!"

Dottie turned around. A beautiful young woman wearing a purple mini dress and "caged" sandals with platform soles stood by the table. A tall dark-haired man stood next to her. "My name is Yvette Gagnon." She glanced up at the man. "This is my partner, Pierre Tremblay."

Dottie and Mabel introduced themselves, and they all shook hands.

Pierre's brows furrowed.

"You are staying in Maison Francais? Is that right?"

"Yes. We arrived a few hours ago."

"The waiter knows we speak English," Pierre said. "He asked us to speak with you. He said the phone in the house is broken, and you need to get it repaired."

"There's no phone in the house," Dottie laughed. "My French needs a lot of work. D'you know where the nearest payphone is?"

"It's just down the road, the only one in St. Siffret." Pierre paused. "We'll take you to it. Why don't you finish your drink and relax for a few minutes." Unlike Yvette's, Pierre's English bore no trace of an accent.

Dottie hesitated. She didn't want to tell strangers they'd found what looked like illegal drugs in a suitcase, and she was anxious to call the police.

Yvette's dark eyes locked with Dottie's. "This is a private party for Francois Trepanier's 75th birthday." Yvette pointed to a large man with a bushy beard chatting with a band member. "Francois 'as relatives in Quebec. 'e will be 'appy to know there are two *Canadiennes* at 'is party."

Dottie realized why they'd been ushered to a table and served with appetizers and Pernod. They'd been mistaken for invited guests. "I was born and raised in Montreal," she explained. "The area I lived was very English, so I didn't have to speak French. Now, I wish I'd persevered with it."

"How did you know we're Canadian?" Mabel asked.

"It is—what do you say—a give way?" Yvette laughed. "We see the leaf pins." She pointed to the pin on Mabel's top. "Tomorrow, we 'ave friends for dinner. They will visit Quebec next year." Her eyes lit up. "You will come for dinner tomorrow evening? Suzanne and Louis will like to meet you."

Pierre smiled. "We won't take no for an answer."

"How kind!" Mabel enthused. Dottie remembered the damaged car. "We have some business to take of first. Can we let you know tomorrow?"

A flash of irritation crossed Pierre's face. Before he had a chance to respond, Yvette cut in. "Of course."

Dottie looked at Pierre. "Have you ever been to Canada?"

"Yes, several times."

"I too 'ave been there," Yvette added. "I spend some time in Toronto. It 'as very good theatre."

"Yvette will introduce you to François," Pierre said. "I have to go back to the house. We forgot to bring his birthday present."

Yvette escorted them across the square. They passed the table where Dottie had observed the good-looking man. He and his companion were enjoying a bottle of wine. As the man leaned forward to replenish his glass, Dottie noticed a camera slung around his neck.

She recognized him, even with the longer hair. It was Hans Van Gogh, the documentary filmmaker. He was supposed to teach the photography course she'd taken in Toronto, but he had been called away for a family emergency.

He's more handsome in person than in the brochure photograph, Dottie decided. What's he doing in St. Siffret? If he's going to be around for the next two weeks, we're bound to bump into each other. This could turn out to be a very interesting vacation.

When Yvette explained that Dottie and Mabel were from Canada, François' face broke into a toothy grin. His arms flapped wildly as he chatted away in French, introducing them to his friends. After insisting that the two women sit at his table, Francois signaled a waiter who carried over a tray with glasses of red and white wine.

"Just one," Dottie insisted, taking a glass of red. "Then, we really must go."

François looked puzzled until Yvette translated for him. As they enjoyed their drinks, Yvette told them that she and Pierre lived in St. Siffret and commuted to Uzès each day, where they ran an Internet café. "Uzès, it is charming."

"We're looking forward to exploring it," Dottie replied. "We bought groceries there on our way to St. Siffret." She was about to tell Yvette that someone ran into the back of their car in Uzès when Pierre returned.

He handed François a bottle of champagne. "*Bon anniversaire!*"

"*Merci, mon ami!*" François grinned as he began to remove the wire over the cork.

Pierre turned to Dottie, lowering his voice. "Have a glass of champagne with Monsieur Trepanier. Otherwise, he'll be offended. Then, I'll make up an excuse, and we'll leave."

Dottie accepted the champagne flute out of politeness. Champagne was one of her favorite aperitifs, but she felt too apprehensive about the upcoming phone call to enjoy it. Mabel, she observed, took a hesitant sip. Glancing around to make sure that no one was looking, she poured the bubbly liquid into a pot of geraniums.

At last, it was time to go. After thanking François for his hospitality, the four left the café.

The two women followed Yvette and Pierre. As they reached the payphone, a babble of voices and raucous laughter rose from a nearby bar. Pierre looked at Dottie. "I'm afraid this is the only phone in St. Siffret, but it does work."

Some side windows were broken, and the grimy floor was littered with bits of paper and dead leaves. He showed them how to use the phone and wished them a cheerful goodnight. "We hope to see you tomorrow evening."

As Dottie watched Yvette and Pierre walk away, something nagged her. She slapped her forehead with her palm. Of course! She'd seen this young couple earlier at the airport. Dottie remembered the "caged" sandals the woman had worn. She was wearing the same designer sandals this evening.

She told Mabel who they were. "Something bothered Monsieur Bouchard when he saw them at the airport. He went quite pale."

"I didn't notice, but I do remember he left in a big hurry."

Thanks to Pierre's instructions on how to operate the phone, it didn't take Dottie long to make the call. Using her phrase book, she explained to a *gendarme* about the bags of powder in the suitcase. He instructed her to go back to *Maison Francais* and wait. The two women rushed back to the house, eager to be there when the police arrived. Unfortunately, Dottie caught her sandal heel between the cobblestones, which took a few minutes to release. They arrived just as a police car pulled into the square.

Three men climbed out. Slim built with jet-black hair and a goatee beard, the older man introduced himself and his colleagues in very good English. "I am Lieutenant Piaf, and this is Sergeant Coté." Sergeant Coté, overweight and scowling, acknowledged Dottie and Mabel with a brief nod of his head. The third *gendarme*, Sergeant Chevalier, stood at full attention, arms straight down his sides, as the lieutenant spoke to him rapidly in French. Switching on a flashlight, the sergeant began to search around the square.

Turning back to the two women, the lieutenant said, "Now, please show us the plastic bags." Lieutenant Piaf and Sergeant Coté followed Dottie and Mabel upstairs. Mabel opened her bedroom door, and they all walked in. Dottie drew in a sharp intake of breath. The suitcase was no longer on the bed. It lay on the floor with its lid closed.

Dottie Flowers and the European Caper

"Where are the plastic bags?" Lieutenant Piaf demanded.

Dottie cleared her throat. "Inside the suitcase."

With a nod from the lieutenant, Sergeant Coté opened the lid, revealing an assortment of multi-colored clothing, red sandals, and pink hair rollers. Mabel gasped, "That's my suitcase!"

The lieutenant seemed not to hear. He removed the contents, placed them on the bed, and ran his hands around the inside of the case. "There are no drugs here. You have wasted our time, *mesdames!*"

Boots clumped up the stairs, and Sergeant Chevalier, his face ashen, dashed into the room, speaking in rapid French. Questions were fired back and forth, and the three policemen hurried away.

Mabel looked at Dottie. "What's that about?"

"Let's find out."

By the time the women stepped into the square, there was no sign of the policemen. Sharp voices rose from a side street. Dottie and Mabel turned the corner. The policemen stood by a white Fiat parked at the curb. In the beam of a sweeping flashlight, Dottie read the license plate. It was the car that'd almost run Mabel over in Uzès.

Beside the car lay the body of a man in a pool of blood.

Chapter 4

Lieutenant Piaf ordered the two women to sit at the dining room table. Stroking his black goatee, he bombarded them with questions. "Why did you phone the police? You say you found bags of powder inside a suitcase. Where are the bags of powder? Where is the suitcase that belongs to a man?" His bushy eyebrows joined as he frowned at Mabel. "It is your suitcase, *madame*, that sits on the floor."

Mabel opened her mouth to say something but closed it again.

He leaned toward the two women, his eyes like slits. "Furthermore," he continued, "we find the body of a man in a street near your house."

Dottie sat up straight. "Was he shot?"

The lieutenant slammed his fist on the table. "*Madame*, I will ask the questions!"

Dottie's temper sparked. "Lieutenant Piaf, we've told you what happened. You obviously don't believe us, even though it's the truth."

Everyone turned around as the front door opened with a loud rattle. Sergeant Coté ambled over to the lieutenant and whispered in his ear. After the man left, Lieutenant Piaf glanced uneasily at the two women and made a great production of tidying up the papers in front of him. Stroking his beard again, he looked at Mabel. "I owe you an apology, *madame*," he mumbled. "It seems a suitcase with the clothing of a man has been found in the trunk of the car."

"What about the plastic bags?" Dottie asked.

"There are no plastic bags in the suitcase."

"Well, they must be somewhere. There were at least a dozen."

The lieutenant glared at Dottie. "There was only one bag. It was hidden inside the jacket the man wore."

"Someone must have taken the others."

Ignoring Dottie's comment, the lieutenant gathered the papers and placed them in his briefcase. He stood. "That will be all for now, *mesdames*. If I have any more questions, I will speak with you."

"We don't have a phone."

"We have a contact who lives here in St. Siffret. He will let you know if we need you."

"What's his name?"

Lieutenant Piaf glared at Dottie. "You ask too many questions, *madame*." He turned to leave. As he opened the front door, he looked back. "You must tell no one of this!"

***

Dottie scrunched her eyes, as the sun's rays poured through a gap in the blind. She grabbed her camera off the dresser, pulled up the blind, and opened the window as wide as possible. She looked through the viewfinder and focused on a grove of olive trees, their silver leaves shimmering in the sun. In the distance, the pale green foliage of grapevines contrasted with the dark cypress trees bordering the vineyard. As she clicked away, Dottie found it difficult to imagine that, a short distance from this Provençal scene, a man had been murdered.

Pulling on her black silk dressing gown, Dottie wandered downstairs and put on the coffee. She opened the glass doors in the living room and stepped onto a small terrace overcrowded with a wrought iron table, two chairs, and terra cotta containers of blue plumbago. The terrace overlooked the courtyard. The small parking area was full. Dottie guessed that the cars belonged to St. Siffret residents, as it was too early in the morning for visitors. An old man, slow moving and bandy-legged, led his dog to the monument in the center of the square. He sat down on the ornately carved stone seat, the dog next to him.

Delicious smells of baking bread wafted in the air from a nearby house, and Dottie's stomach began to rumble. With all the excitement last night, she'd eaten only a piece of baguette and some brie. Humming to herself, she set the table with mugs and napkins, with orange juice, croissants, a jar of blackberry preserves she'd found in the kitchen, and the rest of the brie. "Breakfast's ready!" Dottie called, as she returned to the kitchen for the coffee carafe.

The floorboards creaked, and the toilet flushed. Within minutes, Mabel appeared, her hair sticking out like straw. "It's a bit early for breakfast," she muttered, tying the dressing gown belt around her plump waist.

"It's a beautiful morning, too nice to waste indoors," Dottie said. "Come on; we're eating on the terrace. After breakfast, we'll phone the car rental people to report the damage."

Mabel looked at the table set out for breakfast. "This looks wonderful, Dottie." She patted her stomach. "Suddenly, I feel peckish," she said, reaching for a croissant. "We've had almost nothing to eat since our in-flight meal." She broke off a large piece of croissant and popped it in her mouth.

"It was quite the night." Dottie drank her juice. "Let's hope we have a peaceful vacation from now on."

"What are we doing about the dinner invitation?"

As Yvette and Pierre's guests were going to spend time in Quebec, it made sense to invite Canadians for dinner, so why did Dottie have qualms about it? "I'd prefer to get the car business finished before we decide."

"What's that got to do with the invitation?"

"We might have to pick up another rental car. Who knows what that will involve?"

Dottie was about to pour the coffee when they were interrupted by a loud rap on the front door. "I hope it's not the police again." After making sure her dressing gown was securely belted, she opened the door.

Yvette Gagnon stood on the step, wearing a black cotton sundress splashed with white polka dots. Black thong sandals exposed ruby red toenails. "'ello, Dottie. Pierre and me, we 'ear about last night." Her brow creased. "Are you all right?"

"Yes. Tired, but we're fine."

"Our neighbors say they see police cars by your 'ouse, and a man is dead on the street! That is terrible." Yvette patted Dottie on the hand. "Pierre and me, we worry about you."

"Thank you."

"Do they know who the man is?"

"Presumably, he had identification, but they didn't tell us." Dottie chose not to mention the bag of powder the police found in the man's jacket.

Yvette's tapered fingernails curved around a small envelope she handed to Dottie. "Please come to dinner. It will 'elp you forget. I tell Suzanne and Louis about you and Mabel. They are excited to meet you." A sharp beep of a car horn made them both jump. Yvette's red lips curved into a smile. "I go now; we are late. *Au revoir!*" She ran down the steps where a red Peugeot waited, its engine purring. Pierre, in the driver's seat, waved to Dottie, as Yvette swiveled into the car.

Dottie watched them drive away. She examined the cream-colored envelope with their names written in copperplate handwriting and brought it out to the terrace.

Mabel opened the envelope and read the invitation. "It's handwritten. How elegant!" She handed it to Dottie. "I think we would enjoy having dinner with them, don't you?"

With a start, Dottie realized it wasn't the invitation that unsettled her. It was the couple who'd issued it. She frowned. "What do you think of Yvette and Pierre?"

"They've been very kind to us," Mabel replied. "I think we're fortunate to have met them."

Dottie pushed aside her qualms. After all, it was only a dinner party. "I agree. Let's accept. I'm sure we'll have a great time."

Chapter 5

After breakfast, Dottie and Mabel made another trip to the phone booth. Dottie called the rental company and arranged to take the car into Avignon the following afternoon.

Later, they drove to Pont du Gard, a Roman aqueduct built in 12 BC to carry water between Uzès and Nimes. A massive olive tree, said to have been at least a thousand years old, stood near the aqueduct. Dottie took out her digital camera and tried to take a casual shot of Mabel admiring the tree. As soon as Mabel knew the camera was focused on her, she went into 'pose mode.' Shoulders squared and an artificial grin on her face, she waited for Dottie to take the picture. Dottie obliged but sneaked another one when Mabel wasn't looking.

Dottie recalled the day she'd visited Fred Fortune, an old friend and former lover, at the riding academy where he worked. As he lugged hay bales onto a truck, his sweaty T-shirt clung to his skin. Strands of long gray hair escaped from the elastic band secured at the nape of his neck, and they were plastered on his brow. Seizing the moment, Dottie called out, "Hey, Fred!" He turned his head. A wry smile crossed his face when he saw the camera. "Couldn't you at least let me clean up before you start to click?"

"I want to capture you the way you are."

An unexpected feeling of nostalgia swept through Dottie. The photograph had turned out so well that she'd entered it into the local Seniors Photography Contest.

Dottie and Mabel lunched in the medieval village of Castillon-du-Gard, where wooden tables were set out in a courtyard under the shade of plane trees. They enjoyed olives, eggplant with parmesan cheese, and bread drizzled with olive oil, with a glass of pastis. All that was missing from the idyllic scene was a handsome Frenchman.

On their way home, they stopped at the local *carrefour* to buy a few groceries and a bottle of wine for their dinner hosts. Dottie picked up a bunch of asparagus and a jar of capers and followed Mabel as she struggled toward the bakery section with a wobbly shopping cart. They passed a counter where seafood of all shapes and sizes lay on a bed of ice, complete with heads and tails. The only ones Dottie recognized were salmon, halibut, and octopus.

A selection of filleted fish was displayed at the next counter. "I'm glad they sell fillets," Dottie said. "I can't see either of us gutting a fish."

A loud clash of metal drowned Mabel's response. Dottie swung around to find her friend had collided with another cart.

Mabel's face grew pink as she pulled back. "Oh, dear. I'm so sorry!"

"Madame Scattergood, how wonderful to see you again!"

"Monsieur Bouchard!"

"This morning, I heard about the body discovered in the street next to your house." His voice grew serious. "This must be distressing for you both. I hope very much that you will try to put it out of your mind and enjoy the Provençal countryside."

"Thank you, Monsieur Bouchard," Mabel said. "We intend to." She told him about their trip to the Roman aqueduct. "And we've been invited to dinner this evening by a young couple we met in a café last night."

"Oh?"

Dottie Flowers and the European Caper

"They live here, so I expect you know them," Mabel added. "Yvette Gagnon and Pierre Tremblay."

Monsieur Bouchard became very still. Frowning, he asked, "Do you have plans for tomorrow morning?"

The two women glanced at each other. "We have to go to Avignon in the afternoon," Mabel replied, "but the morning is free."

"I must discuss some things with you. Would you come to my house for coffee? Shall we say around ten? I live on the next street to yours. It is the house with the blue door."

Mabel smiled at him. "Thank you. We'll see you in the morning." He inclined his head to Mabel, then Dottie, and disappeared into the crowds of shoppers.

"I think you're right about Yvette and Pierre," Mabel said. "Monsieur Bouchard looked perturbed when I told him we were having dinner with them. What do you suppose he wants to talk to us about?"

"I get the feeling he wants to warn us about something."

***

Dottie glanced at her watch. They were due to arrive at Yvette and Pierre's house for dinner in half an hour, and she was running late. She opened the closet door. Where was that ivory-colored blouse that complemented the long black skirt and high heels she planned to wear? It had to be here somewhere, but she'd already been through her clothes twice. The trouble was they were all crammed together. On her third try, she found the blouse buried under another one at the back.

As she reached for the hanger, her fingernail caught on something in the wall. She traced the outline of a square piece of wood about three feet wide. It appeared to have been cut out of the closet wall and replaced. Curious, Dottie took her clothes out of the closet and laid them on the bed. She picked up the flashlight from the dresser. After removing a metal clothing rod, Dottie managed to pull out the wooden board. Behind it was a shelf built into a brick wall. She directed the beam on to the shelf and saw a bulky shape. Reaching out, she removed a piece of burlap and found herself staring at a machine gun. Dottie gasped. What was a machine gun doing in her clothes closet?

She ran her hands along the shelf. It appeared to be empty, but stretching her arm into the corner, she felt the edges of a box. Standing on two heavy encyclopedias from the bookcase, she slid open the box lid. Her fingers touched the cold metal of a gun.

Dottie exited the closet and called Mabel. "You'd better come in here quickly!"

"What's going on?" Mabel asked, as she walked into the bedroom, hairbrush in hand. "You sound as though you've found a treasure chest or something."

"You could say that. Look at the back of my closet."

Taking the flashlight with her, Mabel went to check. "I don't believe it! That's an AK-47!"

"How do you know it's an AK-47?"

"My Alf owned one."

"What?"

Mabel stuck her head around the closet door. "He was an avid gun collector."

"I thought they were prohibited in Canada."

"If you owned one before January 1995, I think it was, you were allowed to keep it." Mabel's eyes lit up. "Didn't I tell you about the hours we'd spend at a local shooting range? I became a good markswoman, although I say it myself." She sighed. "I miss those times."

"Speaking of guns," Dottie said. "It looks like there's a box in the corner of the shelf."

"I'll check." Mabel emerged a few minutes later, brushing dust off her clothes. "You're right, Dottie," she said. "My guess is at least a dozen assault weapons are in that box, and they look new."

Chapter 6

Dottie and Mabel stared at each other. "Now, what do we do?" Mabel wondered.

"It's *Déjà vu*. Last night, we phoned the police about bags of powder inside a suitcase," Dottie said." How do you think they'll respond when we tell them we've found assault weapons hidden in a closet?"

Mabel pulled a face. "It's a depressing thought."

"We'd better phone them right away and get it over with."

"Is that wise? We're expected at Yvette and Pierre's house for dinner shortly." Mabel checked her watch. "In fifteen minutes, to be precise. What are we going to say to our hosts? 'We've found some guns, so we can't come for dinner, as we're expecting the police at any moment.'"

"You're right. I'll phone first thing in the morning."

"Let's try to forget about guns for now," Mabel said. "I'm looking forward to spending an evening in a real French home. We're fortunate. Not many tourists get an opportunity to mix with the locals."

"That's true. I have my reservations about their motives, but I'm sure we'll enjoy ourselves."

Before dressing for dinner, Dottie glanced around the room. Instinct told her to leave everything the way she'd found it, so she covered the assault weapon, replaced the piece of wood in the back of the closet, and rehung her clothes

***

When the two women arrived at their hosts' house, Dottie handed the bottle of wine to Pierre.

"I hope you like Merlot."

"Very much. Thank you." He smiled. The wine-colored silk shirt and black slacks enhanced his film-star good looks.

He ushered them into the living room. "Suzanne and Louis will be a little late, I'm afraid," he explained. "They phoned us to say they'd taken the wrong road. And Yvette's zipper on her dress broke, so she's looking through her wardrobe for something else to wear. She'll be down in a few minutes. Please make yourselves at home," he urged, before disappearing through an open doorway.

"It's rather stark, isn't it?" Mabel whispered.

Dottie glanced around. A black leather sofa and matching armchairs contrasted with the white walls and dark slate floor. The room was dominated by a magnificent granite fireplace and black marble hearth. She was surprised to see a fire burning in the grate, but it provided much-needed warmth.

Pierre carried in a tray with two champagne flutes balanced on it. As though reading her mind, he said, "It seems strange to have a fire in June, but the evenings can be quite chilly." He handed the flutes to them. "Please excuse me. I'm doing the finishing touches to the *hors d'oeuvres*." He returned to the kitchen.

Mabel took a sip of champagne. "Very nice."

"I thought you didn't like champagne. You poured yours into a flower pot last night."

"I'm trying to acquire a taste for it."

Dottie wandered around the room, admiring the contemporary artwork, which was in black and white with occasional slashes of blue and red. As she sipped the champagne, the tension in her shoulders eased. They had only been in France for a few days, but with all the excitement, it seemed longer.

Suddenly, a hot flash swept over her. Of all the times to have a menopausal moment, as her gynecologist called them. What did he know! She was tempted to take a magazine from the glass-topped coffee table and use it as a fan, but the other guests would be here at any moment. She seldom suffered these furnace-like heat waves anymore. Why it should happen now, she had no idea. Placing the flute on a side table, Dottie opened the French doors leading to the terrace. Periwinkle pots, overflowing with lobelia and ivy geraniums, added a colorful splash to the black wrought-iron railings and white stucco walls. As she stepped out, a welcome breeze brushed across her hot skin.

"Mabel, come and look at this. Isn't it gorgeous?"

Mabel joined Dottie on the terrace. "It's so... French!"

They walked to the railing and looked down. Mabel pointed. "That's the street we walked along last night."

Dottie checked the view from the left side of the terrace. The monument with the iron cross was hidden behind the clock tower, but even in the fading light, she had an excellent view of *Maison Francais* and the side street where the man's body had been found.

"That's weird."

"What is?"

"Yvette said her neighbors told her about the police cars and the murder. You'd think she and Pierre would have heard the siren and come out to the terrace to see what was going on."

"If they were home. Maybe they returned to Francois' birthday party after taking us to the phone booth."

"Of course. That's probably what happened." Dottie glanced over her shoulder. "I think we should go back inside. Pierre will wonder what we're doing."

As they stepped back into the living room, Pierre held out a tray of appetizers. "Try one," he urged. "The mushroom ones have a kick to them, if you like a bit of heat."

Under the right circumstances, Dottie thought, remembering her hot flash. To Dottie's surprise, Mabel took an oyster canapé. "It's time I tried something different," she said, popping the morsel into her mouth.

At that moment, Yvette entered wearing a purple ankle-length dress with silver and amethyst jewelry. Her glossy hair curved around her face, which was pale except for blood red lipstick. "I am sorry I am late." She explained about the zipper. "I find another dress, but I drop an earring!" She shrugged. "It is impossible to find, so I wear another pair." Her eyes fell on the champagne flutes, and she smiled. "I see that Pierre takes care of you."

The doorbell rang, and the Roys, full of apologies for their tardiness, were ushered in. While their hosts were distracted with the arrival of the Roys, Mabel removed the canapé from her mouth, put it in a paper napkin, and placed the napkin in her purse.

Over dinner, Suzanne and Louis kept everyone entertained with amusing anecdotes about their recent trip to China. They spoke with pronounced French accents, even stronger than Yvette's.

Suzanne, her buxom figure wrapped in a tight-fitting animal print dress, kept a motherly eye on Louis. "He drinks the wine too much," she confided to Dottie sitting next to her.

Sipping the Merlot, Dottie smiled. "It's tempting when it tastes this good."

White swan candles floated in a black bowl in the center of the glass dining table. Square white plates sat on black tablemats, and across each plate lay a folded white linen napkin, a black swan embroidered across the center. Silver cutlery and crystal wine goblets sparkled in the candles' glow. *Yvette and Pierre have expensive tastes*, thought Dottie. *Surely, an Internet café in a small Provençal town wouldn't bring in that kind of money.*

With Pierre's help, Yvette served chilled melon soup, followed by a medley of seafood and roasted vegetables. Although she was gracious to her guests and smiled at Suzanne and Louis's stories, Yvette seemed nervous. Her hands trembled as she served the soup. When she spilled some on the table, she quickly dabbed it with a napkin.

After dinner, everyone returned to the living room, where they were tempted with chocolate-dipped strawberries and petit fours. Dottie answered the Roys' questions about Quebec, as they all relaxed in front of a roaring fire. She told them about the custom of taking one's own wine into many restaurants and about the Winter Carnival.

From the corner of her eye, Dottie noticed that Yvette was pressing her palm against her forehead. "Are you all right, Yvette?"

"I am feeling a little dizzy." She stood. "Excuse me." She swept past Dottie and walked out onto the terrace.

"Don't worry about Yvette," Pierre assured his guests. "She enjoys wine, but sometimes, it goes to her head."

Pierre served coffee and liqueurs. Dottie chose a brandy. "A woman after my own heart!" Pierre smiled at her. "You must try one of my special brandies. I have several types. I'll show you, and you can choose."

Mabel didn't care for brandy. She chose a Cointreau.

After a few minutes, Yvette returned, smiling and looking relaxed for the first time that evening. "The fresh air, it 'elps. The dizzy 'ead, it is gone." She helped herself to coffee, adding a low-cal sweetener. "I am so 'appy you and Mabel are 'ere," she said. "Pierre and me, we do not entertain much. We travel or work at the café."

Dottie was about to ask if their travelling was for business or pleasure when Pierre spoke. "It's market day in Uzès the day after tomorrow. It's well worth dropping by. And there's an excellent restaurant in the market square where you can have lunch."

"You must go!" Suzanne joined in. "Louis and I went two years past. We talk about it many times."

"That seems like a good idea," Mabel said. "What do you think, Dottie?"

"It sounds great." Dottie smothered a yawn. It had been another long day. She finished the brandy, wondering how they could leave soon without seeming rude.

As though on cue, Suzanne spoke. "It is time to leave, Louis." She fished in her large handbag and retrieved a set of keys. "We have the long drive."

Dottie checked her watch. "I can't believe it's already eleven-thirty. We must go as well." She placed the empty brandy glass on the coffee table.

Mabel stood. "We've had a wonderful evening. Thank you for your hospitality."

They left at the same time as the Roys. After bidding their hosts goodbye, they walked home, glad of the fresh air after the wine and liqueurs. Within half an hour, they were in bed.

***

The next morning, Dottie woke with a slight headache. Rubbing her temples, she took two aspirins and swallowed them with a large glass of water. She hoped they would stop the development of a migraine. She lay back on the pillow and closed her eyes. Just as she was about to fall asleep, Dottie remembered the weapons.

She leapt out of bed and rushed to Mabel's room. Mabel wasn't there. Thinking she'd be downstairs having a cup of tea or reading one of her romance novels, Dottie called out several times, but there was no answer. She did a quick check around the house and noticed that Mabel's walking shoes were not in their usual spot by the front door.

The front door banged open. "Cooee!" Mabel sailed in, a big grin on her face. "Guess where I've been!"

Dottie was in no mood to play games. "I've no idea."

"I phoned the police. They're on their way."

"Why didn't you wait for me?"

"You were asleep. Lieutenant Piaf speaks good English, so I knew I wouldn't have a problem communicating with him."

Dottie looked at Mabel. "What did he say when you told him?"

"Well," Mabel sat down, "I didn't tell him exactly."

"What do you mean?"

"I said we had important information and that he must get here as quickly as possible."

"And?"

"He was very rude. Said to stop wasting his time."

"But you said the police are on their way."

"I told him it was a matter of life or death."

"Why didn't you tell him about the weapons?"

"I thought this sounded more dramatic. It got his attention anyway."

Dottie kept quiet. She didn't understand how Mabel's mind worked half the time, but at least the police had taken her seriously. To prove Mabel's point, Lieutenant Piaf, with Sergeant Coté and two other *gendarmes*, arrived fifteen minutes later.

Dottie told the lieutenant about her discovery of the automatic weapons. His goatee twitched as he barked at the two women. "You say on the telephone that it is a matter of life and death. When I come here, you tell me you have found some weapons!"

"My friend got a bit carried away, I'm afraid, Lieutenant. Even so, finding a cache of weapons is pretty significant." Dottie paused. "I discovered a box on a shelf in my closet. Come with me, and I'll show you."

She led the way upstairs to her bedroom. The lieutenant raised his eyebrows when he saw the pile of clothing on the bed. "I cleared the clothes to make it easier for you to search," Dottie explained. She opened the closet door and pointed. "You see that piece of wood inserted in the back wall? Behind it is a shelf where you'll find a box filled with weapons."

She stepped back and waited as the lieutenant, with the aid of Dottie's flashlight, removed the board. After a few minutes, he emerged from the closet. Hands on hips, his eyes flashed with anger. "There is nothing there. The shelf—it is empty!"

"That's impossible!"

He spoke slowly and deliberately. "There is no box. There are no guns on the shelf. Madame Flowers, you have wasted my time again! What is this crazy game you and Madame Scattergood are playing?"

Chapter 7

Dottie felt Lieutenant Piaf's eyes burn into her. "I found a box of guns and a rifle on that shelf, Lieutenant. I swear to you."

"How is it that they are not here anymore?" he demanded.

"Someone must have broken in while we were out."

"There is no forced entry, *madame*! Are you telling me that this thief has a key?"

"Yes, just like the man who was murdered. He must have used a key to get in the house when he exchanged the suitcases." Dottie met his eyes. "I have a theory."

Lieutenant Piaf gave an exasperated sigh. "So, tell me your little… theory, as you put it."

"Lieutenant," Mabel flared, "we are not two old biddies with vivid imaginations who enjoy getting attention from the police!"

"In fact," Dottie added, "calling the police is cutting into our vacation time." She took a deep breath. "I believe *Maison Francais* is being used to store illegal drugs and guns. As there's no sign of a break-in, it makes sense that those involved have keys to the house."

The lieutenant strode to the window and stared out. Hands folded behind his back, he rocked back and forth on the soles of his shiny black boots. Finally, he turned to the two women. "I will authorize a house search. In the meantime, *mesdames*, we will take statements from you."

He looked at each woman in turn. "It is imperative that you tell no one of this! Do you understand?"

They nodded.

***

It was late morning by the time the women were free to go. Mabel glanced at her watch. "We were supposed to have coffee with Monsieur Bouchard at ten. He's probably given up on us."

"Let's hurry over there."

Mabel panted as she struggled to keep up with Dottie's long strides. "What excuse are we going to give?"

Dottie thought about it for a moment. "It's no use saying we slept in. By now, about everyone in St. Siffret will know about the police coming to the house again."

"Why don't we tell him they're looking for more clues in the murder investigation?"

"Perfect!"

When they arrived at the house, they found the door slightly ajar. Dottie tapped lightly. "Monsieur Bouchard?" There were no sounds from inside. She knocked again, harder this time. "I don't think anyone's here." She pushed the door open and peered in. Once her eyes adjusted to the dark interior, she saw that the tiny entrance hall led into a living room crowded with furniture and bookcases. "Come on, Mabel. We'd better check inside."

In the living room, they found a newspaper spread on the sofa. A half mug of coffee and a croissant with a bite taken out of it sat on the coffee table. Dottie dipped her finger in the coffee. It was stone cold. "Why would he leave in the middle of breakfast?"

"We don't know for sure he's left," Mabel said. "I think we should take a quick look around." They looked in every room, but there was no sign of him.

"I wonder if his next-door neighbor has seen him this morning."

"I'll pop around and ask," Mabel volunteered. She paused. "On second thought, you'd better go, Dottie. I can't speak French. At least, you know the basics."

Dottie pulled a face. "A fat lot of good it's done me so far. Let's hope he—or she—can speak some English."

The neighbor's crimson door had a wrought-iron knocker. As Dottie reached for the knocker, the door flew open. Hans Van Gogh stood in the hallway. "*Bonjour, madame.*" He introduced himself, grasping her hand in a firm handshake. "And you are Dottie Flowers."

His gravelly voice with its slight European accent sent heat through her veins. She swallowed hard. "How do you…?"

"I saw you the other night at the café," he interrupted. "I made it my business to find out your name."

Dottie cleared her throat. "Have you seen your neighbor, Monsieur Bouchard, today?"

"As a matter of fact, I have. I heard a car pull up about seven o'clock. When I looked out of my bedroom window, he and another man were climbing into the backseat of a Citroen. He did not appear to have any luggage with him."

"That's strange. My friend and I were supposed to have coffee with him this morning." He scratched his head. "It is not like Monsieur Bouchard to forget appointments."

"I'm sure there's a simple explanation." Dottie turned to leave. "I must go. Thanks for your help, Mr. Van Gogh."

He reached out and took her hand, closing strong fingers around her own. "Call me Hans." He cocked his eyebrow. "I am sure we will get to know each other in the next few weeks." Dottie snatched her hand away. "You seem to be taking much for granted, Mr. Van Gogh!"

"Hans, please."

"I prefer to call you Mr. Van Gogh, if you don't mind."

An amused smile hovered on his lips. "As you wish."

***

"Arrogant creep!" Dottie stormed, as she walked into Monsieur Bouchard's house. "Who does he think he is!" Embarrassed, she remembered how she'd fantasized about him after seeing his photo in the photography course brochure.

"Who's an arrogant creep?"

"Hans Van Gogh. The man next door. Talk about conceited!"

"Does he have any idea where Monsieur Bouchard is?"

"No, but he saw him get into a car first thing this morning." Dottie tensed. "If he were going away, wouldn't he order a taxi?"

"Maybe it was a taxi," Mabel replied. "Just because this Van Gogh chap used the word *car*..."

"Of course, I'm overreacting."

Mabel pursed her lips. "I'm not so sure about that. Why would Monsieur Bouchard invite us for coffee if he was going away?"

"Maybe something unexpected came up."

"Oh, it's no use speculating," Mabel sighed. "Let's go home and have lunch."

At the house, Mabel prepared open-faced sandwiches with slices of brie cheese and grilled red peppers. She served them on the terrace with a pot of Earl Grey tea. Dottie added half a teaspoonful of sugar to her tea and stirred. "It's difficult to believe how much has happened since we arrived in France. If we told anyone, they'd think we'd invented it."

They concentrated on the meal, lost in their thoughts. Afterward, Mabel piled the empty dishes on a tray. "I think we need a day out, Dottie. It's market day in Uzès tomorrow. Why don't we take Pierre's suggestion and spend the morning looking around?"

"I'd like that," Dottie said. "Right now, we have to drive to Avignon to see the car rental people. We can look around the town, maybe go to the Palace of Popes. It's supposed to be well worth a visit."

"And the bridge, of course." A loud rap interrupted their conversation. Mabel answered the door.

It was Pierre. "I can't stop. Here's an advertising brochure about *Monsieur Jacques*, that restaurant in Uzès I told you about."

"How thoughtful!" Mabel said. "Dottie and I were just talking about Uzès. We're going tomorrow morning."

"Excellent idea. You must have lunch at Monsieur Jacques. You need to reserve a table, but I know the owner, Roy, very well. Why don't I make a reservation for you around one? He'll see that you receive the best service."

Mabel smiled. "That would be very nice."

Pierre grimaced and put his hand up to his cheek. "I must go to get a tooth filled." He ran down the steps. Opening his car door, he called out, "One more thing! Get to Uzès before ten. It's very crowded on market day."

They watched Pierre drive away. "That was kind of him," Mabel said. "Going to all that trouble to get us a table. We're lucky to have met Yvette and Pierre."

Dottie bit her lip. "I'm not so sure."

"You worry too much. Come on; get your jacket, and we'll drive to Avignon."

***

When she woke the next morning, Dottie knew she was in trouble. Spots danced in front of her eyes, and she felt nauseated, the sure signs of a migraine headache. She suspected the chocolate dessert she'd eaten in Avignon the day before had caused the attack. She'd allowed Mabel to persuade her to order the rich confection against her better judgment. This time, aspirin wouldn't be enough. She took two migraine pills and settled back in bed, knowing the only remedy was a darkened room and plenty of rest. She'd been looking forward to shopping in the market today, but now Mabel would have to go by herself.

Her friend was adamant. "Go without you? I won't hear of it."

"Mabel, I don't need looking after."

"You can't be left alone when you're sick."

"I'm not sick." She decided to try another approach. "I'd like you to get some fresh veggies, so I can make us a pot of soup. We can go to *Monsieur Jacques* another day."

After much persuasion, Mabel agreed to go to Uzès by herself.

"By the way, when you park, don't forget the replacement car the rental company gave us yesterday is a Peugeot, not a Fiat."

Mabel laughed. "That's good advice, since both cars are blue." She turned to leave. "I'll drop by and cancel the restaurant booking."

As soon as the car pulled away, Dottie sank back on the pillows. Having Mabel fussing over her all day would have made the headache worse.

***

Dottie lounged on a silk couch. A knight in shining armor on a white steed galloped across the drawbridge and into the castle to rescue her from Mabel, who was trying to make her drink some vile-tasting soup. When the knight drew near, she knew it was Hans Van Gogh. He bowed courteously to her but lost his balance and, with a rattle of armor, fell off the horse.

Dottie sat up in bed and gulped some water. Migraine headaches always gave her crazy dreams.

Feeling a good deal better, she headed to the washroom. She was about to flush the toilet when she heard a loud creak, then another one. The noises seemed to come from Mabel's room. A thud startled Dottie. She imagined one of Mabel's large economy jars of skin cream had fallen off the shelf. Suddenly, a man's angry voice cried out, *"Merde!"*

Chapter 8

Heart pounding, Dottie leaned on the bathroom door. What was an intruder doing in Mabel's bedroom? Maybe he was a burglar in the process of searching the room for valuables. A cold shiver ran down her spine. What if he had a gun?

She couldn't hide in the washroom all day. The man might want to use the facilities, and it would be game over. She must find out what he was up to. Edging open the door, Dottie peered out. She heard muffled voices coming from Mabel's room. So, he wasn't alone.

Fortunately, the landing was carpeted. Praying the floorboards wouldn't creak, she tiptoed back to her bedroom and pulled on slacks, a sweater, and a pair of loafers. Her eyes darted around the room. She needed a weapon. Her eyes fell on the flashlight at the corner of the dresser. Gripping the flashlight, she eased out of her bedroom and crossed the landing.

The door was slightly ajar, so she didn't have to worry about squeaky hinges. As she peered through the crack, Dottie smelled cigarette smoke. This was the second time she'd smelled the pungent odor of Gauloise cigarettes since they'd been in Provence.

Two men stood in the far corner of the room, staring at the floor. One wore a red bandana around his head. A cigarette dangled from his mouth. His heavily tattooed arms caught Dottie's attention, particularly a large tattoo of a machine gun on his right forearm. The other man, taller and leaner with straggly black hair, appeared much younger. Hitching up his jeans, he bent toward the floor and pulled up a section of floorboard, which he placed on the bed next to another board Dottie hadn't noticed. Both men got down on their haunches. After a few moments, she heard swishing sounds and light thuds. Burning with curiosity, she pushed the door open a little wider.

The bedside rug had been shoved aside. Numerous small plastic bags filled with white powder were lined up by the opening created by the missing floorboards. The bigger man took two quick drags of his cigarette, issuing directions in rapid French. His companion was reaching down inside the opening. Face red with exertion, the man struggled as he hauled out more bags.

The front door latch clicked. Dottie's heart leapt as she rushed to the top of the stairs. Mabel stood in the hallway, arms loaded with groceries.

"Mabel!" Dottie whispered as loudly as she dared.

Her friend looked up in amazement. Dottie placed an index finger over her lips and beckoned. Mabel placed the groceries on the bench by the door and started to climb the stairs. As she climbed, the stairs creaked. Dottie signaled her to slow down.

"What's going on?" Mabel muttered as soon as they'd entered Dottie's room and closed the door. "And what's that thudding noise?"

"Keep your voice down!" Dottie hissed. "Two men are in your bedroom. They're retrieving bags of drugs from under the floorboards."

"Oh, my goodness!" As though on cue, they could hear men's voices, followed by scraping noises.

"We have to do something. They probably have guns."

Mabel's eyes lit up. "We can lock them in for a start."

"How?"

"There's a bolt on the outside of the door."

Dottie shook her head. "It won't hold them for long."

"What about that chest on the landing? We could barricade them in."

"They could escape through the window."

"It's a long drop to the ground," Mabel said. Loud hammering made them jump. "Let's get on with it while we have the chance. They'll never hear us over that racket."

After closing the bolt, they dragged the chest across the carpet until it blocked the door. Mabel stood slowly, rubbing the small of her back. "I must pay a visit to my chiropractor when we get home."

Dottie frowned. "We'll have to go to that telephone booth again and phone the police."

"One of us had better stay."

"No way," Dottie retorted. "These men are drug dealers. Who knows what they're capable of."

Mabel and Dottie crept down the stairs. "Can you imagine what Lieutenant Piaf will think?" Mabel whispered. "He's already convinced we're a bit crazy."

"I don't care, as long as he gets here as fast as possible. That chest won't hold them for long."

***

Dottie phoned the lieutenant and rolled her eyes at Mabel while he lectured her. "Madame Flowers, I am a busy man. I rush to *Maison Francais* to look for drugs. When I arrive, I do not find drugs. I find a man shot dead. You tell me to look for guns hidden behind a wall, and what do I find? Nothing! Now, you tell me that two men are removing the drugs from under floorboards, and that you and your friend Mrs. Scatterhead have locked these men in the bedroom. You are reading too many thrillers, *madame*!"

Dottie let him ramble on, wondering if his flub of Mabel's name was intentional. When he seemed to have run out of things to say, she said calmly, "I can see your point, Lieutenant."

"Humph!"

"The thing is," Dottie continued, "we have a problem." "Pardon?" "We have two dangerous men locked in the bedroom. What are we going to do with them?" "I warn you, *madame*," the lieutenant growled. "My patience is—how you say it—growing narrow. This must not be another wild horserace. We will be there in fifteen minutes."

Dottie smiled at his misquotes. "Thank you, Lieutenant."

"And remember, Madame Flowers, tell no one of this!"

***

The two women sat in their car with the windows rolled down and waited for Lieutenant Piaf. "This is embarrassing, Dottie. It's the third time in the space of a few days that the police have been to the house."

"And in a small place like this, rumors spread like crazy. I don't know why the lieutenant bothers to caution us not tell anyone. Everyone will know within hours."

"I must admit I'll be glad when the police get here," Mabel said. "I'm feeling nervous about those two men. What if they break down the door and come looking for us?"

Dottie shook her head. "I can't see them coming after us. They'll be too busy trying to escape. If they do, we'll just drive off."

"D'you think the police will get here in time?"

"I expect so. Capturing a couple of drug dealers would probably boost the lieutenant's prospects of promotion."

Dottie Flowers and the European Caper

The roar of an engine broke into Dottie's speculations, and moments later, Pierre's red Peugeot swung into the square and pulled up beside them. Pierre climbed out of the car and walked over to them, his forehead creased in a frown. "I thought you two were going to the Uzès market today."

"Mabel went by herself." Dottie told him about her migraine. Instinct told her to say nothing to Pierre about the two men locked in Mabel's bedroom. Pierre's eyes darted around the houses and square.

"Are you all right?" Dottie asked. "You seem a bit nervous."

"You look pale as well," Mabel added, fanning herself with a folded map. "I daresay it's the heat."

"Pardon?" Pierre stared at Mabel as though seeing her for the first time.

"I wondered if the heat was bothering you."

"I'm fine. I must go." He almost ran to the car and drove off in such a hurry that his tires screeched and sent swirls of dust into the air.

Mabel looked over at Dottie. "What's got into him? He has a bee in his bonnet about something."

Two police cars turned in to the square. The lieutenant and two of his men jumped out of the first. He barked an order, and the men rushed to the back of *Maison Francais*. The three policemen from the second car followed Lieutenant Piaf into the house.

"Come on, Dottie. Let's go after them."

"We'll be in the way."

"I want to see the look of surprise on those drug dealers' faces," Mabel grinned. "And when the lieutenant arrests them, he'll realize we're not making things up."

Dottie and Mabel hurried after the lieutenant and his men. As they reached the top of the stairs, they found the police pushing the chest away from the door. Dottie saw that the bolt was still in place. She chewed her lip. Either the men hadn't realized they were locked in, or they couldn't break the door down. Would they have risked serious injury by jumping out the window? Dottie's heart raced, as she watched the lieutenant pull away the bolt. Signaling his men to get behind him, he drew a gun. He flung open the door and burst into the room, followed by the three *gendarmes*. He shouted something in French.

"What did he say?" Mabel hissed.

"No idea."

Everything fell quiet. "Something's wrong," Mabel said. "Let's go and look."

As they entered the bedroom, a warm breeze from the wide-open window wafted over them. Avoiding eye contact with Lieutenant Piaf, Dottie crossed the room. Everything looked normal. The floorboards had been replaced, and the bags had disappeared. She peered out. The wall was covered with a creeping vine, some of which was pulled away. It didn't take much imagination to guess how the drug dealers had escaped.

Chapter 9

Dottie stole a glance at Lieutenant Piaf. Eyes squeezed shut, he took in long breaths, his goatee twitching each time he exhaled. Perhaps the man didn't feel well, but more likely was trying to calm down.

He opened his eyes and looked at the two women. "*Mesdames*, I wish to speak with both of you down the stairs, *maintenant*!"

"Would you care for some herbal tea, Lieutenant?" Mabel inquired. "It's good for the nerves."

"Madame, I do not want the tea! I do not want anything, except to be rid of the two of you!" He rubbed a hand across his brow. "I have the headache. It never leaves."

The women made their way downstairs. "We might as well let him vent, Mabel," Dottie said. "We've caused him a lot of aggravation."

"What were we supposed to do? Let those men get away?" Mabel looked sheepish. "Well, they did get away, but at least, we didn't make it easy for them."

"Lieutenant Piaf won't care about that. As far as he's concerned, we're busybodies trying to be detectives. If they'd captured the drug dealers, it would have been a different matter."

The three gathered in the living room. Lieutenant Piaf paced the room, hands folded behind his back. "From your description, I believe those two men are part of a drug ring we've been watching for many months." His left eye twitched. "You, *mesdames*, with your amateur detective work, have ruined everything."

"All we did was lock them in the room!" Mabel protested. "I don't see how that constitutes wrecking your plans!"

He stopped in his tracks and glared at Mabel. "When the men discovered they were locked in, they knew that someone was over them..."

Dottie cleared her throat. "On to them."

The lieutenant looked at Dottie, a puzzled frown on his face. "What?"

"The men knew someone was on to them—you know—knew they were in trouble."

"*Précisément, madame*! Now, where was I? Ah, yes, because they had—er—troubles, they escaped through the window. Otherwise, they escape through the back door of the house."

"But what difference does it make how they escaped?" Dottie wondered aloud. "They would still have gotten away."

The lieutenant's face reddened. "Not true! Two of my men were at the back door." He wagged a finger at the two women, his voice rising a few octaves. "It is all your fault, *mesdames*! If they hadn't suspected anything, they would not leave in such a hurry, and we would have caught them with the red hands."

"Lieutenant," Dottie began, making an effort to sound matter-of-fact. "I understand your frustration."

"You do not understand!" he thundered. "You cause everything that has gone wrong. We have been hot on the trails of these men. Now, we have to begin over."

"We didn't choose to get caught up in this, Lieutenant!" Dottie fumed. "We came to Provence for a holiday."

"I no longer care, *madame*!" The lieutenant's eye twitched. "I am going home, and I do not wish to see either of you again!" He marched to the front door and grasped the handle. The house shook as he slammed the door behind him.

"Our lieutenant is not a happy man," Mabel commented.

"That's an understatement!" Dottie sank into the plump cushions of the living room sofa. "I don't know about you, Mabel, but I'm pooped. Let's have an early supper. A good night's sleep will do us both good. With all the goings-on, we haven't done much sightseeing. We haven't even been to Orange or Arles yet."

"You're right, and I'd like to see the amphitheater at Nîmes. Yolanda raves about it."

Dottie raised a mental eyebrow. Mabel's niece raved about everything. Talk about a pain in the butt!

Mabel yawned. "It's stuffy in here. I'm going outside to get some fresh air." She opened the terrace doors and stepped outside.

Dottie joined her. The scorching heat had eased a little, and the air felt smooth like velvet. Not a cloud marred the late afternoon sky. She glanced at Mabel. "There's a bottle of Chardonnay in the fridge. Why don't you pour us a glass, and we can drink it out here."

"That's a good idea, but if I'm going to spend time out here, I need to spray myself with insect repellent. I was bitten the other day."

After Mabel left, Dottie sat down at the small table, opened a new pack of cigarillos, and shook one out. Striking a match, she lit the cigarillo and inhaled deeply. It was good to indulge without feeling guilty for a change. She'd been surprised at the number of people who smoked in France. People smoked as they drank their morning coffee or strolled along the sidewalks.

Her musings were cut short by Mabel's return. "Look what I just found." Holding the insect repellent container in one hand, she held out a scruffy piece of paper with the other.

"What's that?"

"I don't know. It's got some writing on it." She handed it to Dottie. "I borrowed your flashlight to look under the bed for the insect repellent spray. I thought it might have fallen off the dresser and rolled underneath. It had. When I reached under the bed to retrieve it, I found this scrunched up in a ball."

Dottie squished the cigarillo. Putting on her rhinestone-framed glasses, she examined the paper. "It says *Lucca*, and there's a name—*DaVinci*, or is it *DaVino*, and a number 12. It looks like a street address. There are two letters in the corner. One looks like an A. I can't make out the other one."

"One of those men must have dropped it," Mabel replied. "It wasn't there this morning. I keep my bedroom slippers under the bed, and I would have seen it."

Removing the glasses, Dottie looked at Mabel. "I think we should hold on to this."

"According to our lieutenant, those men belong to a drug ring," Mabel said. "Maybe this is some sort of code."

Dottie remembered the lieutenant saying that they read too many crime thrillers. "Let's not get carried away." She smiled. "What happened to that Chardonnay? A glass of white wine would go down well right now."

"Coming right up! How about some brie and crackers?"

"Now, you're talking!"

Mabel returned a few minutes later and placed a tray on the wrought-iron table. The women settled down to enjoy their predinner drink and snack.

Dottie sat back and savored the crisp chilled wine. "You know, Mabel, I've been thinking."

Mabel, feet propped on a chair and a plate of brie and crackers on her lap, glanced at Dottie. "About what?"

"The cache of guns hidden in a secret compartment; the drugs hidden under the floorboards; the obvious intent of the man with the case to drop off drugs at the house. Think about it. Who owns *Maison Francais*?"

Mabel munched on a cracker. "Tom. You think he's involved?"

"Why not? We know from our experience that he's a thief and a con artist."

Mabel dismissed Dottie's words with a flick of her hand. "There's a big difference between that and being involved in the sordid world of illegal drugs and guns, Dottie."

Dottie chewed her lip. "I don't like the idea that Tom could be in this any more than you do."

"I feel it in my bones he's innocent." Mabel sipped her wine. "Well, innocent of drug trafficking."

"You might be right," Dottie sighed. "Even so, it seems too much of a coincidence it's his house that's being used."

"When we picked up the keys, Tom told us that he hasn't stayed here for more than a year," Mabel said.

"Who put the bottle of wine and the welcome note on the table?"

"Marcel checks the house," Mabel replied. "Tom probably asked him to buy the wine."

"But what about the note? It's in Tom's handwriting."

"Tom could have dropped it off. He spends a fair amount of time in Europe."

Dottie stared at Mabel. "Someone in the drug trade must have known that the house was empty."

"Maybe Marcel is mixed up in the business."

Dottie nodded. "It's a possibility. Speaking of Marcel, it's strange we haven't seen him yet."

"He might be away."

A vehicle labored up a hilly road that snaked through the village; in the square, children's laughter and the occasional dog bark drifted to the balcony. "I've got an idea," Dottie said. "Why don't we phone Tom and ask him if there's a backup person we can call in an emergency?"

Mabel's face lit up. "In other words, does someone other than Marcel have a key to the house? Clever thinking, Dottie!"

"We can see how Tom responds. Let's do it tomorrow when we're fresh."

***

The incessant blaring of a car alarm awakened Dottie. Annoyed at being woken up so early, she yanked on her dressing gown and rushed to the window. Her jaw dropped. Men and women in jeans and T-shirts stood around the square, chatting and smoking. Two large cameras had been placed in front of the monument, which was lit up with spotlights. An old man sat on the stone bench, his hands gripping the top of a walking stick. Next to him was an attractive young brunette in a black pantsuit and white blouse. Hand resting on the back of the bench, the young woman chewed gum, a bored expression on her face.

After pulling on a pair of Capris, a cotton shirt, and sandals, Dottie stomped downstairs. Filming at this hour of the morning! Some people didn't give a darn about anyone else.

Armed with her French dictionary, she marched up to a young man who lounged against the wall of the square, a cigarette dangling from his fingers. *"Parlez-vous anglais?"*

The man squished his cigarette and straightened. "A little."

"Could you tell me who is in charge here?"

"Charge?"

Dottie quickly referred to the dictionary. *"Où est le directeur?"*

The man's face broke into a smile. "Ah!" He pointed to a large trailer parked down the street next to *Maison Francais.* "He—'ow you say—*manger*—er—eat!"

Dottie remembered the French for breakfast. "P*etite déjeuner?"*

"Oui, oui!"

Thanking the man, she hurried to the trailer. She heard dishes clattering inside and someone—presumably the film director—whistling. Dottie gritted her teeth. He won't be so cheerful when he hears what I have to say. She rapped on the door. A chair scraped on the floor, and a few moments later, the door opened.

Hair tousled, Hans Van Gogh shaded his eyes from the sun, as he peered at his early morning visitor. He wore a yellow open-necked shirt that hung loosely over a pair of blue jeans. The jeans were rolled above the ankles, exposing bare feet. A silver ring decorated one of his toes. Dottie's determination to keep Hans Van Gogh at arm's length wavered. "So, you're the director."

His face crinkled with amusement. "We meet again, Dottie. You remember I said we would see a lot of each other over the next week or so."

The blood rushed to her face. "You didn't tell me you were making a film here!"

"There was no need. I knew you would find out soon enough."

"I don't appreciate being awakened at the crack of dawn!"

He scratched the back of his neck. "Look, I am preparing espresso coffee. Come in, and I will explain everything."

Dottie hesitated. This could be a dangerous move on her part. Besides, her hair was a mess, and she didn't have on any make-up.

"I do not bite."

"What?"

He grinned. "I will leave the door open if that makes you feel more comfortable."

Dottie squared her shoulders. "All right, I'll have some coffee." She climbed the steps and followed Hans into the trailer.

The exterior of the trailer was dusty and in need of a coat of paint, but inside, the ocher walls and white trim looked freshly painted. She could smell furniture polish and a faint odor of lemon-scented cleaner. A blue-and-white bowl filled with apples, oranges, and pears sat in the center of the pine kitchen table, reminding Dottie of a Dutch painting.

"Make yourself at home, Dottie, while I finish preparing the coffee."

Beyond the kitchen, paintings of country scenes hung from the living room walls. She crossed into the living room where a glass-topped coffee table sat in front of a gray leather sofa. Dottie leaned over a pot of hyacinths on the table, breathing in the heady perfume.

Everything looked perfect, but something was missing. Personal stuff, such as photographs, that was it. Maybe they were somewhere else—in his house or his bedroom, perhaps.

"Sit down; make yourself at home!"

Dottie didn't know whether it was thoughts of Hans's bedroom or the power of his voice, but she headed back to the kitchen, took hold of the nearest chair, and sat.

Dottie Flowers and the European Caper

She took the tiny cup he handed her. Sipping the rich bitter brew, Dottie began to appreciate why espresso was so popular. "You have a house close by, so why do you live in a trailer?"

He sat at the kitchen table opposite her. "My house is up for sale. Living in the trailer gives my agent the freedom to show clients the house whenever she wishes." He sipped his coffee. "That day you came to my door to ask about Monsieur Bouchard I was packing some of my personal items to bring here."

"Speaking of Monsieur Bouchard, has he returned home yet?"

"No." He paused. "It is not like him to leave without a word. I will be at my house later today. I will check to see if he has returned."

Dottie nodded. She glanced around. "Your trailer is luxurious."

He raised his eyebrows. "You are surprised." He placed his coffee cup on the coffee table in front of him and looked at Dottie. "Spending weeks away from home, a man must have his comforts. Don't you agree?"

Dottie's grip on the cup tightened. Although she wore light clothing, the room felt too warm suddenly. A brisk rap on the trailer door brought Hans to his feet. He looked at Dottie. "Excuse me for a moment." The door rattled open, and a woman's voice called out, "We'll be ready for the shoot in ten minutes, Mr. Van Gogh."

"Thank you."

He returned to the kitchen. Pouring himself another coffee, he waved the pot at Dottie, who shook her head. "Now, where was I?" he began, settling back in his chair. "Ah, yes, the joys of living on the road." He sipped his espresso. "I like the freedom, but I miss home-cooked meals."

Until he mentioned home-cooked meals, it hadn't occurred to Dottie that Hans might be married. Somehow, he didn't strike her as the marrying kind.

As though reading her thoughts, he added, "My sister is an excellent cook."

"Your sister?"

"She makes the very best *Hollandse hazenpeper met kruidkoek.*"

"What's that?"

"Dutch hare stew. When her husband died a few years ago, she moved in with me. I have a house in Amsterdam. We have a—mostly—satisfactory arrangement. She does the cooking and housework, for which she receives a generous allowance, and I pay all the bills."

It sounded rather Victorian to Dottie. "What are you filming?"

"It is a documentary. Have you heard of Boris Romanoff, the Russian author?"

"He defected from the USSR years ago, didn't he?"

"In the 1950s. He lives here in St. Siffret."

Dottie recalled the old man with the walking stick sitting on the bench. "But why start so early in the morning? Why not film at a decent hour?"

"It was the only way we could get Mr. Romanoff to agree. He is a bit of a recluse."

"I understand, but a warning would have helped."

Hans nodded. "You are right, and I apologize, Dottie." His voice dropped almost to a whisper. "Let me take you out for dinner tomorrow evening. I know this delightful little restaurant on a hilltop not far from here. The food is superb. It has a terrace overlooking the vineyards, and if we get there early, we can catch the sunset."

A surge of excitement ran through her. "It sounds very appealing. Is it casual or upscale?"

He reached for her hand, his blue eyes piercing her. "It is a place where lovers meet."

Chapter 10

Dottie made her way back to *Maison Francais* in a daze. She could still feel cool fingers circling her wrist and soft breathing in her ear. "Until tomorrow, my dear," Hans had whispered.

"Where on earth have you been?" demanded Mabel as Dottie walked in.

"Out."

"Well, I know you've been out! That racket in the square woke me, and I checked your room. As you weren't there, I decided to make breakfast, but that was half an hour ago." She peered into Dottie's face. "You look a bit dazed. What's wrong? I hope you aren't coming down with some foreign disease."

Dottie smiled. "Nothing's wrong." She patted Mabel's arm. "I'll tell you about it over breakfast. Come on; let's eat. I'm hungry."

The little table on the balcony was set with a red-checked tablecloth, matching napkins, and white china. Fresh raspberries with thick cream, assorted cheeses, and croissants greeted Dottie as she sat. "This looks so good."

"So, tell me," Mabel urged as she poured coffee. "Where did you go?"

Dottie closed her eyes as she bit into a flaky croissant. "Mmm."

"Well?"

"I had coffee with Hans Van Gogh."

"Hans Van Gogh! Isn't he the fellow who lives next door to Monsieur Bouchard?"

"That's right." Between sips of coffee, Dottie explained what happened and how she came to be invited into the trailer.

"You took a chance. What if he'd tried to seduce you?"

Dottie flipped her hand. "It was nothing like that. He just wanted to explain why he was filming so early in the morning and to apologize for the noise."

"Hmm."

"What's that supposed to mean?"

"It sounds suspicious to me. Besides, I seem to recall that you weren't very impressed when you met him the other day. You called him an arrogant creep."

"Yes, well, he was very polite this morning." She lifted the carafe. What had Hans said about the restaurant? 'It's a place where lovers meet.' Was that just a throwaway line or a gentle hint...?

"Dottie, you're spilling the coffee!"

Putting down the carafe, Dottie blotted the spilled coffee with a napkin. "Just as well the tablecloth's plastic."

"You were miles away."

"Was I?" Dottie replied, concentrating on the spill.

"I think you're smitten with Hans Van Gogh."

Dottie glared at her friend. "All I did was have coffee with him! Your imagination is working overtime, as usual."

A mischievous grin crossed Mabel's face. "What's that line from *Macbeth*? 'Methinks the lady doth protest too much' or something like that."

The idea of Mabel, who read cheap thrillers and romances, quoting Shakespeare made Dottie smile. "OK.

I'll admit I find him attractive." She piled her dish with raspberries and added a small blob of cream. "He's invited me to dinner tomorrow evening."

Mabel was about to place a large spoonful of cream in her mouth. Hand frozen in midair, she exclaimed, "I knew it! Where's he taking you?"

"I don't know." Dottie squirmed. She wasn't about to tell Mabel what Hans had said about the place. "I'm sure it will be somewhere—nice."

"Nice? That sounds like little old ladies dining out on a beef and two veg special. I daresay it will be a place where you'll dine by candlelight, and waiters will hover over you..."

"OK, Mabel, that's enough. Let's clear the table and get on with our day."

It didn't take them long to do the dishes. Mabel dried her hands. "Well, now that's done, I think we should decide whether to drive to Arles or Orange. Any preference?"

"Before we make any plans, let's phone Tom."

"Good idea." Mabel rooted in her handbag and produced a dilapidated address book with pages sticking out of it. How can she find anything in there, Dottie wondered, as her friend leafed through the dog-eared sheets.

Mabel gave a triumphant cry. "Got it!"

They made their way to the phone booth. Staring at the broken window and battered door, Dottie was reminded of the frustrating phone calls she'd made here, mostly to Lieutenant Piaf. Mabel held the door open as Dottie made the call. After several rings, an impersonal voice said that the person at this number was away from the phone, but a message could be left. Dottie looked at Mabel. "No answer. Should we leave a message?"

"I don't see the point."

Dottie hung up the phone. "You're right. The whole idea of phoning was to ask Tom if anyone else has a key to the house and to see how he responded."

"We don't have a cell phone, so he can't call back," Mabel said. "We can try again before we leave for Italy." Glancing at her watch, she drew in a deep breath. "It's just as well Tom wasn't there."

"Why?"

"It's about four a.m. in Quebec."

"Shoot, I forgot about the time difference."

"Let's drive to Arles," Mabel said. "It's market day. Think of all the fresh vegetables and cheeses we can buy!"

Dottie linked arms with her friend. "That's the best idea you've come up with since we've been here."

On their way out the door, Mabel grabbed the straw basket hanging behind the door. "I read somewhere that you should always take a straw basket to the open-air markets in Provence."

"I've got our sun hats. Let's go."

***

After finding a parking space, they headed toward the market along narrow streets filled with restaurants. Outdoor cafes, shaded with awnings or umbrellas, were already packed with people.

They could hear the vendors' cries as they neared the market. As they turned in to the street, they breathed in the intoxicating fragrance of lavender. The colors, noisy chatter, and earthy smells surrounded them, as they moved through the crowded stalls. They feasted their eyes on row after row of fruits, vegetables, cheeses, meats, clothing, fabric, and livestock that stretched down the street, and as they would discover, around the corner.

Vendors, mostly local farmers, handed out free samples of cheese and freshly picked plump tomatoes. One man had attracted a small crowd by demonstrating the cutting ability of a special knife he was selling. An artistic arrangement of onions and sweet peas, seedless melons, lemons piled high next to deep purple plums and green peppers was displayed next to a counter that sold colorful sun hats.

Dottie noticed a lineup of people waiting to buy straw baskets. "I'm pleased you brought our basket, Mabel," she said. "It's obviously the thing to do."

The two women walked quickly past rabbits and chickens in small cages. They reached a souvenir stall and couldn't resist buying aprons and tea towels in Provençal colors of periwinkle and deep yellow as gifts for family and friends.

By the time they stopped for lunch at a tiny outdoor café on the outskirts of the market, their basket overflowed with peppers, tomatoes, ripe strawberries, and an assortment of cheeses. Three bottles of a local red wine filled the string bag Dottie always carried with her.

They passed a pottery shop on their way back to the car. Dottie's eyes fell on an earthenware wine jug displayed in the window. The brown glazed jug, decorated with two leaf motifs, was round with a short, narrow neck. It would look perfect on her windowsill in the conservatory filled with dried grasses. Inside the shop, she bought a jug similar to the one in the window, except this one had three leaf motifs instead of two.

***

They stopped at the *carrefour* for a baguette and crackers to go with the cheese, along with some frozen canapés. "We'll have the canapés before dinner with a glass of wine," Mabel said. "They won't take long to heat up."

"We might as well climb to the terrace on the third floor. We can watch the sunset while we enjoy our snack."

"I can't wait. Today was fun, but with the heat and crowds of people, I'm whacked."

As they drove up the winding cobblestoned street to the square, Dottie spotted Pierre's car parked near the top of the hill. They turned the corner to find Pierre and Yvette sitting on the steps of *Maison Francais.*

Pierre stood, as Dottie climbed out of the car. "We wanted to see you before it's too late."

Dottie frowned. "Too late for what?"

"We know you leave for Tuscany soon, and we might be going out of town in the next day or so. We'd like to invite you for a drink."

"It's our turn to invite you," Dottie said. "Are you free this evening?"

Pierre frowned. "It seems an imposition. You've only just got home."

"Nonsense! We've picked up some interesting cheeses at the Arles market and wine. Shall we say around seven?"

After helping Yvette to her feet, Pierre turned to the two women. "Thank you." He flashed a warm smile. "We'll see you later."

Mabel carried the basket into the kitchen. "I thought we'd planned a quiet evening," she grumbled, unpacking the vegetables and cheeses, "and here you invite people for drinks."

Dottie removed a bottle of white wine from the string bag and placed it in the fridge. "I have an ulterior motive."

"Oh?"

"Didn't you think it was strange they were waiting for us when we got home? They could have left a note. And

Pierre made an odd remark when he said something about catching us before it's too late."

Mabel's eyes lit up. "By inviting them for drinks, maybe we'll find out if something's going on. Good thinking, Dottie. We'd better get organized."

***

Their guests arrived on the stroke of seven. Yvette looked stunning in a simple black linen dress and high-heeled bronze sandals, but the pendant, a copper snake dangling from a long chain, caught Dottie's attention. The snake's green eyes glittered in the evening light. Pierre took Dottie's hands, kissing her lightly on each cheek. "You look *très élégante*," he remarked.

Yvette agreed. "That color really suits you."

Dottie smiled. "Thank you." The teal pantsuit was one of her favorites. The fabric was a soft silk-like fabric that flowed as she walked. "Mabel's busy in the kitchen," Dottie said. "Let's have some wine."

An assortment of wines, cheeses, and pâtés were set out on the dining room table. Pierre examined the bottles. "I see you have a Pinot Noir. Very nice."

"I'm glad you like it."

"Why don't I do the honors?"

"Don't pour red wine for Mabel. She prefers white."

Right on cue, Mabel appeared, carrying a tray of delicious-smelling canapés. "Sorry about the delay. I had a problem with the oven." She waved the tray under their noses. "Try one!"

As Pierre poured the drinks, Yvette's blood red fingernails curled around a shrimp canapé, which she popped in her mouth. "Divine!" she murmured and gave the two women a dazzling smile. "It is so sweet of you to invite us."

Dottie chose one with a spinach stuffing. "I'm glad we had a chance to see you before we leave."

"Where are you staying in Tuscany?"

Dottie explained about the farm. "The nearest town is Pescia."

"We know that area well," Pierre said.

"Many of those farms are far away from the tourist areas," Yvette cried. "The roads—they climb high. They wind and wind. There are not many fences. You can fall off the edge."

"Not all the roads are like that," Pierre admonished. "I'm sure Dottie and Mabel know what they're doing."

"I 'ave an idea." Yvette's throaty voice commanded attention. They all turned to look at her. "We 'ave a friend, Antonio Morelli, who lives in a villa near Lucca. It 'as a pool 'ouse, which 'e sometimes gives to *ses amis*. Antonio and his family do not swim, so you 'ave the pool by yourselves. I will phone 'im tonight." Yvette turned to Pierre. "It is good, *n'est-ce pas?*"

Pierre's fingers tightened around his wineglass. "I'm not so sure."

"Nonsense, *cherie*." Yvette kissed him lightly on the cheek. "It is very comfortable in the pool 'ouse."

"Please, don't concern yourselves," Mabel said, "because we can't possibly accept. Tom's friends are expecting us."

An image of Mabel negotiating hairpin bends in the dark made Dottie shudder. "All we have to do is phone them, Mabel. I'm sure they'll understand."

Yvette flung out her arms in a dramatic gesture. "The pool 'ouse, it is perfect for you!"

Pierre's dark eyes flashed.

"What if Mr. Morelli says no?" Dottie asked, feeling a bit uncomfortable. "It's very short notice, and he might not appreciate having two strangers living on his property."

"'e is a good friend. 'e likes to help." Yvette cocked her head. "Can you do one little favor?"

"Of course."

"It is Antonio's birthday next week. We 'ope to go to Tuscany for the celebration, but we might miss the party. Would you please take our gift...?"

Pierre's sharp voice cut in. "Yvette, I need to speak with you!" He glanced at Dottie. "Please, excuse us for a moment." He took Yvette by the arm and guided her into the kitchen.

Mabel turned on Dottie. "What's got into you, Dottie Flowers? We already have a place to stay in Italy, and here you are arranging to stay with this Morelli chap. You can see that Pierre isn't fussy about it."

"I don't like the sound of those hairpin bends," Dottie said, "and it would be great to have a swimming pool."

"You can't swim."

Mabel was right, of course. Dottie had taken lessons over the years but never managed to overcome her fear of water. "I can swim a bit as long as I stay in the shallow end. Anyway, you love water, and you'd make good use of it."

"A pool sounds appealing, I must admit, but we can't let Tom's friends down."

"Tom told us they are very laid back about everything. If we explain we've decided to stay closer to Lucca, I'm sure they'll understand."

Pierre and Yvette returned to the living room. "I apologize, but I'm afraid we must leave." He headed for the front door. As Pierre passed the fireplace, he stopped in front of the wine jug Dottie had placed on the hearth. "May I ask where you purchased the earthenware jug?"

"In Arles."

He got down on his haunches to look more closely. "At the market?"

"In a small pottery shop close to the market. They had several designs."

"I see. I particularly like this leaf motif." He looked up at Dottie. "Were there any more like this?"

"There was another one in the window."

"You have good taste." Pierre stood and looked at Dottie. "I suggest you move it away from the hearth. It could be knocked over."

"You're right. I'll put it in the bedroom, inside my suitcase. It'll be safe there."

Pierre and Yvette bid them good night. As she followed Pierre out of the house, Yvette paused to whisper in Dottie's ear. "Don't worry. I will arrange things with Antonio and bring the gift to your house tomorrow morning. Pierre is a bit—what is the word?—*stuffed*—*stuffy*, sometimes."

Or maybe Pierre has other reasons for not wanting us to stay there, Dottie thought. Who is this Antonio Morelli? Why is Yvette so keen for us to stay with him? Picking up the jug, she took it upstairs to her room.

Chapter 11

Golden light bathed the tiny stone kitchen as the women prepared breakfast the next morning. A sliced baguette, with assorted cheeses left over from the previous evening, was set on the tray ready to be carried outside. "So, what do you think?" Dottie asked, as she spooned coffee into the French press.

Mabel, busily hulling strawberries, looked distracted. "About what?"

"Mabel! Haven't you listened to a word I've said? Are we going to stick with the original plan and stay at the farm or stay in the pool house? Yvette will be here soon, and she'll need to know our decision, assuming she spoke with Mr. Morelli last night."

"And assuming he said yes."

"Of course."

Mabel continued to hull. "I think we should stay at the pool house."

"You're sure about that? Last night, you were adamant that we should go to the farm."

"I've changed my mind."

"Mabel Scattergood, I know you too well. There's something you're not telling me."

Placing the knife carefully on the counter, Mabel pushed her winged glasses back to the bridge of her nose. "We can't go to the farm, even if we wanted to." She looked up, a guilty expression on her face. "I can't find the address or phone number. I could have sworn it was in the zippered pocket of my handbag."

Dottie opened her mouth to say something, and then thought better of it. "Let's hope Yvette managed to get in touch with Mr. Morelli last night."

When the doorbell rang, Dottie headed to the door. Yvette stood on the doorstep, a parcel decorated with red bows in her arms. "Good morning, Dottie. I cannot come in as I work early today." She smiled. "I make arrangements with Antonio for you to stay in the pool 'ouse."

Dottie breathed an inward sigh of relief. "Thank you. We've already talked it over and decided to accept."

"Excellent!" Yvette held out an envelope. "Inside, you find the directions, the address, and the phone number, also a road map of Italy. Pierre 'as marked the best route for you."

How would Yvette have responded if they'd declined the offer, Dottie wondered. "So, Pierre isn't...?" She paused. "Pierre doesn't mind our staying with Mr. Morelli?"

Yvette looked at Dottie coquettishly. "Sometime, 'e needs to be persuaded." *And I daresay you know how to do that*, Dottie thought.

Yvette placed the parcel in Dottie's outstretched arms. "'ere is the gift for Antonio. Pierre and I leave for St. Tropez this afternoon." Her eyes sparkled. "We 'ave friends who give their 'ouse while they are away. We stay for four days."

"Sounds great. Have a wonderful time."

"*Merci*. We 'ope to see you at the villa next week." Yvette ran down the steps and climbed into the Peugeot beside Pierre. Waving, he revved the engine, and the car pulled away.

Dottie closed the front door and set the parcel on the dining room table. "Yvette's arranged for us to stay in Antonio Morelli's pool house."

Mabel whooshed a sigh of relief. "Good!" She glanced at the parcel. "So, that's the gift for Mr. Morelli. I like the red ribbons."

Dottie's mind was on other things. "The first thing we have to do is let our families know our change of address and phone number. I'll phone Hettie. She's easier to get hold of than Jeremy is. Let's walk to the phone booth now and get it over with."

"I'll phone Yolanda," Mabel said. "I don't know how I'd manage without that niece of mine. And Arnold dotes on her. She's got him wrapped around her little finger."

Dottie sighed inwardly, thinking back to last summer. When she'd realized that her friend Arnold was smitten with Yolanda, Dottie had advised him how to win the heart of his beloved. He'd persevered, and they married in the fall. Within weeks of their marriage, Yolanda became pregnant. Now, Dottie wondered if she'd made a mistake by encouraging him to get involved with the bossy, know-it-all Yolanda.

After breakfast, they walked to the phone box next to the bar. Dottie left a message on her daughter's answering machine. She tried Jeremy and, to her surprise, he answered. Mabel phoned Yolanda next. From her monosyllabic responses, Dottie surmised that Yolanda was probably talking about babies and wouldn't let her aunt get a word in edgewise. Finally, Mabel interrupted and gave her the new address and phone number.

"Yolanda does go on sometimes," Mabel sighed, as she hung up the phone.

"Baby talk?"

"Yes, she's trying to persuade Arnold to take her away for a holiday before the baby arrives but isn't having much success."

When they got back to the house, Dottie turned her thoughts to the upcoming dinner date with Hans. Since waking up, she'd been in turmoil about what to wear. Black was safe, of course, but boring. She wanted to be exotic, exciting, alluring. Her teal blue outfit might work, but it was full length with a high collar and long sleeves. It had been perfect for dinner with Yvette and Pierre, but not for a date with Hans.

Dottie hunted through the wardrobe. As she rooted through slacks, skirts, and fancy tops, her fingers touched a silk dress. Removing it carefully from its hanger, she held the dress to her body, smoothing its soft folds with her hands. The dress was a rich shade of copper with gold thread running through it. After stripping down to her bra and panties, she slipped it on and looked at herself in the mirror behind the door.

The swirls of silk accentuated her slim hips, while camouflaging the spare tire around her waist that no amount of exercise would eliminate. Midcalf length, the dress was split on one side from hemline to thigh and revealed her legs as she walked. She'd bought a pair of high-heeled bronze sandals from Holts, just before leaving Canada. Those, with her amber jewelry, would accessorize the dress to perfection. Satisfied, she took off the dress and laid it on the bed.

Hair was a problem. Normally, her auburn hair—courtesy of Monique, her stylist—was long, but because of split ends, she'd had a drastic haircut shortly before the trip. It was long enough to wear in a bun, the style she preferred for work, but too short for a dramatic effect when worn down over her shoulders.

Monique had insisted that she needed a human hair extension. "They are all the rage, *mon amie*. You must take one with you to Europe. You might meet the man of your dreams, and men like long, shiny hair." Dottie removed the hair extension from the dresser. Monique had demonstrated how to wear it, assuring her it was easy to attach. Dottie wished she had Monique's confidence. She sighed. Never mind, as long as she allowed enough time to get ready, it should all work.

The two women drove to Uzès and spent a delightful morning exploring the tree-lined streets. Dottie, her camera slung around her neck, found plenty of opportunities to take pictures: a small boy, his face covered in chocolate ice cream; geraniums tumbling out of a window box; a red bird perched on a wrought-iron railing. They drank espresso in a local café, watched by stray dogs that wandered in and out looking for food scraps. In the town square, Mabel lined up for slices of thin-crust pizza while Dottie searched for somewhere to sit. She found two empty chairs at a table with an umbrella. While she waited for Mabel, Dottie watched people as they milled around enjoying the balmy air.

They spent the afternoon sunbathing on the top balcony of *Maison Francais*. Mabel smoothed suntan oil over her face, arms, and legs. Cautious about the dangers of skin cancer, Dottie smothered herself with sunblock. She looked beyond the adobe roofs of the little houses. Olive groves and rows of grapevines dotted the landscape, broken occasionally by fields of poppies. A light breeze offered welcome relief from the sun that blazed in an azure sky.

"This is paradise," Mabel declared, taking a few sips of mineral water.

Dottie stretched on the chaise lounge, a large hat shading her face. "Mmm," She dozed off, dreaming of Hans.

***

After a luxurious bath in perfumed oils, Dottie put on black lacy underwear, applied makeup with extra care, and spent a frustrating ten minutes trying to attach the hair extension. She finally got the hang of it. She slipped on her dress, sandals, and jewelry. Dare she put on those contact lenses she bought a while ago that changed her eyes from dark brown to green? She wore clear contact lenses for social events and weekends, but she had never plucked up the courage to wear colored ones.

She checked her watch. Hans would be here in fifteen minutes. Hadn't she read in a magazine that men found women with green eyes very sensuous? She removed the lens case from her purse, and using her index finger, popped in the lenses. A look in the mirror assured her that the green was perfect with the copper dress and amber jewelry.

She waltzed down the stairs.

"You look different," Mabel said.

"Different?"

"Well, you know, younger. You look fantastic, Dottie." A car horn honked. "I think he's here." Mabel rushed to the window, craning her neck to look.

"Already?"

"A man wearing a navy blazer and driving an open-top sports car has just pulled up. He's climbing out of the car."

"Darn, I forgot my evening bag." Dottie rushed up the stairs.

"Don't be long. He's heading to the house."

***

A fancy sports car, a handsome man at her side, the wind in her hair—what more could a woman ask for? Well, she could have done without the wind. It lifted her hair and flung strands in her face, as Hans maneuvered the car up a curving mountain road. She wouldn't have minded—in fact, she would have enjoyed the experience—if she hadn't been afraid of losing the hair extension. To make matters worse, dust flew in her eyes, causing them to sting.

They finally arrived at the restaurant. As Hans helped her out of the car, he squeezed her hand. His hazel eyes locked on hers. "You look exquisite, Dottie. The dress complements your green eyes. You will make all the women in the restaurant jealous."

Green! Why did he have to say green? Her eyes felt gritty, and they began to water. She blinked a few times, which didn't help.

"Here, take this." He produced a snow-white handkerchief from his blazer pocket.

She accepted it gratefully. "Thanks." She dabbed carefully, hoping the mascara she wore was as waterproof as the manufacturers claimed.

He guided her toward a flight of wooden steps. Blinded by tears, she gripped the railing and followed Hans. They'd almost reached the top of the stairs when Dottie's heel caught between two wooden slats. As she struggled to release the heel, it snapped off. The force flung Dottie backward. Her hair caught on something, then suddenly released. She slid down the stairs, headfirst, landing on all fours in the dust.

Chapter 12

Hans crouched by her side, his face creased with worry. "Are you all right?"

"I'm not sure." Dottie didn't think any bones were broken. In fact, she felt surprisingly pain-free, except for her eyes, which were on fire. The sexy slit in her dress, on the other hand, was now a gaping hole. She patted her head. At least, her hair was in one piece—or was it? Her fingers searched for the hair extension, but it was gone. Had it blown away as they'd driven to the restaurant?

Hans helped her to her feet. "I think I had better take you home." A smile played on his lips. "Or maybe I will take you to my trailer for a brandy."

Dottie managed to smile back. "A brandy sounds like a better idea."

Out of the corner of her eye, she saw strands of auburn hair dangling from the stair rail. The hair extension! It must have caught on the wrought iron as she fell. As far as Dottie was concerned, it could stay there.

***

As soon as they entered the trailer, Hans switched on the CD player. The voice of Andrea Bocelli filled the living room with its seductive charm.

"I have some Harry Connick CDs, if you prefer."

"Oh, no, this is perfect." *Except for my eyes*, she thought.

"I am going to turn the oven on. I will be right back."

Hans returned to the living room. Settled on the leather sofa, Dottie watched him pour two generous measures of brandy into crystal snifters. He handed one to her. "Well, Dottie, it has been an interesting evening so far."

She sipped the golden liquid. "That's one way of putting it."

"He looked at her curiously, looked away for a few seconds, and turned back.

"What's wrong?" Dottie asked.

"Your eyes. One is green, the other brown."

Dottie's face heated. "Would you excuse me for a moment?"

"Of course. The bathroom is over there," he said, pointing to a door next to the bedroom.

Why did I ever decide to wear colored lenses, Dottie wondered. She picked up her purse and escaped to the bathroom. As she suspected, one lens had slipped under her lid. She removed both lenses and returned to the living room.

"Are you all right?" Hans asked.

"I'm fine."

"You probably dislodged the lens when you fell down the steps." Laughing, he sat down next to her. "I have never had a woman fall at my feet in such a dramatic fashion."

"Don't let it go to your head. Men usually fall at **my** feet." *Oh, dear,* thought Dottie, *did I really say that? Here I am, my eyes red-rimmed and my hair like a crow's nest, giving Hans Van Gogh the impression I'm a femme fatale!* She suppressed the urge to giggle.

"I am sure they do." His voice dropped to almost a whisper. "You are a very attractive woman." Placing his brandy glass on the coffee table, he leaned forward and grazed her cheek with his lips. "Such soft skin," he crooned, "and mysterious dark eyes..."

Dottie felt heat rush through her body. Unfortunately, it wasn't because of Hans's sexy voice. It was the beginning of a hot flash.

A beeper went off in the kitchen. Hans drew away, a frown on his face. "Terrible timing!" He kissed the top of her head.

Dottie picked up a magazine to fan herself. By the time he came back a few minutes later, her temperature had returned to normal. Hans placed a tray on the coffee table. "I don't know about you, but I'm feeling rather hungry. We will start with these. The hot canapés will be ready soon."

As her eyes feasted on Roquefort cheese, rolls of smoked salmon stuffed with cream cheese, and raw oysters, her stomach started to rumble. "This looks delicious." The tray had been prepared in advance, she realized. Inviting her to his trailer for a brandy had not been spontaneous, as she'd first thought.

Hans tipped his brandy glass. "To a beautiful night," he whispered, his blue eyes piercing hers.

Dottie's voice went up an octave. "Night?"

His cool fingers caressed her arm. "You are not in a hurry to go home, are you, Dottie?"

"Well, no..."

"That is good. Now, let me serve you some fresh oysters."

Lifting a shell to her lips, she tipped the oyster down her throat, savoring its distinctive flavor. "It's been a while since I've eaten raw oysters. I'd forgotten how good they are."

"You are a woman after my own heart," he whispered. "Did you know that raw oysters are an aphrodisiac?"

Dottie could feel heat creeping through her veins, but it wasn't a hot flash this time. She took a big gulp of brandy.

A timer pinged. "One moment." Hans retrieved the canapés from the oven and arranged them on a plate. "Try one of these," he said, offering the plate to her. "They are from a little bakery in Uzès."

Thankful for the distraction, Dottie took one. The warm flaky pastry with a rich crabmeat filling melted in her mouth. "I hope the food's this good in Tuscany."

"When do you go?"

"At the weekend." She told him about their decision to stay near Lucca. "It will be much more convenient."

"I know Lucca well. It is an old walled city. You will love it."

"I'm sure we will." Dottie finished her brandy. "Anyway, enough about my plans. I want to hear about you. Do you travel a lot?"

"Too much." He talked about journeys to Africa, Asia, and Australia. "Lately, I have been filming in Thailand." He took a stuffed mushroom and popped it in his mouth.

Dottie remembered a television series about a young woman being arrested and thrown into prison in Bangkok. She'd been tricked into carrying heroin in her luggage. "Have you ever seen anyone caught trying to smuggle drugs?"

Hans began to cough. He took a large sip of brandy. "Sorry about that. Piece of that mushroom filling must have gone the wrong way," he said, dabbing his mouth with a napkin. "Now, what were you saying?"

Dottie repeated the question.

"No, I have not seen anyone caught, but I hear about them. In fact, last year, someone I knew from university days was caught trying to smuggle cocaine into Brazil."

"What happened to him?"

"Her. It was a woman. She is languishing in prison, waiting for a trial."

Dottie thought about the parcel Yvette had given to her earlier that day. Her stomach tightened. What if it wasn't a birthday gift at all, but a container filled with heroin or other illegal drug?

"Dottie?"

"What?"

"You were miles away." He pointed to the brandy bottle. "Want some more, or can I tempt you with a glass of Chardonnay?"

"No, thanks, but that coffee smells good."

"It is a special blend of Brazilian coffee. I think you will like it. Help yourself to some Belgian chocolate while I pour us both a cup." Hans walked to the kitchen.

Dottie selected a smooth dark chocolate. As the delicacy melted in her mouth, she lay back on soft leather cushions and closed her eyes. The evening, which started as a disaster, had turned out well. She smiled to herself, feeling a bit like—what was that saying of Mabel's?—'The cat that got the cream.' All this pampering could go to a woman's head.

A loud rapping on the trailer door jolted Dottie out of her reverie. A draft of cool air blew into the trailer, and the door slammed shut.

A husky female voice cried out, "My dear Hans!"

"Wilhelmina, what are you doing here!"

The voice snapped back. "I come a long way to see you, and all you say is 'what are you doing here?'"

"I have told you not to drop in on me like this!"

"Oh, don't make such a fuss. Pour me a drink, will you? It's been a long day. I'll have the usual, but no soda water this time."

Dottie had heard enough. Grabbing her shoes and handbag, she tiptoed to the back door. She opened it slowly to lessen the chance of squeaks. Raised voices could be heard from the trailer as Dottie crept barefoot along the gravel path to the square. Was the unexpected visitor Hans's ex-wife or ex-girlfriend—or worse, the woman currently in his life? Whoever she was, Dottie didn't want to be involved.

Chapter 13

Praying Mabel was asleep, Dottie slipped into the house, wiped her feet on the doormat, and crept upstairs. She'd just reached the bedroom door when Mabel called out. "Is that you, Dottie?"

Who in the heck does she think it is? "Yes, it's me."

Mabel, her hair in pink rollers, opened her bedroom door. "Well, how did it go?"

"I'd rather not talk about it."

"Oh, dear! Let me make you some chamomile tea. You look as though you... what on earth happened to your dress?"

Dottie sighed with exasperation. "Make the tea, and I'll tell you."

Curled up in an armchair in the living room, Dottie sipped her tea and gave Mabel a brief outline of the night's events. Mabel chuckled. "Getting the hair extension caught on a nail reminds me. Did I ever tell you the story of my Aunt Matilda and her false teeth?"

"Yes, several times." Dottie wasn't in the mood to listen to one of Mabel's stories.

She stretched out her arms and yawned. "I'm bushed. I think I'll go to bed."

"Poor Dottie." Mabel drained her teacup. "I wonder who Hans Van Gogh's fancy woman is."

"Who knows? She obviously didn't tell him she was coming."

"By the way, I popped into your room to close the window. It looked like rain," Mabel said. "I noticed the parcel on the dresser. I wonder what's in it. It's quite heavy."

Dottie stood. "A book, I expect."

As she undressed for bed, Dottie stared at the parcel. What if the police stopped them for a routine check and found drugs inside? She shuddered, remembering what happened to Hans' friend.

There was no point in worrying about it now. What she needed more than anything was a good night's sleep. She crawled into bed. They would open the parcel tomorrow.

**

Dottie knew something was wrong when she stuck her head out of the bedroom window next morning. Hans Van Gogh stood in the square, surrounded by his film crew. She couldn't catch what he was saying, but the crew stood in silence, and most had extinguished their cigarettes.

Dottie dressed quickly. Her feet were tender after walking on gravel the previous night, so she eased her way down the stairs.

She found Mabel in the kitchen, making coffee.

"Something's going on in the square, Mabel. Hans is talking to his crew. Judging by their serious expressions, it must be bad news."

The women craned their necks through the kitchen window to see what was happening. The crew was moving cameras and other film paraphernalia into waiting vans. "I thought they were filming here until the end of this week," Mabel said. "It looks like it's over."

"I don't suppose we'll ever find out."

"Unless you ask Hans."

Dottie shook her head. "No way. I'm going to keep a low profile until we leave."

"Suit yourself. Why don't you set the table on the balcony for breakfast? I'll follow as soon as coffee is ready."

Dottie, glad of the distraction, busied herself with the tablecloth and cutlery. The bright morning sun promised another glorious Provençal summer day. They intended to drive to Nîmes after breakfast and spend the day sightseeing.

Later, they'd planned a quiet dinner on the top terrace, watch the sunset, and be entertained by the swallows dipping back and forth in the square.

A hammering on the front door interrupted Dottie's musings. She heard the clatter of Mabel's shoes on the stone floor and the click of the latch as the door opened. Straining to hear who was visiting so early, she made out a man's voice.

Mabel called out, "Do come in!"

Peering through the French door, Dottie saw to her consternation that their visitor was Hans. Khaki shorts and shirt complemented his tanned skin and white hair. His eyes locked on Dottie's, then glanced away when she glared at him.

After trying to decide if she should ignore him, curiosity got the better of her. She opened the door and stepped into the living room.

"Good morning, Dottie," Hans began. "I was just telling Mrs. Scattergood..."

"Mabel, please."

He smiled. "I was explaining to Mabel that we will not be filming here anymore. Boris Romanoff died during the night."

Dottie drew in a sharp intake of breath. "I'm sorry."

"It has been a shock to everyone." Hans paused for a moment. "We had become rather attached to the old gentleman."

"Does this mean all your work here is wasted?" Dottie asked.

"No, I had hoped to get more of Mr. Romanoff's insights on how literature has changed over the years, but I think we have enough footage."

"I've just made coffee," Mabel said. "Would you like some?"

"Thank you."

As soon as Mabel headed for the kitchen, Hans turned to Dottie. "Why did you leave in such a hurry last night?" Dottie felt her face burn. "When I realized you had gone, I searched for you. I peeked through your living room window so I knew you were safe." Hans cleared his throat. "It was a pity you left. I wanted to introduce you to my sister."

"Your sister?"

"Wilhelmina prefers to make surprise visits. I try to discourage her, but she is very strong-willed." Dottie couldn't think of an appropriate response. After an awkward pause, Hans spoke. "I will be starting my next documentary soon. It is about the master chefs of Tuscany."

Dottie was relieved to move on to another subject. "With the popularity of Italian food, that sounds like a great idea."

"We will begin to film earlier than planned because of Boris Romanoff's death."

"Where?"

"We are concentrating on four Tuscan cities." He smiled. "The first is Lucca."

"That's where we're going."

"I know." He handed her a business card. "This has my cell phone number. May I have your phone number and the address where you are staying?"

Dottie found the information in her wallet. After jotting down the details on a Post-it note, she handed the yellow square to Hans. As he read it over, his face paled. "Who recommended this villa to you?"

She paused. How much should she tell him? "Friends of ours. They rave about the place." She looked at him. "Is something wrong?"

"Not at all." He cleared his throat. "It can be very hot in Tuscany this time of the year. Having a swimming pool all to yourselves will be a bonus."

"Yes."

"I would like to take you out for dinner one evening to my favorite restaurant." He took her hand. "This time, we will make it inside; I promise."

After Hans left, she wondered why he'd been upset when he saw the villa address. When she'd challenged him, he denied anything was wrong. How did he know that she and Mabel would not only have a swimming pool, but also that they would have the pool to themselves?

Dottie blew out a long breath. She pushed all unsettling thoughts to the back of her mind, determined to enjoy the last few days in Provence.

Chapter 14

After a tour of the Nîmes amphitheater, the two women stopped for lemonade at an outdoor café. Wincing with pain, Mabel removed her sandals. "I think I've developed blisters."

"I'm not surprised. You should have taken my advice and bought Mephistos."

Adjusting the winged sunglasses that had slipped to the end of her nose, Mabel retorted, "I refuse to pay such an exorbitant price for footwear."

Dottie clenched her teeth. What was the point? Mabel wouldn't dream of paying for a good pair of shoes, even though cheap ones hurt her feet.

The waiter brought two large glasses of lemonade. Mabel settled back in the chair and sipped the cold drink. She gazed at the majestic Roman structure towering before them. "I can't get over how well preserved this amphitheater is. It's difficult to imagine it was built more than two thousand years ago."

Dottie shuddered. "Think of all those blood-thirsty people who cheered as the poor victims were torn to pieces by wild animals."

"These days, people flock to bullfights, circuses, and concerts instead," Mabel commented. "Elton John is performing here next month."

"Not during a bullfight, I hope."

"Ha! Ha! Good one, Dottie."

Enjoying the lemonade, Dottie watched people as they strolled along the sidewalk. "I'm glad cars aren't allowed in the old part of Nîmes..."

"There's Monsieur Bouchard!" Mabel cried, pointing to a long flight of steps near the amphitheater. Halfway up the steps, a bearded man in a French beret peered at the monument, hand shading his eyes. Mabel buckled her sandals. "I'm going after him. You pay the bill and follow me!"

Oblivious to glares and rude hand signs, she pushed her way through a group of tourists heading to the amphitheater and ran across the street. Dottie left money on top of the bill and raced after Mabel.

"Are you sure it's Monsieur Bouchard?" Dottie asked, as she caught up.

"I'd recognize him anywhere."

They rushed up the steps. When they reached the top, the two women stopped to catch their breath.

Beads of perspiration dotted Mabel's forehead. "I must go back to the 'Y'."

"And what about the diet you keep threatening to go on?" Dottie teased.

"I'm going on the South Beach Diet as soon as we get home," Mabel huffed. "You'll see!"

Dottie glanced around. "Monsieur Bouchard has disappeared. He must be at the back of the temple."

"We can't lose him now. Come on!" Mabel led the way, with Dottie close on her heels.

"Slow down a bit," Dottie urged. "You're going to knock someone over!"

Her advice came too late. Weaving around surprised tourists, Mabel crashed into her quarry. The man's beret fell to the ground with a pair of sunglasses. "But you're not Monsieur Bouchard!" Mabel exclaimed. The man was probably in his late forties. His narrow face and dark eyes bore no resemblance to their friend.

"Watch where you're going, lady!" the man protested. "I don't know anything about your Monsieur Bourdez or whatever his name is, but you almost knocked me over."

"I'm terribly sorry," Mabel said. "I'm afraid I got a bit carried away."

"That's an understatement!" Retrieving his beret and glasses, he marched away.

Mabel pursed her lips. "It was an accident. You'd think he'd be more understanding."

Noticing a few curious onlookers, Dottie took her friend by the arm. "Let's go."

When they reached the bottom step, Mabel sat. Her hands hung limply between her legs. She looked up at Dottie. "I suppose there's no word about Monsieur Bouchard from Hans?"

"No," Dottie replied. "He's asked the next-door neighbors to let him know when Monsieur Bouchard returns. They're concerned as well, because he never goes away without telling them."

"We're leaving for Italy in a few days' time," Mabel said. "If he doesn't show up before then, how will we find out if he's all right?" Her eyes lit up. "Maybe Yvette and Pierre know where he is."

"We can't ask them. They're in St. Tropez." Dottie chewed her lip. "That reminds me. When we get back, we have to open the parcel."

"Whatever for?"

Dottie explained her concerns. "The chat with Hans the other night made me realize we can't take any chances. If drugs are inside, we could be in serious trouble."

"You're right. We'd better get some wrapping paper. Fortunately, it's plain gold paper, so that will be easy to find. And we'll get extra ribbon, in case we need it."

"We need to find a stationery store." Dottie said. "A stroll around the town will help work up a good appetite for dinner."

"I won't be able to walk far."

"Of course, I forgot about your sore feet."

"We walked past a stationery store this morning. It's close by." Mabel indicated a narrow side street, crammed with shoppers. "There's a pastry shop next to it. We can choose a dessert for tonight. I noticed they have chocolate éclairs."

Dottie smiled to herself. Food was a sure way to get Mabel's mind off unpleasant things. There'd be enough time over dinner to speculate on what might have happened to Monsieur Bouchard.

***

After dinner, Dottie fetched the parcel from her bedroom. "I feel uncomfortable doing this, but we don't want to take any chances."

"I agree, so let's get started."

Dottie removed the wrapping paper. Underneath was a cardboard box sealed with clear tape, which she slit open with a kitchen knife. "Here goes!" She opened the box and pulled out a copy of *The Provencal Countryside*.

She flipped through the pages. Photographs of lavender fields, tiny villages, vineyards, and olive groves filled the book. "This is beautiful. I'm going to buy myself a copy." Putting on her glasses, she removed the jacket and examined the hard cover. Finally, she put it down. "Everything seems to be in place. Now, you look through to make sure."

Mabel held the book by its spine and shook gently. "Maybe there's some kind of hidden message," she explained when Dottie gave her an odd look. Nothing fell out. Satisfied, she returned the book to Dottie. "Well, that's a relief. I'll wrap it again. The paper we found is almost the exact shade of the original. Yvette and Pierre need never know what we've done."

Dottie watched Mabel rewrap the gift. Her fear was unfounded. It was just an innocent birthday gift for a friend.

So, why did she have this uneasy feeling in the pit of her stomach?

***

Over the next few days, they visited Aix-en-Provence and Orange and drove to Avignon again. Wearing her most comfortable shoes and covering the blisters with adhesive bandages, Mabel managed to walk around well. The day before they were due to leave St. Siffret, they spent a few hours strolling around nearby Uzès, picking up a few souvenirs. As they wandered in and out of stores, Dottie looked for a copy of *The Provencal Countryside*. She finally spotted one in a small gift shop. Later, they ate dinner on the upper balcony of their house and celebrated their last evening with a bottle of Châteauneuf-du-Pape.

They packed their suitcases after dinner. "We have to phone Tom and explain why we aren't staying at his friends' farm and give him our Tuscany address and phone number," Dottie said.

"And ask him to let his friends know that we won't be staying with them after all."

"Let's call now and get it out of the way," Dottie said. "We'll leave a message this time, if he doesn't answer. Then, we can take one last walk around the village. It's a bit windy, but we won't have time in the morning. I'll bring my flashlight."

They walked to the phone booth, and Dottie punched in Tom's cell-phone number. Again, she got the answering machine. She explained that they had mislaid the address and phone number of his friends who owned the olive farm and would stay near Lucca instead. She gave all the details. "Please phone us as soon as possible," she said. "We have something important to tell you." Telling Tom that his vacation home was being used as a safe house for smuggled guns and drugs was not something Dottie relished, but it had to be done—or had the police already been in touch with him?

There was something creepy about strolling around the village late at night. The moon was obscured by cloud and many houses were dark, so they used Dottie's flashlight to guide their way. Along the narrow stone streets, the wind swirled dried leaves in the air, while small creatures rustled in flowerpots and ornamental bushes. As they walked past the old church, bats swooped down from the belfry, just missing their heads. Mabel cringed. "Bats give me the shudders. Perhaps this walk wasn't such a good idea after all."

They reached the street where Hans Van Gogh and Monsieur Bouchard's houses stood. Was it Dottie's imagination, or was the street darker than the others they'd walked along? She wasn't keen on walking past Hans's house but wasn't sure why. Maybe she was afraid that another car would be parked by his house, a car belonging to a woman friend perhaps. It could just as easily belong to a male friend, Dottie reminded herself. Besides, Hans had lived in his trailer since he'd put the house up for sale.

The slap of Mabel's crepe-soled shoes echoed down the silent street. As they neared Hans's house, a creaking noise made Dottie stop in her tracks. She directed the beam of the flashlight over the house.

"Oh, shoot."

"What is it?"

"Hans's front door is open."

"Maybe there's been a robbery."

"Let's hope not," Dottie said. "Old doors don't always close properly. If that's the case, it would only take a strong gust of wind to drive it open."

"There's only one way to find out."

After looking up and down the street to make sure no one was around, the two women approached the house. Dottie pushed the door wide open, and they stepped inside.

"Hello!" Mabel called out. "Anybody home?" The only sound came from the ticking of a clock. As she directed the beam around the room, Dottie breathed in the faint lavender scent of furniture polish. A crystal wine decanter with six matching goblets stood on top of the mahogany sideboard. A small velvet sofa and two wing chairs sat around a leather coffee table. Woodcarvings and exotic artwork decorated the window ledges and side tables. Over the fireplace hung a large tapestry of an elephant and its rider, woven in gold thread.

"Let's check the kitchen and bathroom, and then head upstairs," Dottie said.

"Why do we need to check?"

"I have a feeling something's not right."

Satisfied that nothing seemed out of place on the ground floor, they headed to the staircase. The creaking of the uneven stairs seemed to grow louder as they climbed. They paused at the top. The open door of the bedroom that faced the stairs revealed a queen-sized bed covered with a rich maroon silk spread. This, Dottie decided, was Hans's room. "Mabel, you look around this room. I'll check the other one."

"I'll need to switch on the light."

"Go ahead. I don't think we need to worry about anyone seeing a light. The bedroom shutters are closed."

Moonlight shone through a small window at the end of the landing, guiding Dottie as she made her way to the other room. Holding the flashlight in one hand, she turned the handle and opened the door.

The sickly sweet smell got to her first. She pinched her nostrils to keep the odor at bay. Then, she saw the body lying on the bed, the white candlewick bedspread splattered with congealed blood. Bile rose into her throat, and she fought the urge to throw up.

Mabel called from the other room. "There's a mural of a naked woman over the bed and other nude photographs all over the walls. I think this Hans Van Gogh is a bit of a voyeur."

"Mabel, come here quickly!"

Mabel dashed along the corridor to join her friend. "What's wrong? And what's that dreadful smell?"

Dottie directed the flashlight's beam on the body.

Mabel's hand flew to her mouth. "It's Monsieur Bouchard!"

They stared at the inert body on the bed. His throat had been slit. The look of terror in the wide-open eyes told its own story.

The two women stood transfixed, unable to drag themselves away. Finally, Dottie turned to her friend. "Let's get out of here." She took Mabel by the arm and guided her downstairs.

Once they stepped outside, Dottie closed the front door. She leaned against the house and took slow deep breaths. After a while, the nausea subsided. "We have to phone the police."

"Yes."

"Just when we thought we'd seen the last of Lieutenant Piaf. Unfortunately, we've no choice in the matter."

***

After calling the lieutenant, Dottie's energy drained. She plopped herself on the grass verge by the phone box, next to Mabel.

"How did it go?"

"Once I explained what happened to the policeman on duty, he transferred me to Lieutenant Piaf. The lieutenant recognized my voice, even though he was half-asleep. I told him what had happened. He asked if I knew the victim, and of course, I told him it was Monsieur Bouchard." She paused for a moment. "It was strange."

"What do you mean?"

"The way he responded. He became very quiet. He asked me if I was sure if it was Monsieur Bouchard. Once I assured him there was no doubt about that, he said in a very subdued voice, 'I will meet you at Mr. Van Gogh's house in fifteen minutes' and hung up."

"Maybe they were friends." A sob caught in Mabel's throat. "Who could have done such a terrible thing!"

"You remember the lieutenant telling us he had a colleague in St. Siffret who would let us know if the police needed to speak with us again. I'm sure it was Monsieur Bouchard."

"What makes you think that?"

"When Monsieur Bouchard invited us for coffee, he said he had something important to discuss. It was right after we told him we were having dinner with Yvette and Pierre, remember?"

"Go on."

"I think he wanted to tell us something about them, maybe warn us. I wouldn't be surprised if they're mixed up in the drug and gun smuggling operation." She bit her lip. "I've never trusted those two. It just seems too much of a coincidence that Monsieur Bouchard disappeared before he had the chance to talk to us." She stood. "Come on, we'd better be at Hans's house when the lieutenant arrives." She looked at Mabel who hadn't moved. "Are you OK?"

Mabel took out the handkerchief and blew her nose. "I'll be fine." Dottie helped her to her feet. "Thanks, Dottie. Come on, let's get this over with."

Chapter 15

Shortly after the two women returned to Hans's house, Lieutenant Piaf and his men arrived. Dottie led them upstairs to where Monsieur Bouchard's body lay. She answered a few perfunctory questions before returning downstairs.

Dottie heard the clatter of dishes. Marching into the kitchen, she found Mabel arranging mugs and a teapot on a tray. "I think you should wait until the lieutenant comes down, Mabel. He might want to have fingerprints taken."

The front door rattled open. Dottie stuck her head around the kitchen door. Hans stood in the doorway, his face haggard. "I received a call from a Lieutenant Piaf telling me about Monsieur Bouchard. I cannot believe it!" He strode into the living room.

Dottie joined him. "I'm afraid it's true. I think he's been dead for a while. Not that I know about these things, but the smell's overpowering, and the blood on the bedspread is definitely not fresh." She gave Hans a brief summary of what had happened

Hans's voice trembled. "I have known Monsieur Bouchard for many years. He is—was—a real gentleman." He ran his hands through his hair. "I had better go upstairs and let the police know I am here."

A few minutes later, he returned. "A *gendarme* informed me we are to wait in the living room for Lieutenant Piaf."

"Did he mention anything about fingerprints?"

"Not a word."

"I might as well go ahead with the tea," Mabel said. She turned to Hans. "Would you like some?"

"That sounds good." He sat down in a wing chair.

Weariness crept into Dottie's bones. Would this night never end?

"Are you all right, Dottie?" Hans's concerned voice broke into her thoughts.

"I'm wiped." She blew a long breath and plopped on the sofa. "I'm glad Mabel's making tea. I could do with a hot drink right now."

A ghost of a smile crossed Hans's face. "I agree."

Within minutes, Mabel bustled into the living room carrying a tray with three steaming mugs, a plate of assorted cheeses, and half a packet of crackers. "Help yourself. I couldn't find any bread," she explained to Hans. "I realize you wouldn't have fresh bread, as you're not living in the house, but you should have some in the freezer for emergencies."

Hans snapped. "Had I known I would have guests in the middle of the night, in a house I no longer live in, I would have purchased fresh baguettes, smoked salmon, pâté, and chocolate desserts—and maybe a bottle of champagne."

Mabel blushed. "Oh, dear, I've upset you."

Rubbing his eyes, Hans sighed. "Sorry, Mabel, that was uncalled for. This is all a bit of a shock."

"Of course," Mabel said. "It was thoughtless of me. I'm trying to keep my mind occupied."

"I understand."

She sat in the other wing chair and stirred two spoonfuls of sugar into her tea. "Have some," she urged, pushing the bowl toward them. "It's good for shock."

Dottie took a heaped spoonful. Hans took three.

They all looked up when they heard voices on the upstairs landing. A man with a strong British accent said, "He's been dead for two to three days, no more."

"How can you tell?" the lieutenant asked.

"In this heat, decomposition happens rapidly. I can confirm more accurately once I've examined the body at the morgue."

"That must be the pathologist," Mabel said.

"It is more likely the *officiel en charge de déterminer les causes d'un décés*," Hans replied.

"The what?"

"The coroner."

Lieutenant Piaf clumped down the stairs, followed by two policemen. He addressed the women. "My men will take statements from you now." His eyes grazed over the contents of the tray. "*Mon dieu! Que faites-vous*? What is this?" he demanded.

"Tea," Mabel responded. "Tea with lots of sugar is the best thing for shock."

Blotches of red appeared on the lieutenant's cheeks. "*Madame*, nothing should be touched in a murder investigation, nothing!" He took out a white handkerchief from his breast pocket and dabbed his face. "You might have destroyed valuable evidence."

"I'm sorry," Mabel responded, "but you didn't say anything."

"Yes, well." He cleared his throat. "No doubt I should have told all of you not to come into the house until we conduct a thorough examination." He sighed. "It is too late now."

"Lieutenant, we`re supposed to leave for Tuscany tomorrow morning." Dottie checked her watch. "Well, this morning. May we leave as planned?"

"*Absolument!*" He sounded relieved. "As long as we have your statements, that is all we need."

He turned to Hans, his face taut. "Monsieur Van Gogh, I presume."

"Yes."

"You will accompany me to the police station." Dottie's heart skipped a beat.

"What for?" asked Hans.

"I have questions to ask you."

"Surely, you can ask your questions here. Why do I need to go the police station?" Hans stifled a yawn. "I have had a very frustrating day."

"Mr. Van Gogh, you are pushing my patience!"

In a resigned voice, Hans replied. "If I have to accompany you to the police station, I think I have a right to know why."

Lieutenant Piaf's voice hardened. "I want to know why a note addressed to you concerning what is almost certainly a drug shipment was found on the floor near Monsieur Bouchard's body."

The color drained from Hans's face. "I do not know what you are talking about. I know nothing about this."

"We will see. You will accompany me to the police station. *Maintenant!*"

Chapter 16

Dottie zipped her summer jacket. The wind had grown stronger, and sudden gusts whipped through narrow alleyways between the rows of houses, sweeping lids off garbage pails and lifting pieces of paper and cardboard into the air. As she and Mabel trudged home, images of the past few hours swam in her head, however hard she tried to push them away. The note found near Monsieur Bouchard's body had serious implications. She swallowed hard. Could, Hans be involved in drug smuggling?

When she saw the familiar stone cross outlined against the night sky, the tension in her shoulders and stomach eased a little. Home at last. What they needed was a good night's sleep before the long drive to Italy. Yet, how could they sleep after tonight's gruesome experience?

A light from her bedroom window cast its glow on the cobblestones as they crossed the square. "That's odd," Dottie muttered to herself. "I don't remember leaving the light on."

Mabel rooted in her bag for the house key and opened the front door. "I don't know about you, Dottie, but I keep seeing Monsieur Bouchard lying on that bed."

"It's horrible." Dottie shuddered as she followed Mabel into the house. "We could both do with a drink."

"Is there any brandy?"

Dottie checked Tom's sideboard. Inside, she found a brandy bottle. "There's enough for two small shots." She poured the brandy and handed a glass to Mabel. They sank down on the living room sofa.

Mabel swirled the golden liquid around. "I can't believe they arrested Hans."

"He wasn't arrested," Dottie snapped. "They want to question him; that's all."

"I daresay you're right. Still, I wonder what that note was about?"

"Maybe it's a red herring."

"What do you mean?"

"The note could have been written by the drug smugglers to make the police think Hans is involved."

"It's possible." Mabel turned to Dottie. "If the police think Hans is a drug smuggler, he'll also be a murder suspect."

The brandy seared Dottie's throat as she swallowed a large mouthful. "I'm convinced Yvette and Pierre are involved somehow."

"That's one good thing about staying in Mr. Morelli's villa."

"How so?"

"If those two make it to Italy, we can keep our eyes on them." A clicking sound made them jump. Mabel put down her glass. "What was that?"

"It's the wind rattling the back door. The latch is a bit loose."

"Let's hope that's all it is."

Dottie stood and drained her glass. "I'll go check, just to be sure. Then, I'm off to bed. We've a long day ahead of us."

After placing the glass in the sink, Dottie checked the door. To her consternation, it wasn't locked. "Mabel, would you come here?"

Mabel joined Dottie. "What's the problem?"

"When we first got here, we checked to make sure this door was locked."

"Yes. I remember."

"Well. It isn't now."

"Oh dear, it's my fault," Mabel said." I opened the door yesterday morning to shake the kitchen rug. I must have forgotten to lock it."

"So, it was only left unlocked for a short while. That's something to be thankful for." Dottie opened the door and glanced around. A stray dog was sniffing a heap of wet leaves. Otherwise, the square was empty.

Dottie reentered the house and locked the door. "Everything seems fine. I'm going to bed," she called out.

"Me too. See you in the morning."

***

Big gray rats scurried around the pitch-black room. She huddled in the corner, numb with fear. A narrow beam of light flickered on the wall, and a voice rasped, "You can't escape!" A gust of wind blew through an open window and lifted the ragged curtain. For a few seconds, the room was bathed in moonlight, revealing the silhouette of a tall thin man in a cloak. She glimpsed a flash of steel as he raised his arm. With a bloodcurdling howl, he lunged toward her.

Dottie screamed.

"What on earth's the matter!" Mabel cried as she rushed into Dottie's room and switched on the light.

Dottie lay back on her pillow, her face damp with perspiration, willing her heart to slow. "I've had a nightmare."

Using a hair clip, Mabel secured a roller about to fall out of her hair. "I'm not surprised with all that's happened. I'll stay for a few minutes until you're feeling better."

"I'll be fine in a minute."

"Well, if you're sure…"

"I'm sure. Thanks, Mabel."

Leaving the light on, Dottie lay back in bed. Her heartbeat gradually returned to normal. It had been a long time since she'd had a nightmare as scary as that. What had triggered it, she wondered. Finding the bedroom light on when they returned to the house had caused a few moments of uneasiness, but it was more than that. Something wasn't right.

Dottie sat up and peered around. Everything seemed in order. Her eyes rested on the parcel sitting on the dresser, carefully wrapped for Antonio Morelli. As she stared at it, her mouth went dry. Her velvet jewelry bag that had sat next to the parcel had disappeared. She climbed out of bed for a closer look, but there was no sign of the bag. It was just as well she hadn't brought anything of value on vacation. The thief would be disappointed when he discovered the loot was inexpensive costume jewelry.

Spooked by the thought that someone had been in her room, she checked in her suitcase, relieved to find the wine jug hadn't been stolen. After checking in the closet and under the bed and making sure the bedroom window was closed, she climbed into bed. It was pointless waking Mabel to tell her about the break-in. She tried to read but found her mind wandering to the events of the past few hours. Lying back on her pillow, she closed her eyes and focused her mind on their trips to Arles, Avignon, and Uzès and the souvenirs they'd purchased. Her eyes grew heavy.

"Thump!"

Dottie sat bolt upright, her heart racing. What was that? She looked around and saw the book she'd been reading lying on the floor. She sighed. Now what? Then, she remembered the crossword puzzles. Rooting through the dresser drawer, she took out three, with her erasable pen. Concentrating on crossword clues would keep her mind occupied—and, just maybe, it would help her fall asleep.

***

Dottie told Mabel about the robbery over breakfast the next morning. Mabel's eyes opened wide in alarm. "You mean to tell me that a thief broke into the house and stole your jewelry while we went for a walk? How creepy!" She shuddered. "I don't know how you managed to sleep after that, Dottie."

Dottie poured a second cup of coffee. "It took a while, but I finally dozed off about two."

"I wonder if that rattling noise we heard last night was the thief escaping through the back door."

"Dottie nodded. "That makes sense."

"I definitely locked the front door when we went for our walk. I pushed the door to make sure. So, either the thief used the back door to get in and out, or else, he—or she—had a key."

Dottie sighed. "I won't be sorry to leave. We've had nothing but trouble since we got here."

"It's really too bad. It's such a picturesque place."

After breakfast, they packed the car, did some last-minute tidying, and drove away from St. Siffret. "We're finally on our way to Italy," Mabel said, steering the car down the winding road toward Uzès. "Let's hope we've left stolen guns, drugs, murders, and break-ins behind us."

They'd just crossed the bridge on the outskirts of St. Siffret when a red car with an open sunroof headed toward them at high speed. As it drew closer, the car veered left, forcing Mabel onto the grass verge at the roadside.

"Crazy driver," Mabel fumed, bringing her car to a halt.

Dottie Flowers and the European Caper

The car pulled up beside them, and the driver, wearing a flowing yellow scarf and over-large sunglasses, stuck her head out the window. It was Yvette. "Mabel! Dottie! Are you all right?"

Dottie glared. "Do you always drive like that?"

"When I drive Pierre's car, I open the sunroof, and I feel the wind in my hair, and it makes me go fast."

"You could have killed us!" Mabel retorted.

Yvette removed her sunglasses. Her face grew serious. "I'm sorry I frightened you."

"Hmm." Dottie glanced at the fancy leopard skin print suitcase on the passenger seat. "Did you have a good time in St. Tropez?"

"Magnificent! We had four wonderful days." She sighed with pleasure. "Pierre and I are—what is the word—cloudy."

"On cloud nine."

"Yes."

"Where's Pierre?"

"I drop 'im off in Uzès. He meets some business people."

Mabel snapped. "If you continue to drive like that, you won't be around to enjoy any more romantic escapes!" She put the car in first gear. "We must be on our way. We've a long drive ahead."

"Of course! We 'ope to see you at Antonio's next week." Yvette waved as she sped away. Within a few seconds, all they could see was a cloud of dust.

"Doesn't that woman have any common sense?" Mabel muttered, easing the car onto the road.

"Yvette is all charm when it suits her. I think she deliberately ran you off the road, just so she could remind us they'd been away. And for how long."

"Why would she do that?"

"Remember that coroner telling Lieutenant Piaf he believed the body had been there for two, maybe three, days max."

"I see what you're getting at. Yvette and Pierre were away when the murder happened. So, they're in the clear."

"Unless they hired someone else to do their dirty work."

***

They stayed overnight in a charming B & B near Grasse and detoured to a hilltop village for morning coffee. Negotiating the steep, winding road proved a challenge. Mabel changed gears so often that, after a while, they could smell burning rubber. "It's the clutch, I'm afraid," she said. "Let's hope I haven't done any serious damage."

Once they reached their destination, they found a café that overlooked the peaks and valleys. They enjoyed the glorious panorama spread before them as they sipped their coffee.

"It's tempting to stay longer," Dottie said, "but we really should hit the road if we want to get to Lucca before dark."

"I agree."

Once they reached the highway, the rubbery smell had almost disappeared.

***

By Dottie's count, they'd driven through well over one hundred tunnels by the time they reached the Italian border. The hilltop villages, rugged grassy outcrops, and sleepy towns of Southern France gave way to a more rural landscape, where terraced gardens grew in the steep hillsides above towns and villages. Far below the motorway, they caught their first glimpse of the azure-blue

Mediterranean. Little red-tiled houses huddled along a shoreline crowded with sunbathers.

"I'll open the windows so we can enjoy the sea air," Mabel said.

Dottie closed her eyes. "This is heaven!" she murmured as a light breeze caressed her skin. A few minutes later, Dottie's nose twitched as an acrid smell filled the air. She looked out the window. No telltale smoke curled from a garden or hillside. "Mabel, can you smell rubber?"

Mabel sniffed hard a few times. "Oh, dear! I'm afraid it's that clutch again."

They stopped at an Italian rest area for a light meal. It was a challenge to choose from the wide selection of pastas, meats, and sandwiches displayed in big glass cases. In the end, they both chose paninis. Mabel took a bite. "Good food."

"Mmm," Dottie agreed, her mouth full. After they'd finished, Dottie noticed Mabel gazing into space, her brow furrowed. "What's the matter?"

"I'm concerned about the car."

"I don't think we need to worry. We aren't far from Lucca, and the villa's only a few miles from there."

Dottie's optimism was short lived. The rubbery smell grew stronger. By the time they'd reached Lucca, it was obvious that they had a serious problem. Mabel managed to find a parking space near the old city walls. "I think we'd better let the car cool down a bit, Dottie."

"Why don't we take a short walk around Lucca? It'll give us a chance to stretch our legs a bit. We can phone the rental company from the villa."

The two women made their way through the imposing gates of the walled city. Once inside the gates, they noticed a market on a side street. Laughter and shouts rose in the late afternoon air as vendors stacked away their wares before counting the day's takings. The meat and fish vans had already closed, Dottie noted, and the bakery van owners had packed away most of their leftover goods. A few loaves of bread remained.

"I'll buy a loaf for breakfast," Mabel said and rushed off.

A large swarthy-complexioned man wearing a black T-shirt and bandana around his head leaned against a fish van. Smoking a cigarette, he chatted with a vendor. At one point, the two men began to laugh, and the man flung an arm around his companion. His arm was covered in tattoos. Dottie froze. A large tattoo of a machine gun was imprinted on his forearm.

Mabel returned, carrying a loaf and a large string of onions. She held up the onions, a wide grin on her face. "I couldn't resist. They were a bargain. Thought we could make some French onion soup. Oh, we're in Italy, aren't we, but I daresay they eat onion soup here."

"See that man by the fish van," Dottie pointed. "The one with the tattoos. It's one of the men who took those bags of drugs from under the floorboards in *Maison Francais*."

Mabel pushed the sunglasses back on the bridge of her nose and peered at him. "I got only a very brief look, but I remember that tattoo. I wonder what he's doing here in Lucca."

At that moment, the man threw his cigarette butt on the ground and began to walk away.

Dottie made up her mind. "Come on, let's follow him!"

"You can't be serious. We've just arrived in Italy and already you want us to chase after a criminal. Really, Dottie! Besides, I've got my hands full…"

"Here, I'll carry the bread. We need to know what he's up to. Hurry before he disappears into one of the buildings."

Chapter 17

Hands thrust in trouser pockets, the man lumbered away. Dottie and Mabel scurried after him, down a warren of narrow side streets, dodging tourists, bicycles, and scooters, as they struggled to keep him in sight.

"It's a wonder people aren't killed, the way they drive those scooters," Mabel complained, pausing to catch her breath. "They think everyone will automatically get out of their way."

"You need your wits about you, that's for sure—oh, no!" A sharp bend in the street hid the man from view. "Quick, Mabel!"

As they rushed forward, people spilled out of a small church onto the street and blocked their path. By the time they wove through the crowd, the man was nowhere to be seen. They found themselves in a large square where outdoor cafes were doing brisk business. Laughter and chatter filled the air, as waiters dashed back and forth with food and drink orders.

"He must be here somewhere," Dottie said, her eyes darting around the square.

"Dottie, we're leaving, this minute!" Mabel declared. "I'm tired of chasing some drug dealer around a strange town. What are we trying to do? Catch him? It's time we started looking for Mr. Morelli's villa."

"All right, all right," Dottie soothed. They turned around and began to walk back.

Just as they left the square, Mabel poked Dottie's arm. "Isn't this a charming little café!" Striped umbrellas and waiters dressed in scarlet aprons gave the establishment a cheerful air. As they scrutinized the menu, the aroma of garlic and basil made Dottie's stomach rumble. "We must come here one day for lunch," Mabel said.

"For sure. Let's find the car. We're close to the gates, so we haven't far to walk."

***

Mabel held her breath as she turned the key in the ignition. She blew out a long sigh when the engine roared to life. "Let's hope the clutch holds out for a while."

Dottie studied Pierre's map. "It won't take long to get to the villa."

They found it without difficulty because Pierre had highlighted the road on his map. Not wishing to do more damage to the clutch, Mabel drove the car slowly up a steep hill. At the top, they pulled up in front of a black wrought-iron gate where a wooden sign with the words *Villa Lorenzo* carved into it swung from a tall post. They climbed out of the car and peered through the gate.

The villa resembled a small pink castle complete with a moat. It reminded Dottie of her trip to Disney World years ago. She half expected to see Mickey Mouse waving from a turret. A high brick wall surrounded the grounds, with iron spikes protruding along the top. Fierce barking punctuated by growls greeted them, as they climbed out of the car. Dottie tensed. She had bad memories of being bitten by a large black dog as a child. She looked through the iron gate to see if the animal was chained up or roamed free, but couldn't see it.

"Now, what?" Mabel wondered.

Dottie spotted a phone by the gate. A notice was posted next to it. The message was written in Italian, but a number 3 appeared in the middle. "I'll try pressing '3' and see what happens."

A woman answered in Italian. Dottie cleared her throat. "My name is Dottie Flowers."

"Ah! Mrs. Flowers and Mrs. Scattergood," a woman's deep voice answered. "Mr. Morelli— he expect you. Drive through the gateway," she commanded. Her accent, though strong, was easy to understand. "You park by swimming pool."

The gate swung open. Windows down, they drove along a graveled driveway, passing lush manicured lawns bordered with colorful flowerbeds. In the center of the garden, the spray of water from a white marble fountain sparkled in the late evening sunshine.

Dottie spotted a red clay tennis court at the far end of the grounds. "It must be nice to own your own tennis court."

"If you play tennis."

"Someone does," she replied, as a young couple holding racquets walked onto the court.

Mabel parked the car by the pool as instructed. Even though the barking had stopped, Dottie scanned the grounds before opening the car door. To her relief, there was no sign of a dog. She walked to the pool house. It was a simple structure—white, modern, with picture windows overlooking the pool and the gardens. The gentle whir of the air-conditioning unit pleased her. Even on a hot day, they would be assured of a good night's sleep.

Through one window, she spotted a comfortable-looking sofa and a round dining table with four chairs. In the middle of the table sat a large flagon of red wine and a basket of fruit. She peeked through the other windows. A bedroom lay on either side of the living room, one painted in lemon and the other in mint green. Each room had twin beds with floral duvets. White terrycloth robes were laid out on each bed with a single yellow rose.

Mabel, who had been testing the pool temperature with her hand, joined Dottie by the pool house. She glanced through the living room window. "This looks nice and cozy."

"'Allo!" Mabel and Dottie turned around quickly. A tall heavyset woman wearing a navy-blue dress and white apron stood by the pool holding a basket of towels. "I am housekeeper, Maria Tomasino," Dottie recognized the deep voice of the woman who had answered the intercom at the gate.

When Dottie and Mabel introduced themselves, Maria smiled, but the smile didn't reach her eyes. "You do not use front gate. That is the one you use." She pointed to a chain-link gate on the right-hand side of the villa. "Next to big gate is door. You use that door if you wish to go for walk."

"Do we need keys?"

"Yes. I give to you." Placing the basket on the patio table, Maria fished a set of keys out of her apron pocket. She held three keys between her fingers. She pointed to the largest key. "This is key to pool house." She pointed to the other two. "These are keys to big gate and door."

She handed the set to Dottie. "Now, you choose linens." She waited, arms folded, as the two women selected towels and bedsheets. Once they'd finished, Maria picked up the basket. Cocking her thumb at the villa, she said, "Mr. Morelli said you come for dinner. At eight." Before they had a chance to reply, she turned and marched across the lawn toward the villa.

"What an odd woman!" Mabel remarked. "And what a strange invitation. Still, it will be interesting to meet our host."

Dottie glanced at her watch. "Let's tidy ourselves up. We'll unpack the car later."

***

Dottie was struck by Antonio Morelli's likeness to Aristotle Onassis. His steel-gray hair contrasted with a deep tan and vivid blue eyes. Stocky and of medium height, he wore a white linen shirt and navy slacks. As he strode across the hallway, Dottie recognized the distinctive Gucci crest on his leather moccasins.

Smiling, he shook hands with each of them. "Welcome to *Villa Lorenzo!*"

Dottie introduced Mabel and herself. "We look forward to our stay with you, Mr. Morelli."

"My friends Yvette and Pierre speak highly of you. They are coming to visit at the end of the week, so we will all be together." He paused. "I have a small favor to ask. Can we dispense with the formalities, do you think, and use first names?"

"Of course," Mabel replied.

"I trust you had a good journey?"

"Pretty good, thank you," Dottie responded. She hoped Mabel wouldn't decide to go into detail about the car problem. It would be pleasant to have an evening without talking about it.

"Please come with me."

He led the two women into a spacious living room, where crimson silk drapes hung from high arched windows. On the hardwood floor lay a richly woven Oriental rug. A light brown leather sofa and two armchairs, decorated with crimson and gold silk pillows, sat in front of a marble fireplace. Dottie smiled to herself. The exterior of the castle with its ramparts and fake moat did not reflect the sophisticated taste of its owner.

"Do sit down. Make yourselves at home."

"Thank you." Dottie settled in an armchair. "How long have you lived here, Mr. Morelli—er, Antonio?"

He paused for a moment, frowning a little. "I believe it is now—let me see—eight years. The location is perfect for my business. The design of the villa is not to my taste, but I content myself with making sure the interior is beautiful."

"It is. That image beside the fireplace… it's captivated me."

"That is one of Picasso's linocuts, which he created in 1958." His voice was full of pride. "It is hand-signed." As he smiled, his even white teeth glinted in the candlelight. "But now, I believe dinner is served, so please let me escort you and Mabel into the dining room." He turned to Dottie. "Yvette has told me that you do not eat meat. I think you will enjoy tonight's menu. There are four courses, but do not worry. The portions are small."

A long table set with white linen dominated the cavernous room. An exquisite arrangement of white roses in an ornate gold bowl sat in the center. Delicate china with a crimson and gold flower motif, accentuated by crimson silk napkins, gave the table an elegant, yet understated look. He had excellent taste, or maybe she was giving him too much credit. Did he have a wife? Somehow, she didn't think so.

Unsmiling, Maria Tomasino served an assortment of antipasti, while a young man poured the wine. His hands shook a little as he poured the first glass, and he spilled some liquid on the tablecloth. Maria had a few words with him, and he poured the rest of the wine without further mishaps.

Dottie took a few sips. "This is excellent." She didn't know much about wine, but appreciated its smooth taste.

"I'm glad you approve," Antonio said. "It is a Chianti Classico Reserva." He leaned forward, his eyes sweeping over them. "While we are enjoying our wine, I must explain something to you. The villa is a busy place. I have a consulting business and people drop by all the time. Day

Dottie Flowers and the European Caper

and night. I trust they won't disturb you too much." He cocked his head. "Now, let us enjoy our evening." He lifted his wineglass in a toast. "May you both enjoy a wonderful holiday here in Tuscany. If there is anything you need or if you have any questions, please let Maria know. I will do my best to accommodate you." *Every inch the charming Italian*, Dottie mused.

Cheese ravioli with a butter and sage sauce followed the antipasti. Antonio poured Mabel another glass of wine. "Good wine must never go to waste."

"I agree," replied Mabel, whose face, Dottie noticed, was becoming rather flushed.

As they enjoyed the ravioli dish, Antonio asked them about their life in Canada, explaining that he visited Montreal and Toronto regularly. On discovering that Mabel had emigrated from the United Kingdom, he wanted to know where she grew up.

"The Cotswolds."

"What is the name of the town or village?"

"Chipping Campden."

Placing his hands on the table, he exclaimed, "But this is such a coincidence! I have a nephew who lives near Chipping Campden."

Mabel's face beamed. "It's a beautiful town."

"The whole area is beautiful. It is my favorite part of Britain." Antonio brushed back a stray lock of hair. Dottie noticed an angry-looking scar across the top of his forehead. *Nasty*, she thought. *I wonder how that happened.*

The main dish arrived. "Sogliola alla Fiorentina," said Antonio. "It is prepared with spinach, lemon juice, and white wine. Enjoy!"

Dottie savored the delicate fish. "This is delicious."

Antonio smiled. "I am glad you approve, Dottie."

A salad of endive, radicchio, and shaved Parmesan cheese followed the main course. Dottie felt full. Much to her relief, dessert was a small serving of lemon gelato decorated with fresh mint. As she savored its tart flavor, Dottie noticed Mabel stifling a yawn.

Antonio must have noticed as well. "You must both be weary after your long journey, so I will not keep you." He smiled. "You will come over another evening when Yvette and Pierre are here, of course."

After they bid their host goodnight, Dottie and Mabel made their way back to the pool house. Mabel stumbled on the crooked pathway but managed to regain her balance. "Isn't this silly?" she giggled. "My head is spinning. I don't usually drink red wine. And I drank too much of it."

"It's just as well you're not driving. Let's get our luggage. We can unpack in the morning."

When they reached the car, Mabel rooted in her purse for the keys.

Dottie tried the car door. "You don't need them. The door's open."

"Oh, dear, that was careless of me."

Dottie glanced at the high wall surrounding the villa grounds. "I don't think we need to worry. The place is like Fort Knox."

They dragged their luggage into the pool house. Dottie yawned. "Goodnight Mabel."

"See you in the morning."

As Dottie brushed her teeth in the small bathroom, something niggled. She wandered back to the bedroom and rummaged through her suitcases for a nightgown. *Really*, she scolded herself; I *don't need so many clothes. I must try to cut down on the amount of stuff I bring on vacations. Then, I'd have room to bring more gifts back. Gifts*! Dottie thumped her forehead with the heel of her hand. Where was Antonio's parcel? Mabel had put it on the floor of the car, behind the driver's seat.

Dottie checked, but there was nothing on the car floor. Had Mabel taken it in? She knocked on Mabel's door and opened it a crack. Her friend lay on the bed in a pink floral nightdress. She looked at Dottie through bleary eyes.

"Did you bring the parcel in from the car?"

"What?"

"I checked the car, and it's gone." When Mabel's eyes began to glaze over, Dottie covered her with the duvet. Was it possible that the parcel had been stolen at one of the roadside inns? She quickly dismissed that idea, confident that they'd locked the car each time they stopped for a toilet break or a snack.

Snapping off Mabel's light, Dottie sighed. Had their problems followed them to Tuscany?

Chapter 18

Dottie bolted upright in bed. What was that awful crowing noise? It sounded like a rooster. She peered through the window. Nothing. Checking her watch, she saw it was only 5:30 a.m. She got back into bed, and pulled the duvet over her head.

It was late morning by the time Dottie and Mabel got up. Clutching a mug of black coffee, Mabel wandered into the living room and slumped on the sofa. "My head feels achy and thick."

Dottie poured her friend a glass of water and handed over two aspirin. "Here, take these."

"Thanks." Mabel swallowed the pills and gulped down the water.

"Do you remember I told you last night that the parcel has disappeared?"

Mabel's eyes opened wide. "No, I don't. It was on the floor of the car behind the driver's seat."

"I've checked in the car. Do you think you might have taken it into your room last night?"

"I doubt it. Mind you, I don't remember much of anything. I'll look."

Mabel disappeared into her bedroom, but the search didn't take long. "It`s not there."

The parcel must have been taken from the car while they were having dinner with Antonio, Dottie realized. With

Villa Lorenzo's tight security system, it was most likely an employee or someone who lived on the premises.

"We could ask Maria Tomasino," Mabel said. "Maybe she'll have an idea who it might be."

"It wouldn't hurt." Dottie stood and stretched. "I must unpack."

"Me too. Let's go for a short drive later."

"We need to speak with the car rental people first about the clutch."

"Maybe we could get it fixed in Lucca."

"Hmm," Dottie said. "That might work if it's OK with the car rental people."

Their discussion was interrupted by a knock on the door. Maria stood on the doorstep, holding a basket of eggs. "Mr. Morelli, he say you have eggs for breakfast."

"Oh, how kind." Mabel took the basket. "How much?"

Maria shook her head. "This is gift. Mr. Morelli has chickens in back of house. They lay many eggs."

So, a rooster had woken Dottie up! She joined Mabel at the door. "Is there a garage around here, Maria?" Seeing the blank expression on Maria's face, she pointed to their car.

"You need petrol?" Dottie shook her head.

"Here, let me try," Mabel said. She pretended to change gears, then pinched her nose and pulled a face.

Maria half smiled. "Bad smell from car. In Lucca is place for car. Via Del Conce 38. Roberto, he fix for you. You tell him Maria Tomasino send you."

"Thank you." Dottie paused, wondering how to broach the subject of the missing parcel.

Before she had a chance to say anything, Mabel spoke. "Maria, we have something to tell you." Pointing to the car and using hand gestures, she explained about the parcel.

Maria's face paled. She clasped her hands. "I know nothing!" she protested. "Now, I go!" She turned abruptly and hurried away.

"Oh, dear, that wasn't such a great idea," Mabel sighed. "She thinks we're accusing her of theft."

"Or, she knows who took it."

"Let's hope it reappears," Mabel said. "I'll put the eggs in the fridge. We'll have them for breakfast tomorrow."

It didn't take Dottie long to unpack. She hung as many items of clothing as the small wardrobe could hold and managed to find space for everything else in the chest of drawers. After a quick shower, she dressed in beige cotton capris and a short-sleeved linen blouse.

She found Mabel in the living room, decked out in a yellow polka-dot sundress. Instead of the usual purple-winged sunglasses, she wore an identical orange pair. "That hot shower has done the trick," Mabel smiled. "I feel much better."

"So do I, even though I was woken at 5:30 by a rooster."

"What rooster?"

"Never mind," Dottie said, remembering how soundly Mabel slept. "Let's go phone the car rental company."

Dottie made the call from the phone box near the villa's main gate. The representative explained the company would be happy to arrange for a replacement car. If she preferred to have the clutch repaired, they would reimburse up to 250 euros. He reminded Dottie to keep the bill.

"While Roberto fixes the car, we can do some sightseeing," Dottie said. "Lucca looks like an interesting place."

"And we can have lunch at that dear little café we found yesterday. My treat."

"Sounds great. All we've had this morning is coffee."

***

The garage was easy to find. A short man with black curly hair watched as they climbed out of the car. "*Buongiorno!*" he called out. His broad smile revealed two missing front teeth.

"Are you Roberto?" Mabel asked.

"*Si.*"

"Maria Tomasino recommended you."

His eyes lit up. "Maria, she is my cousin." Mabel explained the car problem. He promised to do a good job and assured them his garage was the best in Lucca. "You go. I fix car."

Reassured, Dottie and Mabel wandered through Lucca's narrow streets. The tall houses provided shade, so it was cooler there than the large open squares, where the intense heat encouraged many tourists to relax in outdoor cafés under umbrellas. They discovered gift shops filled with postcards and souvenirs and art shops with original paintings of famous Italian sights, including Lucca—and a bakery where they feasted their eyes on cream-filled pastries and iced cakes and inhaled the mouthwatering smell of fresh baked bread.

In one store, Dottie purchased a phone card when she learned from the assistant that it could be used in a public phone box. Too bad she hadn't bought one in Provence. They passed an iron-studded wooden door where an old man sat on the steps smoking his pipe. Three dark-haired children with mischievous grins stuck their heads out the window above the door and waved at Dottie and Mabel before sticking out their tongues.

They searched for the little café Mabel had discovered the day before. By the time they found it, they were tired and thirsty as well as hungry.

Mabel fanned herself with a menu. "I could spit feathers. It's probably a combination of walking up and down those streets and overindulging last night."

They ordered sparkling mineral water. A young waiter, dark and handsome, served them. "You are wise," he said.

Dottie frowned. "Wise? How so?"

"The sun and the wine, it makes people sick. The mineral water—it is better." The waiter cocked his head. "May I recommend the special, a clam sauce over a bed of noodles?"

The two women replied in unison. "Yes, please."

The waiter left. He soon returned with a basket of bread and a bowl containing small green and black olives lying in a pool of olive oil and balsamic vinegar.

Mabel took several large swigs of the water. "This is so refreshing. I'm beginning to feel like my old self again."

"I hope Roberto can fix the problem with the car," Dottie said, breaking off a piece of bread and dipping it in the olive oil and balsamic vinegar. "I don't fancy going through the hoopla of arranging for a new one to be delivered."

Mabel grabbed Dottie's arm and pointed. "See over there!"

Shading her eyes, Dottie turned around. A short distance away, she saw a building that looked like a warehouse, with two large steel doors. A white van was backed up to one, and a thin man with straggly hair appeared in the doorway, carrying a cardboard box. He placed the box in the back of the van. "What am I supposed to be looking at, Mabel? All I can see is a van with *Giuseppe's IMPREND...* something or other written on its side, and a scruffy-looking guy loading a cardboard box into the back of it."

"Just watch!" Mabel said. A big burly man wearing a red bandana climbed out of the van. Within seconds, raised voices could be heard. "I'm sure that's the man we followed yesterday."

Dottie recognized him at once. "You're right, Mabel." From the wild hand gestures accompanying the shouting, it was clear the two men were arguing. "I need to take a closer look."

"Be careful."

Dottie patted her canvas bag. "I've got my camera. I'll pretend I'm taking photos." As she headed toward the two men, Dottie noted the street's name, *DaVinci*. Her heart began to race. That name was on the scrap of paper Mabel had found under her bed. Once she drew close, she sat down at a nearby café table and pretended to read the menu. Now, she had a clear view of the younger man's face. She sucked in her breath. It was the man who'd taken the bags from under the floorboards in *Maison Francais*.

The burly man was shouting. Dottie couldn't understand a word, but when the younger man yelled back, he called his partner Carlos. Carlos took the young man by the shoulder and spat words in Italian that Dottie guessed were four-letter ones. Again, she was in luck when Carlos referred to the younger man as Nico. After locking the warehouse doors with a padlock, Nico climbed into the passenger seat. Carlos slammed the back door of the van. He climbed into the driver's seat and sped off, gravel flying, but not before Dottie memorized the license plate number.

To the side of the warehouse lay a small flower garden. Armed with her camera, she sauntered to the garden and snapped a few unusual-looking specimens. She passed the steel door on the way back and saw the number 12 scrawled across the badly scratched metal.

Dottie returned as the waiter served their pasta dish. She breathed in the garlicky aroma of the sauce. "Mmm! it smells wonderful. First, I must write down the van's license plate number." She sat down, and jotted it on a paper napkin.

Dottie tucked the napkin in her purse. "Those were the men who lifted bags of powder from under the floorboards in your bedroom. The one we followed yesterday is Carlos; the skinny one's Nico."

"I wonder what they're doing in Lucca." Mabel said. "And wasn't the name 'Nico' on that piece of scrap paper I found under my bed after the break-in?"

"Yes, and the street name and the number on the door were also written on the paper." Dottie picked up her fork. "Let's eat."

They ate the pasta, savoring the rich clam sauce. It didn't take long to finish the meal.

"So, what's next?" Mabel asked, mopping the sauce with a piece of bread. "I mean, we know their names, but where do we go from here? Maybe we should call the Italian police."

Dottie finished her last forkful of pasta. "I don't think we need to worry about that. We'll have to tell Lieutenant Piaf that Carlos and Nico are here. He'll let the Italian police know what's going on."

"Of course." Mabel pulled a face. "We can't get away from the lieutenant, even in Tuscany. This time, maybe he'll believe us."

Chapter 19

They ordered coffee to finish off the meal. As she sipped hers, Dottie stretched her legs. "We haven't visited any of the historic sites yet," she said. "I'd like to start with the Duomo."

Mabel consulted a street map. "It's easy to find, by the looks of it. Let's ask for the bill and go there. By the way, did you know that Lucca is Puccini's birthplace?"

Dottie nodded. "You can see the original scores of *Turandot* in the house where he was born."

"You've done your homework, Dottie."

The cool interior of the thirteenth-century Duomo was a welcome relief from the hot sun. The magnificent tomb of Ilaria with its carvings of garlands, cherubs, and soft cushions brought a lump to Dottie's throat.

"So, what's next?"

"The San Frediano church sounds interesting," Dottie replied. "We can stop and look at the Guinigi Tower on the way."

They stared at the oaks growing out of the tower. "There are seven oaks, and they all self-seeded," Dottie said.

"Fancy walking to the top? It's supposed to have a fabulous view of the city."

Dottie looked at her friend in amazement. "Are you serious? That's a lot of climbing. Besides, it's too hot."

"We might never get the chance again."

"There are 130 steps"

"130? You're right," Mabel conceded, fanning herself with the map. "It's too hot. I'll be glad to get back to our pool house for a swim."

They walked to the church and spent several minutes studying the lavish mosaic façade. Inside, they saw the shrine to Lucca's saint, Santa Zita. Mabel checked the guidebook. "It says here that her mummified body is brought out once a year so the devout can touch her."

"Fascinating."

Mabel sighed. "I don't know about you, Dottie, but I've had enough culture for one day."

Dottie knew that old monuments and churches wouldn't keep Mabel occupied for long. "I don't think the car will be ready yet. Why don't we wander around the city walls for a while? We can people-watch if we get bored."

Shaded by chestnut trees and umbrella pines, the walls' wide gravel road was crowded with people enjoying an afternoon walk. Cyclists zigzagged around mothers pushing babies in strollers. Dottie snapped many pictures and hoped one would be good enough to enter in the next seniors' photo contest.

The results of this year's contest were due in another week, she realized. Would her photo of Fred Fortune, competing against snaps of adorable grandchildren, cute family pets, and stunning scenery, stand a chance of winning?

Half an hour later, the women made their way to Roberto's garage. "The car, it is fixed!" a grinning Roberto informed them. "It was not an easy job," he added, mopping his brow with a grubby cloth. "I do not stop for break. I work in hot sun because I promise the car is ready for three o'clock."

"You fixed the clutch?"

Roberto looked puzzled. "*Non capisco.*"

To Mabel's amusement, Dottie pretended to change gears. "You'd never win at Charades, Dottie!"

Roberto nodded his head vigorously. "*Si! Si!*"

Dottie laughed. "I can't be that bad if Roberto understood me." She checked her Italian phrase book. "*Quant e?*"

Roberto stroked his chin. "For my cousin, Maria Tomasino, I give you deal."

A phone rang inside the garage. "I come back!"

"I don't remember his promising to have the car ready by three," Mabel said.

"Nor do I."

"Well, he says he's fixed the clutch and vows he won't overcharge us."

Roberto returned. "200 euros." A wide grin spread across his face. "But for you, 150!"

"We need a receipt," Dottie said.

Looking at Roberto, Mabel pretended to write on her hand. He gave Mabel the thumbs-up sign and disappeared into the garage.

Dottie had no idea whether 150 euros was a good deal. She counted out the money and gave it to Roberto. He handed her an oil-stained receipt. The only thing she could understand on it was the amount.

***

A BMW and a Mercedes were parked on the driveway when they arrived at the villa. "Nice cars!" Mabel enthused. "I expect they belong to Antonio's business clients."

"I'd like to get that call to Lieutenant Piaf over with. Why don't we do that now?"

Mabel parked the car by the chain-link fence, and they made their way to the phone booth around the corner, near the villa's main gate.

"The lieutenant isn't going to be happy when he hears my voice," Dottie said as she removed the phone card from her handbag, "but we have to let him know we've seen Nico and Carlos in Lucca."

She lifted the phone. "Well, here goes." Reading the numbers on the card, she punched them in. When she got through to the station, the receptionist informed her that the lieutenant was away. Dottie felt the tension in her shoulders ease.

"He is back on duty tomorrow," the receptionist added, in heavily accented English. "Do you wish to leave a message?"

"I think it's best if I speak with him directly."

"Is he expecting a call from you?"

"No, but I've some very important information for him."

'Could I have your name, *madame*, and your phone number?"

Dottie hesitated. She could imagine the lieutenant's response. Clearing her throat, she gave her name.

"Dottie... F-L-O-W-E-R-S. I don't have a phone, so please tell the lieutenant I will call him tomorrow morning." She hung up the receiver.

Mabel linked her arm through Dottie's as they walked back to the car. "Let's forget about the lieutenant and organize some more sightseeing for tomorrow. I've been looking through my travel guide. I thought we'd start with Florence. We'll catch an early morning train from Lucca. After we've spent a few hours exploring the city, we can visit the Uffizi and the statue of Michelangelo's *David*."

Firenze, city of Michelangelo, with its museums and priceless works of art was a place Dottie had longed to visit.

Dottie Flowers and the European Caper

"Dottie? Are you paying attention?"

Dottie smiled. "I heard every word you said. It sounds wonderful. I'll phone the lieutenant from the train station when we arrive in Florence."

As soon as Dottie opened the big chain-link gate, the dog began to bark frantically. She rushed to the car and jumped in. "That dog must have eyes in the back of its head."

Mabel chuckled. "It probably heard the gate rattling." She drove through the entranceway. "Don't worry. I'll close it." When Mabel returned, she said, "I wonder if it's a tape recording to scare people away."

"Maybe," Dottie said. "We'll ask Maria."

"Let's get these groceries out of the car and organize dinner."

Chapter 20

Mabel made mushroom omelettes while Dottie prepared an avocado and pear salad on a bed of spinach. They ate at the poolside, lighting citronella candles to keep insects at bay. Dottie poured two glasses of Italian chardonnay and lifted hers in a toast. "Here's to a fabulous holiday in Tuscany."

"We have two weeks," Mabel said. "Let's hope it's trouble-free and relaxing."

A swallow skimmed the surface of the pool, and then swept upward, its wings brushing the pool house roof. The pool looked so inviting in the evening sunshine. As Dottie sipped the light crisp wine, she wished she could overcome her fear of water and learn to swim well.

Sparrows had gathered near their table to peck breadcrumbs Mabel scattered on the ground. When a large black cat with a white nose appeared, the birds flew off in a whoosh. The cat snaked its way along the pathway from the villa to Dottie and Mabel.

"Well, look what we have here!" Mabel said. The cat padded up to her and attempted to jump on her knee. She pushed it gently to one side. "I don't want my allergies to act up. Go make friends with Dottie."

Dottie examined the cat's collar. "His name is Satana."

"Doesn't that mean 'devil'?"

"Yes, I think it does." Dottie stroked the smooth silky fur on his head. "What a beautiful animal. He must belong to the villa."

Mabel glanced across the lawn. "I can't see Antonio with a cat. He strikes me as someone who would own a pit bull terrier."

"A pit bull?"

"I shouldn't worry, Dottie. If there is a dog, it's obviously kept chained up or in an enclosure."

Dottie shuddered. What if the animal escaped?

***

As soon as the train pulled into *Firenze*, Dottie found a public phone box and called Lieutenant Piaf. The receptionist informed her that Lieutenant Piaf had been delayed and wouldn't be back for two days. Dottie hesitated. Should she wait? No, the police needed to know. She passed the information about Carlos and Nico to the receptionist and gave her Antonio's address and phone number.

Firenze captivated Dottie's heart. The *Duomo*, its unusual façade of red, white, and green marble, so familiar in photographs, was far more dramatic in reality. They could not get tickets for the Uffizi, but after spending time studying the Baptistery mosaics, they visited the Galleria dell'Accademia.

Reaching the end of the corridor where Michelangelo's *David* stood, Dottie gazed at the beautiful work of art. She understood why people stood around the statue in silence, many of them with tears in their eyes.

***

By the time they got back after a long day of touring and a hot train ride, they were ready for a swim. They changed into their bathing suits and slipped into the pool. Dottie floated in the shallow end, feeling her body cool down as water lapped over her legs and arms.

They ate by the pool again. "How do you fancy Pisa tomorrow?" Mabel said. "We could stay on a bit and have dinner there."

The roar of an engine drowned Dottie's reply. As the villa gates opened, a silver sports car shot up the drive and stopped suddenly, tires squealing. A young man with long dark hair jumped out and rushed toward the villa.

"I expect that's another of Antonio's clients," Mabel said." He's in a big hurry."

"Do you notice something odd?"

"Odd?"

"The dog didn't bark."

"Perhaps the young fellow is a relative of Antonio's. Or," she smiled mischievously, "perhaps the tape machine broke."

***

It was 2 a.m. Dottie had almost reached the end of her P. D. James novel but kept nodding off. It was no use; she'd have to wait until tomorrow to learn who committed the crime. She turned off the light and snuggled into bed.

In the distance, she heard the distinct rumble of a car engine, which grew louder as the car drew near the villa. She heard the gates swing open. Dottie jumped out of bed and peered through the window. A light activated by the motion sensor swept over a white van as it drove through the gateway. Who could be visiting Morelli at this time of the night? More to the point, why? Gravel crunched as the vehicle eased down the drive. Dottie's heart began to beat fast. It was time to do some sleuthing.

She checked on Mabel. When she heard loud snores, Dottie didn't have the heart to disturb her friend. Dressing quickly in black slacks and sweater and armed with her flashlight, Dottie crept to the door. She opened and closed

Dottie Flowers and the European Caper

it as quietly as possible glanced around. All was silent. She crossed the lawn. The foliage bordering it was so thick that hardly any moonlight penetrated. She flicked on the flashlight. Guided by its beam, she dodged around bushes and trees and struggled through the undergrowth until she reached the tall hedge running down the side of the driveway.

The van was parked close to the villa. Dottie crept along the hedge until she found a gap large enough to squeeze through. She dashed to the back of the van and directed the flashlight's powerful beam on the license plate. When she saw the number, Dottie froze. It was Carlos's license plate number.

In a daze, Dottie stumbled to the gap and plunged through. Using the flashlight to guide her, she moved as fast as the rough undergrowth would allow.

She breathed a sigh of relief when she arrived at the pool house. Once inside, she sank on the sofa and rummaged in her bag for a cigarillo. It took a few attempts to light it. She closed her eyes and inhaled, trying to bring her heartbeat back to normal. Why was Carlos's van in the driveway, she wondered. Had he been driving the van or had someone borrowed it? And, whether it had been Carlos or someone else, what was he—or she—doing in Antonio's villa at two in the morning?

Chapter 21

After a heavy rainstorm overnight, the sun shone from a cloudless sky. The air felt dry and warm, so Dottie and Mabel decided to eat breakfast by the pool.

While she poured the coffee, Dottie told her friend about Carlos's van.

"You went sleuthing in the middle of the night on your own!"

"You were asleep. I couldn't bring myself to wake you."

"That wasn't very smart," Mabel snapped. "What if Carlos had seen you?"

"I was very careful."

"Well, you should have taken me. There's safety in numbers."

"There's something else." Dottie retrieved a piece of paper from her pants' pocket.

She handed it to Mabel.

Mabel looked at the paper. "It's the scrap of paper I found under my bed."

"Yes." Dottie sipped her coffee. "We know who Carlos and Nico are. We also know that the address on the paper is a warehouse in Lucca."

"Go on."

"Take a really close look at the two faded letters in the left-hand corner of the paper. Remember, we couldn't make them out before."

Mabel scrunched her eyes and peered at the letters. "I think the first letter's an 'A.' The other one looks like an 'N.'" She closed one eye and took another look. "No, it's an 'M.'" She glanced at Dottie. "Maybe they're the initials of a company name, A & M something or other. Or perhaps they mean morning, as in 'A.M.'"

"It could also be someone's initials."

"Of course. Antonio Morelli!"

Dottie helped herself to a serving of yogurt and added a spoonful of strawberries. "If they do refer to him, you know what this suggests, don't you?"

Mabel nodded. "That he's involved in the drug trade."

"It certainly looks that way. Why else would Carlos visit him in the middle of the night?" Dottie put down her spoon. "This could put us in real danger."

"How?"

"When I phoned the lieutenant's office and gave the receptionist the information about Carlos and Nico, I also gave her Antonio's phone number, in case the lieutenant needed to speak with me."

"So if he phones and identifies himself... I see what you mean." Mabel paused for a few moments. "What do we do now? Tell the local police about our suspicions or wait and see what happens next?"

"I'd rather speak with Lieutenant Piaf when he returns tomorrow and let him deal with it." She sipped her coffee. "As soon as I finish breakfast, I'll phone the receptionist and stress that the lieutenant must not call that number under any circumstances."

"Good." Sprinkling a heaped teaspoon of sugar over her strawberries, Mabel said, "Don't forget Yvette and Pierre will be here in a few days."

"Exactly."

"What do you mean by that?"

"Well, think about it. Who arranged for us to stay here?"

"Yvette. Pierre wasn't keen, though."

"That's true but, we ended up here, regardless of Pierre's lack of enthusiasm. Doesn't that strike you as a bit strange?"

"Perhaps Yvette was trying to be helpful."

Dottie pulled out a packet of cigarillos. She glanced at Mabel. "Do you mind?"

"Go ahead."

Dottie lit the cigarillo and, closing her eyes, inhaled. She turned her head to one side and blew out the smoke. "I don't think Yvette is the helpful type."

Mabel's eyes sparked. "Why have you taken such a dislike to her? She's self-centered, I'll grant you that, and she drives recklessly. That doesn't mean she's a drug trafficker or arranges for people to be murdered."

Dottie felt a pang of guilt. It was true she'd taken a dislike to Yvette. Was her dislike clouding her judgment? She mulled things over as she smoked. Finally, she squished the cigarillo in the ashtray. "Whether Yvette and Pierre are innocent or not, I'd like to know why Carlos turned up at the villa at 2 a.m."

Mabel's eyes lit up. "I've got an idea."

"Go on."

"Why don't we stay up tonight and see if Carlos appears? Maybe we could confront him…"

Dottie cut in. "Are you crazy? Who knows what he might do?" She chewed her lip. "I must admit, it would be interesting to see if he does turn up again."

Mabel pushed her chair back and stood. "We're on! I'll clear away the dishes while you phone Lieutenant Piaf's office. We'll go to Pisa as planned and get back early enough to have a nap. We'll need to have our wits about us tonight."

***

Dottie gazed up at the tower. No matter how many pictures she'd seen of the odd-looking structure, they didn't prepare her for the thrill of seeing the real thing. How could a tower possibly lean that far without collapsing, she wondered.

The midday sun beat down relentlessly as the two women wandered through the rows of souvenir stands near the tower. Dottie was glad she'd brought her sunhat. After buying some postcards, they found a café and ordered lemonade.

Mabel fanned herself with the menu. "Whew! This heat is a bit much."

"Why don't we head home after our drinks? Then, we can relax for a few hours."

"Suits me," Mabel said, mopping her brow with a tissue. "We've seen the tower; that's the main thing—and the last thing I feel like is eating."

As they drove back, dark clouds gathered, blotting out the sun. Thunder rumbled overhead. Within minutes, rain hammered on the windscreen like tiny pebbles. The rain continued throughout the afternoon and into the evening, but Dottie didn't mind, as she planned to catch up on some reading. Both women settled in the living room. Curled in the leather armchair, Dottie buried herself in the P. D. James novel, determined to finish it this time. Mabel lay on the sofa with a copy of the *National Enquirer*, and a bowl of potato chips resting on her stomach.

***

Over a supper of Dottie's minestrone soup, the women made plans. They decided to take turns watching out for Carlos, starting at 10 p.m.

Dottie lifted a spoonful of soup to her lips. "It's a bit ridiculous."

"What is?"

"The odds of Carlos visiting Morelli a second time. He probably made the drug deal last night."

Mabel's face fell. "You think it's a waste of time?"

"Probably."

"Well, it won't hurt to look out for him. We won't confront him—that's a stupid idea." Mabel leaned forward. "Even if Carlos doesn't come back, maybe another dealer will make a clandestine visit."

From the excitement in her voice, Dottie knew that the idea of hiding in the bushes and looking for a drug dealer in the middle of the night had caught Mabel's imagination.

"We both know something's going on," Mabel continued. "Maybe we'll discover what it is."

"You're right."

"Besides, we've nothing to lose."

"Who's taking the first watch?" Dottie wondered. "I think we should do two hours on, two hours off."

"I will."

"OK. Let's clear up and rest for a while. And don't forget to wear dark clothing."

"I packed an extra sweatshirt at the last minute. It happens to be black, thank goodness. And I have some navy-blue pants."

"What about shoes?"

"I have a pair of sneakers I found in a sale just before we left. Did I tell you about them?"

"Are they comfortable?"

"I expect so."

"Did you try them on at the store?"

"I didn't have time."

Dottie shook her head. "I give up!"

***

Time dragged. By the time 2:30 a.m. rolled by, Dottie decided she'd had enough. She wandered into Mabel's room and shook her gently by the shoulder.

Mabel rubbed her eyes. "Is it my turn?"

"I think we should call it a night…"

Dottie's sentence was cut short by the rumble of an engine. "Or maybe not." She dashed to the window. The gate had opened, and a white van pulled onto the driveway. "Let's go, Mabel. I think Carlos has arrived."

The two women crept out of the house. Even though the rain had stopped hours ago, the air felt damp and musty. The *Villa Lorenzo* sign creaked as a sudden gust of wind swept through the gardens, bending trees and bushes in its wake. Looking around carefully to make sure the coast was clear, Dottie and Mabel squelched across the wet lawn and headed into the wooded area.

As on the previous night, the thick foliage blocked most moonlight. The sharp beam of the flashlight made it easier to avoid tripping over roots or broken branches, but every time they brushed against a tree or shrub, they were drenched.

The van was parked closer to the house this time. The two women inched along until they reached the gap in the hedge.

"What now?" Mabel whispered.

"We'll wait to see what happens."

"I'm soaked."

"So am I. Let's hope we don't have to wait too long."

They huddled by the hedge for what seemed ages. The wet wool sweater clung to Dottie's skin, making it itch. "I don't think I can stand this much longer, Mabel."

Mabel's teeth chattered. "Me, neither."

From the side of the house, a door slammed, and raised voices could be heard. Moments later, they heard loud cracks like wood splintering, and a man's angry voice yelled out something in Italian.

Agonized moans pierced the air. "Someone's hurt," Dottie said. " We'd better go check."

They crept through the gap in the hedge and glanced around. Satisfied that no one had seen them, they hurried past the van to a spot where the drive gave way to a narrow footpath. Bordered by a tall hedge, the footpath led to the villa's back porch, which was surrounded by bushes. Light, filtering through a curtained window, illuminated the wooden railing around the porch. A section of the railing lay broken. Posts had split in two, as though someone had fallen or been pushed into them.

The two women stood on the path, uncertain what to do. The wind, stronger now, whipped through the hedge, swirling leaves into the air. For a few seconds, the path and its surroundings were swathed in brilliance as a flash of lightning forked across the night sky.

Mabel whispered. "It's like a scene from a horror movie."

Dottie was barely listening. Her eyes were fastened on something under a bush. She moved closer and, after a quick glance around, switched on the flashlight. The powerful beam fell on a badly scuffed running shoe. Cold fear prickled the back of her neck when she realized the shoe was attached to a foot.

Mabel joined her. "Oh, no!"

They stared down at the foot. The trouser leg was pushed up a little, revealing a man's pale hairy shin and a white sports sock.

Dottie bent down to look more closely. As she reached out to push back the foliage, something squeaked. She jumped back as a field mouse ran over her shoes.

"Let's go before someone sees us," urged Mabel.

As though on cue, the porch light flicked on, bathing the two women in a yellow glow.

They bolted down the path. Dottie's eyes searched desperately for the gap in the hedge. "There it is!" she hissed. They plunged through.

With the help of the flashlight, they struggled back. Exposed tree roots and fallen branches presented a challenge, and Dottie almost tripped a few times. Intent on staying upright, she stepped back in fright when an animal leapt out of the bushes. The flashlight catapulted out of her hand as she stumbled and fell in the mud. "Shoot!"

"Are you all right?"

"I think so. An animal—I'm sure it was a cat—ran in front of me." Dottie struggled to her feet, wiping mud clods off her clothes. "Can you see the flashlight?"

They glanced around, but everything was in darkness.

"It must have broken," Mabel said. "Fortunately, we're almost back."

When they emerged from the woods, a loud meow made them jump. They recognized Satana's distinctive white markings when he appeared from behind a tree. He ran to Dottie, purring enthusiastically and brushing himself against her legs. "So, you're the culprit," she scolded.

"We'd better take our time crossing the lawn. It will look suspicious enough if we're seen out here in the middle of the night but if someone sees us running it will look even worse," Mabel said.

Satana trotted behind them, ignoring attempts to shoo him away. Feeling tired and weary, Dottie longed for bed. As though reading her mind, Mabel commented, "I'm looking forward to a warm shower."

"And a hot drink."

"I'll make us some Earl Grey tea," Mabel said. "Then, I think I'll soak my feet… Ouch!"

Dottie turned. Mabel lay on the ground, cradling her ankle. Her face winced with pain. "I slipped on the wet grass."

Dottie knelt and felt Mabel's ankle, trying to remember the little bit she'd learned about first aid in Girl Guides years ago.

"You're not supposed to press that hard," Mabel complained.

Dottie noticed the tread on the bottom of Mabel's sneaker was almost nonexistent. *Cheap crap*, she thought. *No wonder Mabel had slipped.*

Footsteps crunched on the gravel pathway. Mabel's fingernails dug into Dottie's arm as a beam of light flickered over the lawn.

"It looks as if we've been caught," Mabel whispered. "We'd better do some fast thinking as to why we're prowling around the villa grounds in the early hours of the morning."

"The main thing is to stay calm," Dottie said. "We're not doing anything wrong."

"Satana!" a woman's deep voice rang out. Satana meowed in response but stayed by Dottie.

"It's Maria." Mabel said. "I'd recognize that voice anywhere!"

Dottie Flowers and the European Caper

Maria headed over to them. Dottie shielded her eyes from the glare of the light.

As she drew close, Maria looked at the two women. "Something is wrong?" she asked.

"Mabel's hurt," Dottie said. "I think her ankle's twisted."

Maria turned her attention to Mabel. "You fall," she stated. "I will help you."

She leaned over and to take Mabel's arm. Mabel shook her head. "A man has been injured. He must be helped first."

"What man?"

"We don't know," Dottie answered. "We heard a noise and went to check. He's lying under a bush by the back door of the villa."

Maria shrugged her shoulders. "He is drunk."

"Drunk? But we heard him moaning in pain."

"He come to see Mr. Morelli. I hear him threaten Mr. Morelli. Mr. Morelli throw him out."

As Dottie and Maria helped Mabel to her feet, Dottie heard the faint crunch of gravel as tires moved along the driveway. A minute later, the driver revved the engine, and the vehicle sped away.

The three women made their way to the pool house. The slow progress gave Dottie time to think. The man she'd found under the bushes wasn't dead. He was drunk. He'd threatened Morelli – why? She'd worry about that later. Right now, she needed to come up with a good reason they'd been out so late. We wanted to see if there were any fireflies—but why would they be out so late looking for fireflies? We like to stargaze—but again, they wouldn't need to stargaze at 2:30 a.m.

Once they were inside the pool house, Maria found an elastic bandage from a first-aid kit in the bathroom and wrapped it around the swollen ankle. "Now, you rest."

Wracking her brains for a good excuse, Dottie put the kettle on and made tea for them all. In the end, Maria solved the dilemma.

"So, you see ghost?"

"What?"

"You are—feared?"

"Afraid?" Dottie gave a sheepish grin. "Yes, a little." Out of the corner of her eye, she saw the look of puzzlement on Mabel's face. She prayed Mabel wouldn't say anything.

Maria drank her tea and placed the mug on the coffee table. She stared into space. "My cat Satana see the ghost many times. You must not worry. The ghost is—friend."

Dottie was curious. "What kind of ghost is it?"

Maria waved hands in a gesture of dismissal. "No more talk!" She wiped away a tear that had fallen down her cheek. "Now, I go." She stood, secured the belt of her dressing gown, and walked to the door. "*Buonanotte!*"

Chapter 22

The following morning, Dottie decided to make omelettes for breakfast. "Hope you don't mind having omelettes again. We have plenty of eggs, courtesy of Antonio."

"Or more precisely, his chickens," Mabel said.

Dottie laughed. "That's right." Whisking the eggs in an earthenware bowl, she remembered Maria's cryptic remark about a ghost. "That ghost business last night was strange."

"Very weird," Mabel agreed. "Maria was quite emotional."

"Maybe the ghost is someone she's close to."

Mabel frowned. "What it's all about, do you think?"

"I don't know but I'd like to find out." Did the woman possess extra sensory perception or did she simply have a vivid imagination? Dottie had read somewhere that almost half of Canadians believed in ghosts, and about 18 percent swore they'd seen one. Did the same statistics apply to Italians?

A sharp rap on the pool house door brought Dottie out of her reverie. Maria stood on the doorstep, unsmiling. "You have phone call."

Dottie's heart raced as she followed Maria along the path to the villa. It wouldn't be the lieutenant. She'd made it clear to the receptionist at the police station that he mustn't phone the villa. She hoped it wasn't Hettie or Jeremy, because neither of her children would phone unless it was an emergency.

Maria ushered her through the front door. "There is phone." She pointed to the receiver on the hallstand and left, closing the door with a firm click.

Biting her lip, Dottie picked it up.

"My dear Dottie!"

Dottie's breath caught in her throat. "Hans!"

"I do apologize for phoning so early. I arrived in Lucca late last night and wanted to catch you before you went out." He chuckled. "The last time I saw you I was being dragged out of my house by that odious lieutenant." He cleared his throat. "But I did not phone to talk about that." His voice grew conspiratorial. "I would like to take you out for dinner this evening to one of Lucca's top restaurants."

"Tonight?"

"It is short notice, and I realize you might have other plans, but we begin to film in two days' time," Hans explained. "Once filming begins, I will be extremely busy."

Relieved that the call was not from the lieutenant or her children, Dottie did some fast thinking. Mabel's ankle was much better this morning. She could make tea for herself and Dottie could make her a simple meal.

"So, what do you say? I have some things to tell you, but I would rather do that over a bottle of fine Italian Chianti."

Dottie made up her mind. "I'd like that."

"Splendid! I will pick you up at seven!" She heard the phone click.

As she hurried back to the pool house, Dottie realized he hadn't asked for directions. Then, why would he? From his comments about the swimming pool, it was clear he was familiar with the property. She remembered he looked upset when he learned where they were staying. Or had she imagined that?

"So, who was it?" Mabel asked as soon as Dottie walked in.

"Hans."

"Well, well!"

Dottie let out an exasperated sigh. "What's that supposed to mean?"

"He's an attractive man."

"Let me get started on these omelettes, and I'll tell you about the call."

After adding salt and pepper and finely chopped spring onion, Dottie melted butter in a pan and poured in half the mixture.

She told Mabel about the dinner invitation. "I said yes. I hope you don't mind. He has some things to tell me."

"Of course, I don't mind."

"I'm anxious to find out more about the note found on the floor beside Monsieur Bouchard. I'm also curious about Hans's connection with *Villa Lorenzo*."

"You can't fool me, Dottie Flowers. I've known you for too long. You're thrilled he's invited you for dinner."

Dottie felt a warm blush creep over her face. She shook herbs over the omelette and placed it in the warm oven.

"What are you going to wear?"

"I haven't had time to think about it." Dottie melted more butter and poured the rest of the egg mixture into the pan. "I think we're going to a fancy restaurant, though."

"I'd avoid wearing those green contact lenses, if I were you," Mabel grinned.

"Funny!"

Dottie served the omelettes and poured the coffee. They settled down to eat.

"S and S," Mabel said, as she took a sip of coffee.

"What?"

"S and S. Simple and sexy. Now you have a bit of a tan, that white low-cut bodice with those slinky black pants would look terrific. And what about your silk jacket with the swirly black-and-white design? That would give a spectacular finishing touch."

Dottie couldn't believe her ears. "Since when did you take an interest in clothes? You sound just like Serena!" She pictured her assistant Serena, arms folded across her ample bosom, lecturing her about what to wear.

Mabel smiled. "I haven't. I just think it makes sense to dress up for a man such as Hans."

"You make him sound like royalty."

"Don't get defensive. If he turns out to be on the level, you'll want him to ask you out again."

Dottie cut a piece of omelette with her fork. "Right now, I just want to get on with breakfast. Let's eat while it's warm."

***

That evening, Dottie prepared a chicken salad for Mabel's dinner. "I'm not an invalid," Mabel protested. "My ankle's much better now."

"You don't want to overdo it. Besides, I'm having fun." Dottie sliced fresh tomatoes and cucumbers to accompany the chicken salad and put the plate on the tray with a soft dinner roll and a glass of white wine. As an afterthought, she added a small bowl of strawberries with a dollop of thick cream.

"There's extra chicken salad in the fridge if you want more." She placed the tray on the dining room table. "Now, you can eat whenever you feel like."

"Thanks, Dottie."

"You're welcome. I'd better get ready."

Dottie Flowers and the European Caper

After a long hot shower, Dottie smoothed honey and almond body cream on her legs and arms. Wrapped in the terry bathrobe, she highlighted her tanned face with blush and rose-colored lipstick. She checked her makeup carefully in the mirror. Her almond-shaped eyes were her best feature. She applied eyeliner to enhance them and draw attention away from her slightly hooked nose and pointed chin.

Dottie dressed in the outfit Mabel had recommended, with high-heeled black sandals. "So, what do you think?" She twirled around for Mabel to take a good look.

"Perfect! Now, go and enjoy yourself."

Dottie waited inside the pool house. Through the window, she watched the main gates open. A black sports car pulled onto the driveway. As Hans climbed out of his car, she left the pool house and walked to him.

"Dottie! You look fabulous." He kissed her on the cheek and opened the passenger door. She was about to get in when Antonio Morelli strode over. He greeted them with a warm smile. "Good evening, Dottie." He turned to Hans and shook his hand. "When my housekeeper told me who was at the gate, I was delighted. It is an unexpected pleasure to see you again, Hans. What brings you to this part of the world?"

Hans described the documentary film he planned to make about the Master Chefs of Tuscany. "We will be filming in Lucca first. Then, we go to *Sienna* and *Firenze*."

"You must come for dinner while you are here."

"I do not think that will be possible." Hans's voice sounded flat. "I am going to be very busy once filming starts."

"Even a busy filmmaker such as you has to eat," Antonio laughed. "No matter, we will talk about that later. *Ciao!*"

Once they'd buckled their seatbelts, Hans eased through the open gateway and onto the road. Why was Hans so reluctant to have dinner with Antonio, Dottie wondered.

***

When they arrived in Lucca, Hans parked the car near the Piazza San Michele. He took Dottie by the arm and led her to a nearby restaurant. "I think you are going to enjoy the experience."

Dottie looked at the sign. *"La Buca di Sant'Antonio?"*

"You have heard of it?"

"I read about it in my guidebook." In the book, *La Buca* had been described as 'the premier gastronomic pit stop of Lucca.'

Hans held the door open, and Dottie walked in. The white walls covered in copper pots and brass musical instruments gave the restaurant a classy, comfortable ambience. Once they'd been shown to their table, Hans took over. "I know you are a vegetarian, Dottie. They have divine ravioli filled with ricotta and lightly sautéed in butter, with a wide choice of other pasta dishes. And fish…"

"Wait!" Dottie laughed. "Please let me look at the menu." As her eyes glanced over the pages, she realized why Hans had wanted to make suggestions. There was a large selection of dishes, many of which she didn't recognize.

After discussing options, she chose a mushroom risotto. Hans ordered the spit-roasted kid with roast potatoes and artichoke pudding. He grinned sheepishly. "I order this every time I eat here. I should try something else, but I cannot resist it." He examined the sommelier's wine list. "A Chianti Classico Reserva will complement our meal well, I believe."

"That's the wine Antonio served when he invited Mabel and me to dinner."

A frown crossed Hans' brow. Finally, he said, "Antonio has excellent taste."

Dottie paused. Clearly, something about Antonio troubled Hans. She decided this wasn't the time to pry. "I'm afraid I know very little about wine."

"Wine tasting is a hobby of mine, but that is not what I wanted to talk about tonight."

After the sommelier poured the wine, Hans's face became serious. "First. Let me tell you what happened after I was taken to the police station. Then, we can relax and enjoy our evening together." He cleared his throat. "As I explained to the lieutenant..."

"Lieutenant Piaf."

"Yes. I assured him that I knew nothing about any drugs. When he showed me the note, everything became clear."

"What do you mean?"

"Until two weeks ago, I had a cameraman named Georgio working for me. I discovered he was smoking pot on the job. That was bad enough. Then, I found out he was dealing drugs. I had no choice but to fire him. The note the lieutenant found in Monsieur Bouchard's bedroom was addressed to me. It wasn't signed, of course. Fortunately, I recognized the handwriting."

"Georgio's."

"Yes, he used to drop off notes to me occasionally if he was going to be late or needed time off. His flowery writing is very distinctive."

"So, you managed to convince the lieutenant that Georgio wrote the note?"

"Eventually." He drank some wine. "In the note, Georgio spoke about a shipment having arrived and where we were to meet."

"A shipment of what? And where were you supposed to meet him?"

"The note didn't say what was in the shipment," Hans said. " As to the meeting place, it simply said 'usual meeting place 15:00 hrs. tomorrow.'"

"That sounds contrived."

"Clearly, he wrote the note to implicate me in a drug deal."

"To get even with you because you fired him."

"I suppose."

"How did Lieutenant Piaf react?"

"At first, he was sure the note was genuine. I think he was so overwrought by the death of Monsieur Bouchard that his head was not clear. Later, after I told him about Georgio, he examined the note again. He thought it possible that the note was false. A red halibut, I think he called it."

Dottie smiled. "Our lieutenant gets his idioms mixed up."

Hans raised an eyebrow. "It would seem so."

"So, Lieutenant Piaf let you go?"

"Yes. He arrested Giorgio the following day." Hans smiled. "Now, let us forget about unpleasant things and drink to our evening together."

They clinked glasses. Hans put down his glass and took Dottie's hand. "No matter how busy I get, I will make time to take you out for lunch or dinner. Or both."

Before she had a chance to respond, the waiter arrived with their entrées. "Risotto for you, *signora*?"

"Thank you." He placed the steaming dish in front of her.

"The chef hopes you enjoy the special sauce he has prepared for you, *signore*," the waiter said as he served Hans.

"I am sure it will be exquisite as always, Sergio."

After the waiter left, Dottie picked up her fork and began to eat.

Hans cut into the roasted meat. "What are you doing for the rest of this week?"

"Mabel's taking a cookery class in Lucca on Thursday. I'll probably come in with her and do some shopping. Apart from that, we haven't made any plans."

Hans's face lit up. "Let me take you out for lunch while Mabel is in her cooking class. I know the perfect little spot where we can relax over a Limoncello Mojito. It gets busy, so I will reserve a table for noon hour."

A warm glow filled her heart. Could this be the beginning of a romance?

***

They drove back to the villa about midnight. Always wary of the dog, she felt relieved when Hans insisted that he escort her to the pool house. They reached the door. He drew her toward him and kissed her gently on the lips. "Thank you for a wonderful evening, Dottie. I will phone to let you know where to meet me for lunch."

She watched him leave. As he walked past their rented Peugeot, Dottie noticed a car parked next to it. Puzzled, she walked over to check it out. Moonlight glinted on the familiar Mercedes insignia. *Nice car! It must belong to one of Antonio's relatives, but why would he—or she—park here?* She looked through the car window, but it was too dark to see anything.

Dottie opened the pool house door and almost fell over a large leather suitcase. Filled with apprehension, she opened her bedroom door. In the second bed lay Mabel, on her back, snoring gently. Dottie marched to the other bedroom. The door was ajar. She pushed it open and crept in. On one bed, a man in striped pajamas lay on top of the duvet, his mouth open. She moved closer. In spite of the sagging mouth and disheveled hair, she recognized her friend, Arnold.

Dottie's heart sank. The large mound in the next bed, covered with the floral duvet, must be Mabel's niece, Yolanda.

Dottie's hands curled into fists as she marched back to her room. She shook Mabel's shoulder. Mabel moaned and turned over on her side. "Mabel, wake up!" Dottie ordered.

Mabel rubbed her eyes and sat up. "What's the matter?"

"What's the matter? You have the gall to ask me that? I've just found you in my spare bed and Arnold and Yolanda in your room!"

"I can explain…"

"It had better be a good explanation, Mabel!" Dottie hissed. "What are they doing here, in our pool house, in the middle of the night?"

Dottie glared at Mabel. "Well?"

"Sleeping, I hope."

"Don't try to make light of it, Mabel. This is not funny!"

Chapter 23

Mabel propped herself in bed. "OK, so here's the skinny."

"The skinny?"

"Isn't that what they call inside information these days?"

Dottie huffed. "Go on."

"Yolanda and Arnold arrived here just after you left."

"How did they get in?"

"Yolanda told Maria that she's my niece."

"Did you know they were coming?"

"Of course not!" Mabel snapped. "They're touring Tuscany and thought they'd surprise us with a visit."

"They've certainly succeeded," Dottie said. A thought crossed her mind. "Wait a minute. Isn't Yolanda expecting the baby soon?"

"Yes, Yolanda wanted Arnold to take her on holiday before the baby arrives. He wasn't keen, but he's obviously given in to her."

"Haven't they heard of hotels?"

"By the time they'd had supper—they ate the rest of that chicken salad you made—it was getting late. I just didn't have the heart to turn them out."

With a sigh, Dottie plunked herself on Mabel's bed. "All right, I can see that. Sorry, I got angry with you."

"I don't blame you. They should have warned us they were coming."

"I'll make them a good breakfast in the morning, and we'll see them on their way." Dottie stretched her arms and yawned.

"Did you have a nice dinner?"

"Yes." Her heart gave a little flutter as she remembered the kiss.

"Aren't you going to tell me about it?"

"Tomorrow, after our guests leave. I need to get a good night's sleep. We'll have our hands full in the morning."

***

Dottie felt warm affection for Arnold when he walked into the kitchen the next morning. She'd met him a year ago when they'd taken riding lessons together. Arnold had been a confirmed bachelor until he'd set eyes on Yolanda. Feeling sorry for his pathetic attempts at romance, Dottie had given Arnold advice on how to win Yolanda's heart. The conspiracy had bound them, and they'd become good friends.

She hugged him. "It's great to see you again, Arnold."

"And you, too, Dottie." He smoothed his moustache, a nervous habit of his. "Must apologize for dropping in on you like this. We're going to Lucca after breakfast to find accommodations."

Seeing Arnold's embarrassed face, Dottie said, "You don't have to apologize." She tied an apron around her waist. "Now, I'm going to make breakfast. How does eggs and bacon sound?" Thank goodness, Mabel had bought bacon!

Arnold's face beamed. "Wonderful! Haven't had a good old English breakfast for ages."

"It's too greasy!" a voice boomed.

Dottie turned around. Yolanda stood in the doorway wearing a red tartan dressing gown and matching slippers. "Arnold doesn't need all that artery-clogging food," she declared. "His cholesterol count is too high, so we're eating sensibly these days."

Dottie felt her blood pressure rise. "One unhealthy meal isn't going to do any harm."

"It's a slippery slope," Yolanda pointed out. "Before you know it, we'll be eating cream cakes and French fries."

"I'm sure you're right, dear." Arnold said in a soothing voice.

Dottie snatched the kettle off the countertop and filled it with water. "So, Yolanda, did you sleep well?"

"I never sleep well these days," Yolanda replied, patting her large belly. "Cornelius kicks too much."

Dottie almost dropped the kettle. "Cornelius?"

"Isn't it a perfect name? We were going to tell you over breakfast. Dottie, do you have whole wheat bread?"

"Yes."

"Good. I'll have two soft poached eggs with three slices of whole wheat bread, toasted and lightly buttered. I've given up coffee, so I'll have tea with a drop of milk."

"What about you, Arnold?"

"I'll have the same. Yolanda's right. Fried eggs and bacon are out," Arnold said in a wistful voice.

Chicken, thought Dottie. "Coffee or tea?"

Arnold looked Dottie square in the eyes. "Coffee," he announced.

"I thought you drank tea."

"Used to. Gave it up once I got the taste of good coffee."

"Weak tea is much better for you, Arnold," Yolanda pointed out.

"Maybe so, but I've no intention of giving up coffee."

At least he's sticking to his guns over that, Dottie thought.

"Anything we can do to help?" Arnold asked.

"Yes, you could set the dining room table for breakfast," Dottie said. "Everything you need is in the cabinet."

"Can you manage that, Arnold?" Yolanda asked. "I'd like to get dressed."

"Of course, dear."

As soon as they left the kitchen, Dottie took a deep breath. She checked her watch. In a short while, they'll be gone, she reminded herself. She switched on the kettle and placed a small pan of water on the gas burner.

Mabel wandered into the kitchen, yawning. "What's for breakfast?"

"Poached eggs and whole wheat toast."

"What? No eggs and bacon for Arnold? There's bacon in the fridge."

Dottie pointed her thumb toward Mabel's bedroom "It's not allowed," she mimed.

"Too bad." Mabel glanced at the coffeemaker. "It looks like the coffee's ready."

"You'll need to make tea for Yolanda."

"Tea? She drinks coffee."

"Not anymore, she doesn't. She's given it up."

Mabel found a tea bag. "I suppose that's because of the pregnancy."

"I suppose," Dottie snapped. "Would you pass me the eggs?"

Mabel took the bowl of eggs out of the fridge and handed it to her. "Are you all right?"

"What do you think?"

Mabel sighed. "Yolanda can be demanding at times."

Dottie added salt and a drop of vinegar to the simmering water, cracked open two eggs, and then slid them gently into the pan.

"I'll make the toast."

"Good, these eggs won't take long. Yolanda wants her toast very lightly buttered, by the way."

Yolanda, wearing a red maternity dress with a large navy-blue bow at the neckline, walked into the kitchen. "I see you're busy. I might as well go in the dining room and sit."

Once the slices popped, Mabel buttered them. Dottie lifted the eggs, one at a time, onto the toast. "This is Yolanda's," she told Mabel. "Tell her not to wait. Poached eggs need to be eaten right away. I'll bring her tea. Then, I'll prepare Arnold's eggs."

Dottie placed the teapot on the table with a small jug of milk. Yolanda cut into an egg. "This is overcooked."

Dottie stared at the yolk oozing out of the egg. "That's soft poached."

"I'll give this to Arnold," Yolanda said, ignoring Dottie's comment. "He likes his eggs well cooked, don't you, darling?"

Arnold looked up from a magazine he'd been reading. "Sorry, did you say something?"

Yolanda handed him the plate. "These eggs are just right for you."

"Tell you what, Yolanda," Dottie seethed. "Why don't you cook your eggs? That way, you'll be sure to like them."

Yolanda looked at Dottie. "Oh, heavens, now, I've upset you. It's this pregnancy. It's made me very fussy over food."

Arnold cleared his throat. "I'll make your breakfast as soon as I've eaten mine, if you'd like, dear."

Yolanda beamed. "Oh, Arnold, that would be lovely." She turned to Dottie. "Arnold knows how to make my eggs. He has just the right touch, don't you, dearest?"

Arnold's face grew red. "If you say so, dear."

Dottie and Mabel escaped to the kitchen.

"I think," said Mabel, "that I'll have cereal."

"Great idea. I'll join you."

***

Yolanda and Arnold left for Lucca shortly after breakfast. "I can't say I'm sorry to see them leave," Mabel said.

Dottie looked at her friend in surprise. "I thought you'd be thrilled to see Yolanda."

"I love my niece, Dottie, but she'd take over everything if you let her. She's good company in small doses."

They washed and dried the dishes. "Do you fancy a drive around the countryside?" Mabel asked as she rinsed the last mug. "It's a beautiful morning."

"That sounds like a perfect way to unwind."

They rooted out their sunhats. "Let's go!" Mabel urged. "Do you have the camera?"

Dottie patted her bag. "It's right here."

"We can relax now," Mabel said as she climbed in the car.

Mabel's words failed to reassure Dottie. Somehow, she didn't think they'd seen the last of Arnold and Yolanda.

Chapter 24

The two women drove through the Chianti region, with its craggy slopes and woods of flowering chestnut trees, stopping several times for Dottie to photograph the trees and fields of sunflowers. Reaching Radda in Chianti, they parked the car and strolled through winding streets filled with shops, restaurants, and bars. The cool interiors of the pottery shops offered a brief respite from the blazing sun. Looking at the vast assortment of vases, jugs, and dishes reminded Dottie of her wine jug. She hunted around for a piece of pottery to complement it and found a set of small pasta bowls with a similar glaze, decorated with a flower motif.

Mabel found a vase painted with bright red poppies standing in the corner of the shop. "Isn't this gorgeous!"

"It's definitely you, Mabel, but it's far too large to fit in your carry-on luggage."

Mabel pursed her lips, "I have friends who've brought all kinds of pottery back from Europe!"

"Are you sure they didn't have the items shipped? You could do that, if you've really set your heart on that piece."

Mabel examined the vase. "I don't think I'll buy it after all. There are several flaws in the design."

"Why don't you buy something smaller, like this cute honey pot?"

The glazed periwinkle blue pot with yellow sunflowers painted on it appealed to Mabel. She bought two of them.

Later, they shared an antipasto dish of olives, marinated artichokes, roasted peppers, and cheeses on the terrace of a small bar, with glasses of sparkling mineral water. Sipping her drink, Dottie watched three teenage girls pause next to a souvenir stand. Brief shorts and tops set off their smooth tanned skin. Giggling, they held up T-shirts and tried on hats.

"A penny for your thoughts," Mabel said.

"Watching those teenagers trying on hats brings back memories of my youth."

"So, you weren't daydreaming about Hans."

Dottie took a long sip of mineral water. "Not at that moment."

"How was your dinner date last night?"

"We went to a beautiful restaurant with delicious food."

"Never mind about the restaurant and food. I want to hear about Hans!"

The waiter hovered over them and asked if they'd like another drink.

"I'll have a glass of white wine this time," Dottie said.

"We have Chardonnay, Pino Grigio…"

"Pino Grigio, please."

"Mabel shook her head. "I'm driving. I'll stick with mineral water."

After the waiter served their drinks, Dottie told Mabel what happened to Hans after Lieutenant Piaf had questioned him. She leaned back in the chair and sipped the chilled Pinot Grigio. "The lieutenant was pretty upset over the death of his friend, Monsieur Bouchard. Once Hans explained about Georgio's drug habits, I think the lieutenant realized he'd overreacted."

Dottie Flowers and the European Caper

"Hans must have been relieved when all the questioning was over, and they let him go home." Mabel leaned over to Dottie. "So, let's get back to your date with Hans. You ate, enjoyed a bottle of wine, and he brought you home. Did he kiss you?"

Dottie felt her face grow warm. "Yes."

"Mabel smiled. "How wonderful!"

"Really, Mabel, you're such a romantic!"

"When are you going to see him again?"

"I'm not sure. He said he would phone."

Mabel pressed Dottie's hand. "I'm happy for you, Dottie."

"Don't jump to conclusions. So far, we've only had dinner together. Let's wait and see what happens." Hans's words floated into her head. *I will make time to take you out.*

The waiter brought their bill. Dottie asked him for directions to *Casa Porciatti*, a family-run grocery store she'd read about in her guidebook. In broken English with many hand gestures, he told them the location of the shop. His face broke into a wide smile when he added, "*Il formaggio—benissimo!*" They thanked him and headed to the shop.

The women lingered in the store, with its vast array of cheeses, meats, wines, and honeys, breathing in the sharp, salty smell of Romano cheese and the occasional pungent whiff of gorgonzola. Laden with two bottles of Chianti Classico, two Sicilian whites, pecorino and Romano cheeses, a jar of honey, ready-made spreads for crostini, and fresh olives, they staggered to the car.

"It's just as well we didn't have too far to walk," Mabel muttered as she opened the car door and placed her purchases on the backseat. "My arms feel as though they're coming out of their sockets."

Dottie placed the bottles of wine on their side, on the floor of the car. "I know what you mean." She rolled her shoulders a few times. "That feels better."

Warm and relaxed, they drove back to the villa in the late afternoon. After they'd unloaded their purchases and put them away, Mabel made a pot of tea. "I'm glad I popped a carton of tea bags in my luggage," she said. "Do you remember the day we met? I served you Earl Grey and found out later you didn't even like tea."

Dottie sipped the tart, orange-flavored beverage. "I've developed a taste for it since then."

They heard the crunch of feet, followed by a sharp rap on the door. "I expect that's Maria," Mabel said. "I'll get it."

Antonio stood on the doorstep. "Good afternoon, Mabel. May I come in for a few moments?"

"Of course."

He stepped into the pool house. Smiling, he said, "I won't keep you. I just wanted you to know that I've had a phone call from Yvette and Pierre. They're arriving tomorrow."

Dottie's heart sank. "So soon!"

"Their plans have changed, it seems, and they were able to leave St. Siffret a few days early. It will be good to see my old friends again."

Dottie forced a smile. "Of course."

"They will arrive around six. Would you join us for dinner?"

"That's kind of you," Mabel said.

"Come at seven. That will give us the opportunity to have a drink before we dine." His eyes twinkled. "I'm sure Yvette and Pierre will have lots of stories to tell."

I'm sure they will, thought Dottie. *And maybe some they won't tell.*

After Antonio left, Dottie let out a deep sigh. "Now, we're in a fix!"

"What's wrong?"

"Have you forgotten that Antonio's birthday gift disappeared?"

"Maria knows something," Mabel said. "Remember her strange response when we asked her about it the other morning? She turned very pale and walked away in a huff, as though we were accusing her of stealing it." Mabel tapped a finger on her lips. "A thought's occurred to me. You bought yourself a copy of the same book, remember. Why don't we parcel that? We can buy wrapping paper with red ribbon and a bow. Yvette and Pierre will never know the difference."

"Great idea! They didn't sign the book or put in some kind of birthday message, so that's one less thing to worry about. We'll need a box as well, roughly the size of the other one."

"We can ask the shopkeepers. Or perhaps we'll find one that's been put out for garbage."

"OK. We'll talk to Maria about the missing parcel later."

Mabel smiled. "That's settled then. We'll go to Lucca tomorrow morning."

***

They drove into Lucca after breakfast and purchased wrapping paper almost identical to the original. A local bookstore found them a box. "Let's go straight back," Dottie said. "I'd like to get this giftwrapped. Then, we can relax."

Mabel agreed. "Why don't we spend a few hours around the pool? I have a feeling things might get a bit hectic once Yvette and Pierre arrive."

"I'm sure they will. I'll need my 35 SPF sunscreen. The sun's brutal."

"It's time I concentrated on getting some color on my legs and back," Mabel said. "Did I tell you I found this terrific Hawaiian suntan oil? It was on special at Shoppers Drug Mart."

"You should protect your skin, Mabel, not fry it."

"Sunshine's good for you. Plenty of Vitamin D."

"It is. In moderation."

They headed home. As they began their ascent up the winding hill to the villa, they heard a vehicle close behind them. Mabel glanced in the mirror. "There's a white van right on our tail. I'll try to lose it." She accelerated, but the van caught up and overtook them on a bend.

As it sped by, Dottie saw the name *Giuseppe's* and two words in Italian on the side of the van, with a logo of a man carrying bricks. Dottie's heart skipped a beat. "That's Carlos's van! And I'm almost sure it was Carlos driving. I bet he's on his way to the villa."

"He's asking for trouble driving like that."

They drove past the main villa gates and saw Carlos punching in the entry code. "He's here a lot," Mabel remarked. "He must be one of Antonio's busiest customers."

Dottie shook her head. "I think it's more likely he's working for Antonio. Remember we saw Nico and him at the warehouse putting stuff in the van."

"I'd like to know what's being stored in that warehouse," Mabel commented. "We should try to get inside and look."

"Are you mad? Who knows what they'd do to us if we got caught. Let's leave that to the police."

They drove into the villa grounds through the side entrance, as usual. Dottie's good humor vanished when she spotted the Mercedes parked by the pool house. *So much for a lazy afternoon by the pool.* "It looks like we have visitors."

Before Mabel had a chance to reply, laughter floated through the air, followed by a loud splash. The two women looked at each other.

"Someone's in our pool," Dottie seethed. "And there are no prizes for guessing who it is!"

Mabel parked the car next to the Mercedes, and the women climbed out. They walked over to Arnold, who sat at the side of the pool in his baggy swimming trunks and Tilley hat, watching Yolanda swim.

"Hello!" Arnold stood, smiling broadly. "It's jolly nice of you to let us use the pool. Yolanda's under doctor's orders to exercise while we're away. He recommended swimming—so here we are!"

Wearing a scarlet bathing suit, Yolanda floated on a rubber mattress. "Yoo hoo!" she called, waving at them. She rolled off the mattress and swam to the side. "It's a perfect day to swim. I've managed four lengths so far."

Mabel took Dottie by the arm. "We have to wrap that parcel, Dottie."

Dottie let Mabel lead her into the pool house. "I can't believe this!" she fumed. "Since when did we say that they could use our pool?"

"We didn't," Mabel assured her.

"So, how did they get the idea that they can just mosey in and swim whenever they please? We were having a peaceful Tuscan vacation, and suddenly, we're taken over!"

"It's hardly been peaceful. You do exaggerate, Dottie." Mabel rooted out scissors from the kitchen drawer. "Now, would you get that book, please?"

Dottie stomped into her bedroom and retrieved The *Provençal Countryside* from a suitcase. She handed the book to Mabel. "OK. I need to know what you said to them. Or to Yolanda. She has the idea that we've given her *carte blanche* to come and go as she pleases. And no bloviating, Mabel."

"Bloviating?"

"Expounding to extremes. Exaggerating."

Mabel removed a sheet of wrapping paper and placed the box on top of it. She held the paper against the sides of the box. "That's going to fit perfectly."

"Mabel!" Dottie snapped. "Have you heard even a word I've said!"

Mabel put down the paper. "I told Yolanda that they could come for a swim sometime. I meant when we're here, of course. I had no idea they'd come when we weren't here. I'm annoyed as well." She paused. "I wonder why Maria let them in."

"That's a no-brainer. Yolanda's an expert at getting people to do what she wants."

After placing the book inside the box, Mabel stuffed tissue paper to fill in the spaces. "Don't worry. I'll have a serious chat with my niece when she finishes her swim."

Mabel wrapped the box with the paper, tied it with ribbon, and stuck the red bow on top. "I don't think Yvette or Pierre will suspect that it's not the same parcel."

"You did a great job." Dottie took it to her room and placed it on the dressing table. She was about to return to the living room when Yolanda's voice boomed through the open bedroom window. "Don't be ridiculous, Arnold!" Dottie leaned against the wall next to the window so she could hear without being seen.

"We can spend a day in Florence after we've left Lucca," Arnold said.

"Florence is full of art and history. We need to spend at least two nights there."

"We won't have time. We've booked our hotel in Lucca for five nights, and we're due to fly home two days after that."

"Let's change our booking to three nights. Then, we can spend two nights in Florence."

Arnold's voice was firm. "I see no good reason to change our plans. We haven't even scratched the surface of Lucca yet."

Dottie grinned. *Way to go, Arnold!*

"Lucca's interesting, but I want to see Florence. You are very stubborn at times, Arnold Gateshead!"

"Gallivanting around a busy city in your condition isn't a good idea," Arnold said. "Remember what the doctor said about not overdoing things..."

"That does it! I'm not an invalid, Arnold. And I refuse to be treated like one!" Yolanda declared.

Dottie peeked through the window. Yolanda yanked on her robe and threw her towel into a large straw bag. Grabbing the bag with both hands, she pushed her feet into a pair of sandals and marched across the lawn.

"Where are you going?" Arnold shouted. Ignoring her husband, Yolanda kept walking.

Dottie glanced at the van parked in the driveway. Carlos was sitting in the driver's seat. As the gates began to swing open, he switched on the engine. Yolanda headed toward the van. What was she up to? She spoke with Carlos through the open window, and then strode to the passenger side of the van. Dottie watched in horror as Yolanda climbed in the passenger seat. When the gates were fully open, Carlos threw a cigarette butt out the window and pulled away.

Arnold raced across the lawn. Arms flailing, he yelled, "Stop! Wait!"

The van raced through the gateway. Tires squealing, it disappeared down the hill.

Chapter 25

Dottie joined Arnold as he stared at the dust clouds on the empty road. Mabel ran to them. "What's going on? I heard Arnold shouting and tires squealing." She looked from one to the other. "Something's happened. Where's Yolanda?"

Arnold's voice cracked. "She's gone."

"What do you mean she's gone—gone where?"

"In Carlos's van." Dottie said.

"Whatever for?"

"She probably asked him for a lift to the hotel when she found out he was driving to Lucca," Dottie replied.

"Why would she want to do that?"

Arnold cleared his throat. "Yolanda and I had—words."

"Oh!" Mabel paused. "Even if she was annoyed with you, Yolanda wouldn't ask a stranger for a lift."

"She would have seen the sign on the van," Dottie reasoned, "and figured Carlos was doing construction work at the villa."

Arnold stared at Dottie. "You mean she felt safe hitching a ride with him?"

"Something like that."

"The idiot! Carlos is a reckless driver," Mabel said. "He almost ran us off the road this morning." Dottie flashed a warning glance at her.

"I expect he was running late," Mabel said. "Still, I don't like the idea of Yolanda cadging a lift with a drug dealer."

Arnold's face paled. "Are you telling me that my wife is alone in that van with a criminal?"

Dottie decided it was time to take charge. "OK. Arnold, we're all going to Lucca to make sure Yolanda is safe. Is the Mercedes an automatic?"

Arnold nodded.

"Right. I'm going to drive."

"I'm fine, really."

"No, you're not. Get in the passenger seat." With glazed eyes, Arnold obeyed. Mabel climbed into the back of the car.

After fastening his seatbelt, Arnold rubbed his hands over his face. "What if that man—Carlos, I think you called him—kidnaps Yolanda? You hear of these things…"

Dottie cut in. "Arnold, don't get carried away. Yolanda is probably sitting in the hotel right now, feeling very guilty about running off like that." *And so she should*, Dottie thought. *Mabel's right. What a fool she was to climb into a stranger's van just because she'd had a fight with her husband!*

"How are we going to get back?" Mabel wondered.

"We could take a taxi."

"I have a better idea. I'll drive our car and follow you."

A few minutes later, Dottie eased the car onto the road and headed to Lucca with Mabel following behind her.

***

They arrived at the hotel forty-five minutes later. While Dottie parked the car, Arnold rushed off to find Yolanda. Mabel pulled into an empty space next to the Mercedes. She climbed out of the car and joined Dottie.

"Let's walk around the parking lot while we wait for Arnold," Dottie suggested. "It could be a while."

"Good idea. It might help me to calm down a bit," Mabel fumed. "I can't believe that Yolanda would be so foolish! She's normally very sensible."

"Pregnancy makes people do dumb things sometimes."

Mabel gripped Dottie's arm. "Forget about the walk. There's Arnold by the front door of the hotel."

They hurried over. "Yolanda isn't here." His voice shook. "I've spoken with the doorman and the receptionist, and neither has seen her since this morning. We'll have to call the police."

"I think we should look around Lucca first," Mabel said. "She might have gone shopping. It's market day. Yolanda loves bargains. What do you think, Arnold?"

Arnold removed a white handkerchief from his shorts pocket and mopped his brow. "I'm not thinking too clearly, I'm afraid."

"Of course not," Mabel patted his arm.

"There's no way Yolanda will have gone shopping," Dottie protested. "She knows that Arnold will be looking for her. She could be in a café near the hotel." *Drinking herbal tea and sulking*, Dottie added to herself.

Arnold nodded. "You're probably right. We'd better check the local cafés."

He took a photo of Yolanda out of his wallet. He spoke with the waiters in each café they visited, pointing to her picture. *Ha visto?* Dottie felt a lump in her throat when one by one they shook their heads.

"It wouldn't hurt to try some gift stores," Arnold said. "She loves to bring knick-knacks back from trips abroad."

"We should check the hotel again," Dottie replied.

"Of course!" Arnold sounded hopeful. "No point in searching further until we've done that."

They made their way back to the hotel, keeping a watchful eye on the scooters and bikes that wove their way through the crowded streets. A young woman on a scooter drove so close to the sidewalk she almost knocked Dottie over.

As they entered one square, a white van sped past them and disappeared down a side street. "Quick!" Dottie urged. "I think that's Carlos's van!"

They dashed across the square. A tour group led by a woman holding a *Unitours* sign above her head jammed the narrow street, forcing the vehicle to stop. Dodging her way through the straggling group, Dottie ran ahead. She'd almost reached the van when the tour leader led her flock into an old church. The street cleared quickly as they filed in, but Dottie managed to read the license plate before the van sped away.

Arnold and Mabel caught up to Dottie.

"It was Carlos's van!" she told them, pausing to catch her breath.

"Did you see anyone on the passenger side?" Arnold asked.

"It left before I had a chance to look."

Dottie chewed her lip. "Wait a minute! Did you notice which direction the van was heading?"

Arnold's lips twitched into a half smile. "Toward the hotel!"

"Let's go!" Mabel shouted.

It didn't take long to get to the hotel.

"There she is!" Dottie cried.

Yolanda sat on a bench, her hands folded across her stomach, the straw basket by her side. Her face looked drawn and pale.

Arnold ran to her. "Darling!" He sat on the bench beside Yolanda and put his arm around her. "Are you all right? We've been so worried about you."

Yolanda's face crumpled. "Oh, Arnold," she cried. "I'm so glad to see you!" Sniffing, Yolanda took the handkerchief Arnold gave her.

"Where have you been?" Mabel demanded. "We've been worried sick about you! Do you realize that you cadged a lift with a drug dealer!"

Yolanda blew her nose. "So that's why Carlos seemed so agitated."

"What do you mean?"

"He drove too fast. I told him in no uncertain terms that if he didn't slow down, I might go into premature labor."

"I suppose he thought he'd have to deliver a baby," Dottie said. "No wonder he was jittery."

Yolanda replied, "But that didn't faze him, until I said he might have to call the ambulance and police to get me to the hospital in time. He slowed down the rest of the way."

Mabel laughed. "Good for you!"

"He was supposed to drop me off at the hotel," Yolanda continued. "On the way to Lucca, he got a phone call. From what I could make out, the caller wanted him to come directly to some warehouse."

Mabel looked at Dottie. "We know where that is."

"You do? Well, anyway, he insisted that he had to go there first. When we arrived, a man was waiting. Carlos handed him a package from the back of the van."

"Was the man scruffy and thin with straggly black hair?"

"How did you know that?"

"Never mind," Dottie said. "Go on."

"Well." Yolanda sat up straight. She looked more like her old self. "This is where it gets interesting."

"What do you mean?" Mabel asked.

"I overheard this guy (Nico, I think) telling Carlos that a shipment was due in two days' time," Yolanda replied. "I didn't take much notice until I heard Carlos say something about the last shipment being a 'bad bundle.' Nico told him that the new shipment would be all 'China cat.'"

Arnold looked bewildered. "China cat?"

"It's street slang for high-potency heroin."

"How in the blazes do you know that?" Arnold exclaimed. "You never cease to amaze me, Yolanda."

Yolanda looked a bit sheepish. "I learned about it from a *CSI Miami* episode."

"Did Nico say anything else?" Dottie demanded. "This could be very important."

"Carlos whispered something to him. The way they were both looking at me I think he was telling Nico to be quiet because I speak Italian."

"What happened next?" Mabel asked.

"Carlos drove me here." She looked in Arnold's eyes. "What an idiot I've been, my dearest, climbing into a van with a stranger. You must have been beside yourself."

"You're safe. That's all that matters." He looked at Dottie and Mabel. "I can't begin to thank you for everything you've done."

"The main thing is that everything's turned out well," Mabel smiled.

Arnold looked at his wife. "You're going to bed for a rest, my dear, and no arguing. This has been quite an ordeal for you." For once, Yolanda didn't argue.

Dottie decided this was a good time to leave. "Antonio Morelli, the owner of the villa, has invited us to dinner," she explained. "We'd better get going."

Mabel glanced at her watch. "We should make it in time if we leave now."

***

They arrived at the villa with twenty minutes to spare. "You shower first," Mabel said. "You take longer to get ready."

Dottie closed her eyes as the warm water sprayed over her. What a day it had been! And they had a long evening ahead of them. Swathed in a fluffy bath towel, she opened the bathroom door

Mabel was waiting for her. "While you were in the shower, we had a visitor," she said.

"Oh?"

"It was Pierre. He came for Antonio's gift."

"He didn't waste any time."

"Pierre wasn't his usual charming self. He seemed anxious. His eyes kept darting around the living room. I went to get the parcel from my room, and when I returned, I found him peering into your room. He said he was admiring the décor."

"Hmm."

"Anyway, I gave him the gift, and he left."

"Maybe he and Yvette had a fight."

"Perhaps. We'll find out more at dinner. Speaking of which, I'd better hurry."

Dottie Flowers and the European Caper

As Dottie dressed, her head spun with questions. What was Carlos's connection with Antonio Morelli? Were drugs being stored in the warehouse, and were Yvette and Pierre involved?

Something big was brewing; she could feel it in her bones.

Chapter 26

Mabel rang the doorbell, and Antonio Morelli opened the door with a flourish. *"Benvenuto, signore!"* Dressed in a black silk shirt and cream linen trousers, he ushered them into the living room.

Yvette was draped across a leather armchair, holding a glass of red wine in her elegantly manicured hand. A skimpy black dress and dark stockings accentuated her long, shapely legs curled around the chair leg. Smiling, she rose from the chair and kissed them on each cheek. "*Bonjour*, Dottie and Mabel! It is wonderful to see you again!" She looked them over. "You 'ave got the sun, I think."

Mabel agreed. "The trick is not to overdo it."

"Of course." Yvette glanced back at Pierre standing by the marble fireplace staring into space. "Pierre 'as got the 'eadache. So 'e is drinking soda water." She laughed. "'e was lying by pool this afternoon. The sun, it is too much."

As though on cue, Pierre retrieved his glass from the mantelpiece and strode across the room. A smile flickered across his handsome face. "It's good to see you again, Dottie." He kissed her on both cheeks.

He turned to Mabel, looking guilty. "I was distracted when I dropped by the pool house earlier for Antonio's gift. I wasn't feeling well. Yvette's right—I stayed too long in the sun. I hope you will forgive my rudeness, Mabel..."

Antonio's sharp voice cut in. "I'm sure Mabel has already forgotten about it." He looked at Pierre, his eyes like knives.

Antonio turned abruptly to Dottie and Mabel. Rubbing his hands together, he smiled broadly. "Now, what will you have to drink? I make an excellent martini. Or would you prefer a glass of wine?"

"Red wine for me, please." Dottie replied.

"I'd like a small glass of white wine," Mabel said, "with soda water."

"I'll tell Maria."

Dottie watched Antonio as he disappeared through the doorway. The look he'd given Pierre had been a warning; Dottie was sure of it. A warning about what?

***

The table's centerpiece of yellow roses arranged in a gilded bowl added a splash of color to the wood-paneled dining room. The centerpiece was complemented by delicate white china edged with gold. Dottie was pleased that Pierre sat opposite her. She could observe him without being too obvious.

Once they were all seated, Maria served the first course, a cold mint-flavored soup mingled with spices and yogurt. Mabel looked a bit dubious. She took a small spoonful and tasted it. "Mmm, this is scrumptious."

Yvette's eyes lit up. "*Zuppa fredda alla menta*!" She gave Antonio a dazzling smile. "You know it is a favorite of mine!"

Antonio inclined his head and smiled at her. "Of course."

"A perfect summer appetizer, *n'est-ce pas*, Pierre?"

Pierre took a spoonful. "It's spicy." His eyes focused on Antonio. "Quite potent, in fact." The two men locked eyes.

The same young man who had served the wine the night they'd arrived at the villa poured a chilled rosé. This time, he managed to pour without spills.

Maria served the next course. "This is *tagliatelle* with zucchini flowers and shrimp, my friends," Antonio declared. "The zucchini flowers have a pleasant delicate flavor and marry well with the light creamy sauce. I hope you find it to your taste."

Pierre picked up his fork and moved it around the plate. He finally put it down.

"Not hungry, Pierre?" Dottie asked.

He looked startled for a moment. "I have a headache. I must excuse myself for a few minutes." He stood and left the room.

Yvette turned to Dottie. "Pierre is such a baby when 'e is sick. I go to find the aspirin. 'e will not find it." She followed him out of the room.

"Oh, dear," Mabel said. "I hope he'll be all right."

Yvette returned a few minutes later. "I give the aspirin. Now, 'e is taking a little sleep."

They ate raspberries with gelato for dessert. "I 'ope Pierre will feel better for the birthday party," Yvette confided to Dottie. "It is not just the 'eadache. 'e is bad-tempered, not—'ow you say—Pierre."

"You mean, he's not himself," Dottie replied.

"That is what I mean. *Merci*."

Dottie wondered if Hans had been invited to the celebration. "Apart from Yolanda and Arnold, who else is coming to the party?"

Yvette glanced at Antonio who busily chatted with Mabel. Dropping her voice to almost a whisper, she leaned over to Dottie. "Antonio's niece, Simone, but it is a surprise. She is in Lucca for three days. She comes from Rome for the birthday."

Dottie drummed her fingers on the table. "Is anyone else invited?"

"Yes, Antonio's grandson Fabian will be 'ere."

Her heart sank. Remembering Hans's lack of enthusiasm when Antonio had suggested he come to dinner one evening, Dottie consoled herself with the thought that, even if he'd been invited, he'd probably turn it down.

"Fabian is fond of 'is grandfather," Yvette remarked. "'e visits often. You 'ave seen 'im?"

"I'm not sure. What does he look like?"

"Tall with long dark hair. 'e drives a silver sports car."

"Yes, he visited the other day." As a frequent visitor, Fabian would not pose a threat to the dog, Dottie realized, which would explain why the animal hadn't barked.

Mabel cleared her throat. "I think it's time for us to go," she said, looking at Dottie. "It's been a long day."

Yvette waved at Dottie and Mabel as they left the dining room. "Goodnight, *mes amies*!"

Antonio escorted them into the hallway and opened the front door. "I hope you had a good evening, ladies."

"We did. Thank you." Dottie paused. "I hope Pierre feels better soon."

Antonio replied in a clipped voice, "We will see."

Once they'd left, Mabel breathed a sigh of relief. "I'm glad to be out of there! You could have cut the tension with a knife."

Dottie agreed. "Something's going on between Antonio and Pierre; that's for sure. I'd love to find out what it is."

They reached the pool house. Mabel unlocked the door. "Once I've cleaned my teeth, I'm heading straight to bed."

"I won't be long, either," Dottie replied.

She closed the living room blinds and headed to her bedroom. As she grasped the door handle, Dottie paused.

Why was the bedroom door closed? She called out to Mabel. Toothbrush in hand, Mabel hurried over. "What's wrong?"

"Someone's been inside the pool house."

Mabel frowned. "What makes you think that?"

"My bedroom door's closed."

Mabel laughed. "Oh, Dottie, really. Just because you usually leave it open doesn't mean…"

Dottie cut in. "I always leave the door open. In fact, before we left, I remember checking to make sure. I like the air to circulate."

"All right, but how would an intruder get in? There's no sign of a break-in."

"With a key."

Mabel stroked her chin. "You think it's Pierre."

Dottie began to pace the living room. "Yes. It wouldn't be difficult for Yvette and Pierre to find out where Maria keeps her keys. As for opportunity, I think the headache was just a ruse. While we were eating dinner, he could have sneaked out of the villa."

"Why would he want to search the pool house?"

Dottie shrugged.

"Don't forget that Yvette and Pierre have stayed at the villa before," Mabel pointed out. "Maybe they hid something in the pool house."

"Could be. Anyway, let's go to bed. You have a busy day tomorrow."

Mabel pulled a face. "That cooking class in Lucca! There's so much going on I almost wish I hadn't signed up for it."

"Never mind. It'll be over by three. I'll come with you to Lucca. I want to take more photos before we fly back to Canada."

Mabel looked at her friend. "Aren't you meeting Hans for lunch?"

"He hasn't phoned, so I assume he was caught up with work."

"That's too bad."

Dottie walked into her bedroom and closed the door. She'd been surprised and disappointed not to hear from Hans, after he'd been so insistent that they meet for lunch. Fortunately, she had enough things to keep her busy while Mabel took her class.

She fell into a restless sleep. In her dreams, Carlos and Nico tried to kill her. Lieutenant Piaf, instead of being sympathetic, told her off for interfering with his investigation. As Carlos pointed a gun at Dottie, Yolanda loomed out of the shadows and hit Carlos over the head with her handbag. Dottie turned to thank Yolanda, but instead saw Hans. Pale and feverish, he staggered toward her and collapsed in her arms.

Even though she slept late, Dottie felt as though she hadn't slept at all.

Chapter 27

By the time Dottie emerged from the bedroom, Mabel had already prepared breakfast. A bowl of strawberries, fresh cream, and a jar of apricot jam sat on the table with buttered toast.

Mabel poured the coffee into mugs. "Bad night?"

"Yes. I kept having these stupid dreams." Dottie took several sips of coffee. "Ah, that's better."

"I've got news."

Cradling the warm mug, Dottie murmured, "Something good, I hope."

"Not sure if I'd use the word 'good,' but it's interesting."

"I'm intrigued."

"Antonio's invited Yolanda and Arnold to his dinner tomorrow night."

Dottie put her mug down. "How did Yolanda pull that off?"

"She phoned the villa to speak with me, and Antonio answered." Mabel slathered a piece of toast with jam. "During the conversation, she told him that tomorrow night would be the last opportunity she and Arnold would have to see us, as they're leaving for Florence the next day."

Dottie smiled. "So Antonio asked, 'Why don't you join us for dinner?'"

"Words to that effect. You know what Yolanda's like. If she makes up her mind to do something, then watch out."

Dottie knew only too well. "Did I tell you that Antonio's niece is planning to come? It's supposed to be a surprise."

"Let's hope Antonio and Pierre have resolved their differences by then."

Dottie tapped her fingers on the table. "What do you think Pierre was looking for in the pool house? I've wracked my brains trying to think what it can be."

"I just wish we knew for certain that it was Pierre. It could have been anyone."

"Not likely."

They ate breakfast in companionable silence. "What do you have planned for tomorrow?" Dottie asked. "We only have two days left, I think I'll relax by the pool."

"I'm meeting Yolanda for lunch. I'll bring her back here. Arnold wants to spend the afternoon looking for a gift for her. He told me he'd like to find something special after the ordeal she's been through."

"That sounds just like Arnold."

"He's planning to drive to the villa about 6:30."

"He'll enjoy looking around Lucca. It'll be a nice break." Dottie was tempted to add "from Yolanda" but stopped herself. She piled the dishes on a tray. "Let's leave as soon as we can. We can drive into Lucca and enjoy a stroll around the city walls before your class starts."

"Sounds lovely." Mabel paused. "Speaking of Yolanda and Arnold, there's something I need to discuss with you."

"Go ahead."

"I think they should stay overnight."

"Whatever for?"

"Yolanda is worried about Arnold drinking and driving," Mabel explained, "and he won't let Yolanda drive in her condition."

"You've already discussed it with them?"

Mabel glared. "Of course not! I wouldn't do that without speaking to you first."

It would make more sense if they stayed over, Dottie realized. Arnold could have that extra glass of wine without worrying about the drive home. "OK," Dottie agreed. "On one condition."

"What's that?"

"That we keep breakfast simple. Maybe cereal and toast."

Mabel smiled. "That's fine by me. Definitely no poached eggs!"

***

After arriving in Lucca, they strolled along the wall's tree-lined pathways, enjoying the fresh morning air. Apart from a few joggers and dog walkers, they had the place to themselves. "What are you going to make in cooking class?" Dottie asked.

"We'll learn how to prepare three different kinds of pasta dishes. Then, we choose the one we'd like to make. We're on our own after that, although the chef will keep his eye on what we're doing and give friendly advice if we need it."

"I guess this means we won't have to worry about dinner tonight."

"Don't be so sure. Pasta isn't something I make very often. My last attempt ended up a gooey mess."

Dottie laughed. "I remember. You invited me for dinner, and we ended up ordering Chinese takeout. And we drank that awful red plonk."

"I'll have you know that I bought that wine to complement the pasta dish!" Mabel started to laugh as well.

"Speaking about wine," Dottie said, "We haven't bought anything for Antonio's birthday."

"We can't go wrong with bottle of *Brunello di Montalcino*."

Dottie looked at her friend in amazement. "Since when did you become a wine connoisseur?"

"It was in one of my books. This man is trying to seduce his boss's daughter…

"OK. I get the picture."

"And what about sparkling wine as a thank-you gift for allowing us to stay in the pool house?"

"I hadn't thought of that. We should get a thank-you gift for Maria as well. I'll see if I can find something appropriate."

They found the building where the class was to be held and arranged to meet at a nearby café after. Dottie spent the next few hours taking photographs. Along with churches, old doors, and monuments, she captured pictures of children playing in a narrow cobblestoned street, old men sitting on a bench smoking, and a group of teenagers eating gelato. Satisfied with her morning's work, she put her camera away.

It didn't take long to find a wine store. When she asked the proprietor for sparkling wine, he presented her with a bottle of prosecco from Cartizze, where, he assured her, in broken English, the very best prosecco is produced. He also helped her choose a good Tuscan wine. The cards presented more of a challenge. In the end, with the help of her Italian phrasebook, she found one that simply said *Buon Compleanno!* and a blank one so they could write a personal thank-you.

She tried to find a gift for Maria, but nothing caught her attention.

Dottie decided to have an early lunch and found a café near the old Roman amphitheater. There were plenty of empty tables. She chose one near the front of the café and sat with a sigh of pleasure to indulge in one of her favorite pastimes, people-watching. She ordered crab salad and a glass of sparkling mineral water.

Dottie glanced around. A man and woman sat in the corner of the café deep in conversation. The woman wore a pinstriped suit and white blouse. A briefcase sat on the floor beside her. Her light brown hair, cut in a simple bob, framed her delicate oval face. The man lifted the carafe and poured the coffee. When the woman picked up her cup, Dottie noticed an ugly red scar on the back of her hand. The man's back was turned toward Dottie, so she couldn't see his face, only the white hair curling over the collar of his tan jacket. She wondered what kind of business they were involved in.

Dottie's lunch was served. She was about to start eating when, out of the corner of her eye, she saw the man reach for the woman's hand. Dottie turned her head discreetly for a better look. The woman was crying. Streaks of mascara marred her pale cheeks. Not a business meeting after all. A lover's tiff, perhaps?

 The man suddenly turned around and signaled for the nearest waiter. Dottie's breath caught in her throat. It was Hans Van Gogh.

She turned away quickly. He mustn't see her. She picked up her glass and took several swallows of mineral water. No wonder he hadn't phoned her about meeting him for lunch. He had other plans!

After a futile attempt to eat some of the salad, she pushed the plate to one side. "Excuse me, *signora*." The waiter's voice startled her. "Is everything all right?" His eyes lingered on the salad plate.

"Yes," Dottie snapped. "Everything's fine."

Blinking nervously, he asked, "Would you like a glass of wine?"

Dottie swallowed hard. "No, thank you." Suddenly, she felt her energy seep away. "I'll have a Scotch on the rocks, please."

His eyebrows shot up. "Si, *signora*."

When the waiter left, she glanced at the other table, but it was empty.

***

Dottie found her way to the café where she'd arranged to meet Mabel. "What a fun time I had!" Mabel enthused, as she pulled out a chair and sat. "The chef spoke perfect English. He had a great sense of humor. The morning went by very quickly, and I now have a pasta dish for two, packed in a thermal container, all ready for us tonight."

Dottie tried to mirror Mabel's enthusiasm. "I'm so glad it worked out."

"Much better than I'd expected." A waiter appeared. "I'll have a glass of lemonade, please. What are you having, Dottie?"

"A large glass of sparkling mineral water with lots of ice."

After the waiter left, Mabel peered at Dottie. "Are you all right?"

"What makes you ask?"

"You sound a bit low, and your face is flushed. Maybe you've caught some bug."

Dottie let out a deep sigh. "It's not a bug. It's Hans."

"Oh, dear, do you want to talk about it?"

"Sure."

After their drinks had been served, Mabel leaned across the table. "So, tell me."

"I found him with another woman."

"What!"

"You heard me. I'd just ordered lunch when I noticed this man and woman at another table. The man had his back to me, but when he turned around, I realized it was Hans."

"Because you saw Hans sitting at a table with another woman, you assumed they're…"

"Lovers? Yes, that's exactly what I think." Dottie told Mabel the whole story.

"She could be an employee of his," Mabel pointed out. "Perhaps he'd just sacked her and that's why she was crying. Or she could have been a close friend who'd just found out her husband is having an affair."

Dottie shook her head. "There was something about the way they looked at each other."

"I see."

"Now I know why he didn't phone me."

The waiter arrived with their drinks. Dottie took a few sips of mineral water. "It isn't as though we're in a relationship. I've only dated him once. Well, twice, if I count that disastrous evening when I fell down the restaurant stairs and ended up in a mud puddle!"

Mabel sat up straight. "Dottie, you must speak with Hans and clear this up. I'm sure it's all a misunderstanding. Let's go home. I'll serve dinner by the pool. We'll start with bruschetta, followed by the seafood cannelloni. And I'll open a bottle of Chianti."

On the drive back, Mabel said, "You know that wine jug you bought in Arles. Would you mind if we used it tonight? It seems fitting, as we're almost at the end of the holiday."

"Of course not."

When they returned to the villa, Dottie retrieved the wine jug from the trunk of the car. "I thought it was in your bedroom," Mabel said. "Why did you leave it in the car?

"It seemed the logical thing to do, as the pool house is so small. After I unpacked, I placed the box containing the jug inside my carry-on bag and put the bag in the car trunk." She admired the jug. "It's a lovely piece of art. I like the leaf motif and the brass base with its scalloped edge. It'll look really good on my sideboard."

"You chose well, Dottie."

"Just a minute! Something's wrong." Dottie rooted in her handbag for her glasses. She put them on and studied the jug. "Take a look, Mabel." Dottie pointed to the embossed leaf decorations on its side.

Mabel scrunched her eyes and peered at it. "I can't see anything wrong. All I see are two leaf motifs."

"The piece I purchased had three."

Mabel stared at her. "What are you saying?"

"This is not the jug I bought in Arles."

"The pottery shop must have given you a different jug by mistake," Mabel responded.

"No, I watched them wrap it."

"You think someone stole yours and replaced it with this one? Come on, Dottie, that's impossible."

Dottie shook the jug. Her heart began to race. "I can hear a faint rustling sound! There's something inside it."

Chapter 28

Mabel held the jug to her ear and gave it a good shake. "I can't hear anything."

"Are you sure?"

"Just a minute. That's my bad ear. Let me try the other one." Her eyes grew wide. "There's definitely something inside."

"Do you remember when we invited Yvette and Pierre for drinks just before we left St. Siffret?" Dottie asked.

"I do. Yvette and Pierre were at odds that evening."

"When they were leaving, Pierre noticed the jug. He pestered me with questions. He wanted to know where I bought it and if there was another one like it at the shop."

"He probably showed an interest to lighten the atmosphere."

Dottie shook her head. "I think when he saw the jug and found out there was one like it for sale, he came up with a plan."

Mabel tapped her index finger on her lips. "You think he bought the jug to plant drugs inside."

"Yes." Dottie took another look at the jug. "The neck's very narrow, I'm not sure how we'll get them out."

"Perhaps there's a false bottom."

Dottie turned the jug upside down. "It looks pretty solid."

"I'll be right back!" Mabel rushed off to her bedroom. Dottie could hear drawers being opened and closed.

Mabel returned, holding a magnifying glass. "Now, we can take a close look."

"You brought a magnifying glass with you?"

"I always travel with one."

After peering through the microscope, Mabel pointed to the brass base. "See this scalloped edge. Each of the scalloped bits is shaped like a claw. Well, some claws are bent back."

Dottie took another look. "You're right. It looks like someone's tried to force the base open." She tried to unscrew it, but it wouldn't budge. She fetched a sharp knife from the kitchen. After placing the jug on its side, she inserted the tip of the blade behind the claws, cautiously jiggling the knife back and forth.

"Here, let me hold the jug." Mabel gripped its sides as Dottie continued to jiggle the knife.

"OK," Dottie said. "I'll try again." She gripped the base, and this time, it unscrewed.

"Phew!" Mabel breathed. "That was nerve-wracking."

Dottie looked at her. "Do you want to do the honors?"

"You go ahead."

Dottie put her hand through the opening and removed three plastic bags filled with a white powder.

"Well, well!" Mabel exclaimed. "No wonder Pierre's so agitated."

"I bet this is worth a fortune," Dottie mused.

"We have to tell the police."

"Not right away."

Mabel raised her eyebrows. "Why not?"

"You know that icing sugar you bought the other day?"

"For the cake I didn't bake?"

"Yes. What if we fill three plastic bags with icing sugar and put them in the jug? Pierre won't know the difference. Once he's let himself in the pool house and taken the bags from the jug, we'll contact the police, show them the bags of heroin, and tell them everything we know."

"It'll only work if Pierre searches the pool house again," Mabel pointed out. "He's searched once, so why would he bother a second time?"

"Good question." Dottie bit her lip. "Somehow, we have to let Pierre know the jug's here."

A sharp rap at the door made them jump. "I'll hide these in my room," Dottie whispered, grabbing the plastic bags.

"In case it's Pierre, let's leave the jug on the table. You take the bags and knife, while I put the base back on the jug."

Dottie hurried to her room, placed the bags and knife in the closet, and covered them with a jacket. That would have to do, for now. She glanced out the bedroom window and caught a glimpse of a red polka-dot dress.

Dottie returned to the living room. "It's Yvette."

Mabel grinned. "That's perfect! I couldn't get the base on properly, but it's good enough for now."

When Mabel opened the door, Yvette handed her a white box. "I visit a little bakery and bring you and Dottie some pastries."

"That's very kind of you. Why don't you come in and have some tea with us?"

"I would like that very much." Yvette clasped her hands. "It is a comfort to 'ave such good friends!" She walked into the house.

"I'll go and put the kettle on," Mabel said. She disappeared into the kitchen.

Dottie invited Yvette to sit down. "Is Pierre feeling better?"

Tears welled up in Yvette's eyes. "No, 'e does not speak since 'e woke up. 'e is not 'imself! 'e is not the Pierre I love!" She flung out her arms in despair. "I do not understand what 'appened!"

Dottie handed Yvette a box of tissues. "Have you tried talking to him?"

"Thank you," she sniffed, removing a tissue. She blew her nose. "I 'ave tried. 'e is like a mule."

"Stubborn."

"Yes! 'e walks across the room and back again. When I ask 'im what is wrong, 'e ignores me."

Mabel came in, carrying a tray with three mugs and a pot of tea, and the pastries. She placed the tray on the coffee table. "Here we are." She glanced at Yvette. "Oh, dear, what's wrong?"

Yvette turned a tear-stained face to Mabel. "Everything!" She burst into a fresh flood of tears.

While Yvette fumbled for more tissues, Dottie mouthed to Mabel, "It's Pierre. Try to distract her."

Mabel poured the tea and handed a mug to Yvette. "There's nothing like tea to soothe the nerves," she smiled. Now, tell me, is everything organized for the big night?"

"Oh, yes!" Yvette sniffed a little as she cradled her mug. "Antonio 'as chosen the menu, but the dessert 'e plans is not served."

"Why not?"

Yvette managed a smile. "Simone, Antonio's niece, she order a birthday cake."

"Does he know Simone will be at the dinner?" Dottie asked.

"No, it is a secret." Yvette sipped her tea. "Antonio will be very 'appy. It is several years since they see each other."

"I expect Antonio has been busy choosing wines."

Yvette nodded.

"Speaking of wine," Dottie said, "Don't you love the jug I bought in Arles, Yvette!" She pointed to it. "I can hardly wait to entertain friends with it when we return to Canada."

"It is a very nice jug."

"Pierre really liked the leaf motif design."

"'e has seen it?"

"He admired it when you were over for drinks the night before we left St. Siffret."

"Ah, *oui*! I forgot! 'e spoke of it all the way 'ome."

"When Mabel's niece Yolanda came by, I couldn't resist showing it to her," Dottie continued. "I couldn't find it at first. Then, I remembered I'd packed it in the trunk of the car."

Yvette glanced at her watch. She looked at the two women. "I must go." Putting her mug on the coffee table, she stood up and walked to the door.

"You haven't finished your tea," Mabel said.

"I am sorry, but Pierre is back at two. It is after two." She opened the door and smiled. "Thank you both, for—for everything."

The door clicked shut. They could hear the crunch of feet on the patio, and the tapping of spiked heels on the stone pathway as Yvette headed to the villa.

"Well," Mabel declared. "What do you make of that?"

"She's in a big hurry to get back; that's for sure."

"I bet she can't wait to tell Pierre that the wine jug he's been looking for is here in the pool house," Mabel said

"I'm not so sure about that. She seemed distracted."

"I've got an idea."

"Go ahead."

"You know how we've talked about driving down to the coast," Mabel said. "This is the ideal time to do it. It isn't far. We'll be back in a few hours. And 'while the cat's away…'"

"…the mice will play?'"

"Let's hope so. We'll have to let them know we're going for a drive."

Dottie's eyes fell on a pretty red silk scarf lying on the sofa. She picked it up. "Yvette forgot her scarf. We can drop it off at the villa. We'll tell her we're going out and won't be back for a few hours. And I'll try to think of something to make sure Yvette tells Pierre about the jug."

"Great. We'd better get organized," Mabel pointed out. "You get the icing sugar and bags from the kitchen."

It didn't take long to fill three Ziploc plastic bags with icing sugar. Dottie put them in the jug. This time, she made sure the base was screwed on properly. "Now, we need a good hiding place for the drugs," she said. 'We can't leave them sitting on the closet floor."

"I have the perfect solution." Mabel smiled. "We'll hide them in that bag of flour I bought."

"Brilliant! It's just as well you didn't bake that cake after all."

When Dottie returned the scarf to Yvette, she explained that she and Mabel were going to the seaside and would be away for a few hours. "If Pierre wants to take a second look at the wine jug and still likes it, I'm thinking of giving it to him as a gift."

"But you cannot do that! It is yours."

"The truth is, Yvette, it's an awkward shape to pack and transport back to Canada. I bought it in a hurry without giving any thought to how I would take it home." Now, the trap was set.

"Good thinking, Dottie," Mabel said as they drove away. "Now, she's sure to tell Pierre about the jug."

***

They drove to Forte dei Marmi, a seaside town not far from Lucca. It was market day. After they'd found a parking space, they worked their way through crowded stalls heaped with lace tablecloths and napkins and brightly colored pottery. A stall displaying jewelry and scarves caught Dottie's eye.

"How did you find out about this place?" Mabel asked, as she glanced around. "I suppose you read about it in your guidebook."

"My assistant Serena raves about it. She has family who live nearby. What really cinched it," Dottie continued, as she paused to admire some earrings, "was when I found out that Andrea Bocelli lives here. Well, he did. He may have moved."

"That's impressive! I really like the Romanza CD you gave me a few Christmases ago."

"That's one of my favorites. I figured if Andrea Bocelli likes it enough to live here, it must be pretty special." Dottie picked up the earrings and handed them to the stall keeper, a young man with fair wavy hair. "*Quanto costa?*"

He smiled broadly. "*Ventee.*"

Dottie paid for the earrings.

"Look at this scarf!" Mabel enthused. "It's the perfect gift for Maria." She held up the blue and yellow floral scarf for Dottie to see.

Dottie agreed. "I'm glad you spotted it."

After Mabel bought the scarf, she checked her watch. "We must leave soon."

"Before we head back, let's stroll along the marble sidewalks and get some sea air," Dottie said. "It would be a shame to miss that."

***

As they approached the front door of the pool house, Mabel turned to Dottie. "Well, here goes." She unlocked the door and they walked in.

The jug stood on the dining room table where they'd left it. Next to it lay a parcel wrapped in gold paper and trimmed with a red bow.

Mabel's eyes grew wide. "It's Antonio's birthday gift."

"I thought you gave it to Pierre."

"I did." Mabel said. "This must be the gift that went missing. Which indicates that someone stole it, then thought better of it. How odd!"

"I think Maria knows what happened. Let's not worry about it right now. We need to check the jug."

Mabel picked up the jug and shook it. "I don't think there's anything in there, but I'll check to make sure." Using a knife, she eased back the claws, and unscrewed the base. She grinned. "It's empty. Our plan worked."

Dottie felt a familiar tingling at the back of her neck. "I wish I could share your optimism."

"What do you mean?"

Dottie bit her lip. "If Pierre finds out the bags contain icing sugar, he'll know we've tricked him."

"How?"

"Quite easily. If he's at all suspicious, all he has to do is taste the powder."

Chapter 29

The next morning, Dottie and Mabel sat by the pool. Dottie tried to read, but after her eyes had scanned the same paragraph three times, she put down her book. "It's no use. I can't concentrate." She had images of Pierre storming across the lawn, demanding to know what they did with the drugs.

"The odds of Pierre finding out what we've done are not worth worrying about. You're obsessing," Mabel said, returning to her Nora Roberts novel.

"You're right. I'm going to relax and think about something else."

Dottie slathered more sunscreen over her arms and legs. Pulling her hat down so her face was well protected, she settled back on the chaise lounge and closed her eyes. She concentrated on deep breathing exercises, visualizing waves lapping on a deserted beach, palm trees swaying, and a heart-stopping sunset.

"There you are!"

Dottie sat up, her heart pounding. "Pierre!"

He loomed over her, his face in deep shadow. "I hope I'm not disturbing you," he said. "Yvette will be here in a minute. We have something to discuss with you both." Dottie tensed.

As though on cue, Yvette walked across the path to join them. *"Bonjour, mes amies!"* She wiggled her fingers in greeting. "I am sorry I am late. There 'as been a problem with icing sugar."

"Icing sugar?" Mabel squeaked. Dottie felt sick.

"I will explain." Yvette sat next to Dottie in a pool chair. "The birthday cake Simone ordered 'as arrived. Some of the icing, it 'as broken off. The cupboard where the icing sugar lives is very 'igh. Maria, she is in fear of 'eights, so I climb the ladder and get the icing sugar. Now, she repairs the cake." Dottie's body went limp with relief.

Pierre frowned at Yvette. "Why don't you tell Dottie and Mabel what we've been discussing? I'm sure they don't want to listen to all this nonsense about a birthday cake."

Yvette looked at the two women. "Simone, Pierre, and me, we talk. We think that after dinner is over, we 'ave dessert and champagne 'ere, by the pool, not inside the villa."

"It sounds delightful," Mabel answered. "Don't you agree, Dottie?"

"I do."

"Good!" Pierre replied. 'The staff will set up the tables and chairs this afternoon." He stood. "Now, we'll let you get back to your reading. Come on, Yvette, I'll take you for a drive in the car. We can have lunch at that new restaurant I told you about."

"That would be wonderful, *mon cher*. You go. I 'ave to speak with Mabel and Dottie."

As soon as Pierre was out of earshot, Yvette turned to Dottie and Mabel. "Pierre, 'e is like 'is old self!" she enthused. "'e served me breakfast in bed and gave me orchids! 'e is so romantic!"

Mabel smiled. "I'm glad things are back to normal."

"I will see you both tonight!" She dashed after Pierre.

Mabel pursed her lips and let out a long sigh. "Talk about a fright! When Yvette mentioned icing sugar, I thought it was game over. I don't think my nerves will stand any more shocks like that."

Dottie frowned. "I wonder why Pierre is so keen to have the champagne and cake served around the pool. I know Yvette broached the subject, but you could tell it was Pierre's idea."

"I hadn't thought about it. You're right, though, he did seem keen. And he didn't hang around once we'd agreed to it, either."

Later that morning, Mabel drove to Lucca and took Yolanda for lunch. She brought her niece back to the villa around three.

"Arnold is in his element," Yolanda said as she settled on the living room sofa with a glass of lemonade. "He's spending the afternoon in Lucca, looking for a piece of art. He'll probably visit every gallery and antique store." She sipped the lemonade. "Sometimes, he gets carried away and loses track of time."

"Does that mean he might be late?" Dottie asked.

"Absolutely not! I've told him to be here for cocktails at 6:30."

When Yolanda excused herself to use the washroom, Mabel said, in a lowered voice, "I saw Arnold briefly before he left on his shopping spree. He said he knows which jewelry shop Yolanda likes. He plans to find something special."

"Let's hope he gets here on time," Dottie said. "I wouldn't want to be in his shoes if he's late."

***

Dottie helped Yolanda to get ready for the birthday party. "Ouch!" Yolanda complained. "You stepped on my toe!"

"No wonder. How can I pin this brooch on when you're fidgeting?"

"Sorry. I hate this dress. I feel like a fruit bowl."

The clingy material was covered with large bunches of red, purple and green grapes. "Hmm. I see what you mean," Dottie said. "Why are you wearing it if you don't like it?"

Yolanda sighed. "I can't get into the other 'dressy' dresses I brought with me."

Mabel burst into the living room. "What do you think?" As she twirled, the lime green dress with its full skirt billowed around her, making her waistline and hips look even plumper. Seeing her beaming smile, Dottie didn't have the heart to say what she really thought. "It's you, Mabel."

"I'm glad you think so."

Now, it was Dottie's turn to choose between the black dress and the pumpkin-colored one. Pumpkin wasn't her color. She'd bought it to take on vacation because it was nonwrinkle and drip-dry. Considering the dresses Yolanda and Mabel were wearing, she knew it had to be the latter.

She chose high-heeled black sandals, a jet pendant with matching earrings, and flung a black lacy pashmina around her shoulders. She was pleased to see that the black accessories toned down the dress's vivid color.

Dottie joined her companions in the living room.

"You look cheerful and elegant at the same time, Dottie," Mabel commented.

"Thank you, Mabel." Dottie glanced at her watch. "It's 6:30. Yolanda, shall we wait for Arnold?"

Yolanda shook her head. "There's no need. He knows where we'll be."

"I expect he's racing along the road right now," Mabel said.

Yolanda glared at her aunt. "Racing? He'd better not be. He tends to speed on these winding roads—thinks he's Mario Andretti."

Dottie and Mabel's high heels clicked along the path to the villa. Yolanda plodded along behind them in flats.

A handsome young man wearing a white shirt with purple stripes and black dress pants opened the front door. His long hair curled around the shirt's collar. He greeted them with a warm smile. "*Buonsera, signoras,* and welcome." Pointing his foot in a ballet-like pose, he swept his arm across his waist and bowed deeply. He straightened himself, grinning boyishly. "I'm practicing for a play about Louis XVI and the French Revolution. I'm one of the courtiers." He ushered them into the hallway and shook hands with each. "I'm Fabian. Antonio Morelli is my grandfather." Like his grandfather, he spoke excellent English.

"I thought I recognized you," Mabel said. "I saw you last week on the driveway getting out of your car. I'm Mabel." She turned to Dottie and Yolanda and introduced them. "Dottie and I have been staying in the pool house."

"Of course! Nonno told me he had guests. You are friends of Yvette and Pierre."

"That's right."

"Let's go in, and I'll organize your drinks."

They followed Fabian into the living room. Guests, dressed in evening attire, milled around, sipping drinks and socializing. Dottie spotted Yvette and Pierre looking stunning in black. They were speaking with a group of people, none of whom Dottie recognized. She assumed they were Antonio's friends and family members.

"What would you like to drink?" Fabian asked them. Dottie ordered a Chivas on the rocks, and Mabel, a small gin and tonic.

In a flat voice, Yolanda said, "I'll have a sparkling mineral water, please, with a slice of lime. No ice." Dottie almost felt sorry for her, knowing how much Yolanda enjoyed a glass of chilled Chardonnay.

"I'll tell Maria. She'll make sure you're served right away," Fabian assured them.

At that moment, Antonio, looking every inch the host in a black tuxedo with a red bow tie, walked over to them. "Welcome, my dear friends. My grandson has taken your drink orders?"

"Yes, thank you." Mabel smiled. "What a charming young man he is!"

With pride in his voice, Antonio replied, "Thank you. He wants to train as an actor. I have tried to point out the difficulties of such a profession, but his mind is made up."

At that moment, a waiter arrived with their drinks. "I have other guests to meet, so I will leave you to enjoy your cocktails," With a slight inclination of his head, he walked away.

Removing the glass of mineral water from the tray, Yolanda said, "I think I'll mingle a bit."

"I'll come with you," Mabel said. She took her gin and tonic and followed Yolanda.

As Dottie sipped her Scotch, her eyes wandered to the corner of the room, where Fabian sat next to a young woman, his arm flung casually around her shoulders. As they talked, her eyes never left his face.

After a few minutes passed, Dottie noticed Yolanda glancing at her watch. Dottie checked hers. It was after seven. Through the living room window, she could see the pool house and their Peugeot parked next to it. The extra parking space was empty.

She crossed the room to speak with Yolanda. "I know you're anxious. Why don't you phone the hotel?"

"I was about to do that. Arnold knows I'm not supposed to be stressed out in my condition. He's more than a half an hour late already."

"Do you have the hotel number?"

"It's in my purse. Is there a phone nearby?"

"It's in the hallway. I'll show you."

Dottie waited while Yolanda made the call. From Yolanda's tone of voice, she surmised Arnold wasn't there.

Yolanda hung up the receiver and turned to Dottie, her face drawn and pale. "No one has set eyes on Arnold since he left this afternoon. And there are no messages."

"How would they recognize him?" Dottie asked.

"It's one of these small boutique hotels. We've been staying there for quite a few days, so they know who we are."

Dottie bit her lip, unsure of what to say.

Mabel joined them in the hallway. "So, what's happening?"

"There's no sign of Arnold—no messages, nothing," Yolanda said in a shaky voice, running her hands through her hair.

Dottie urged Yolanda to sit. "I know it's getting late, but he could be caught in traffic."

"Or be lost." Yolanda managed a weak smile. "That man has no sense of direction."

Mabel said, "He's probably wandering in circles around Lucca."

Dottie didn't believe this for one moment. Arnold's sense of direction wasn't very good, but she couldn't imagine anyone getting lost in Lucca. It was a straightforward place to get around.

"I actually came to tell you that that dinner will be served in five minutes," Mabel told them. "I think we should go into the dining room." She tucked her arm into Yolanda's. "You watch. Arnold will walk in just as we're in the middle of the meal, full of apologies."

Yolanda looked at the two women. "There's no point in getting people alarmed. If anyone asks about Arnold, I'd rather you say he's been delayed."

***

The gold centerpiece, shaped like a gondola, was filled with white orchids. A banner in gold lettering that read Buon Compleanno, Antonio! hung over the table from the dining room's high ceiling The white china trimmed in crimson and the gold cutlery, with cream-colored damask tablecloth and napkins, created the perfect blend of opulence and good taste.

Place cards, in calligraphic handwriting, rested against the water glasses. Antonio took his place at the head of the table, and Dottie was pleased to find she'd been seated next to him. If anything interesting happened, she'd have a ringside seat. A large pleasant-looking woman sat on Dottie's right. Dottie smiled at her. "I'm Dottie Flowers. Are you a friend of Antonio's or a member of the family?" The woman shrugged her shoulders and, smiling apologetically, turned away. Mabel sat opposite Dottie. The chair next to her was empty.

The first course, gnocchi with gorgonzola sauce, was served in tiny white dishes. Dottie placed a forkful of gnocchi in her mouth, savoring its soft texture and the sharpness of the cheese sauce.

At that moment, the dining room door burst open. A slim young woman wearing an ivory-colored wool dress walked in and headed toward Antonio. His eyes lit up, and his face broke into a broad smile. "Simone, my dear! What an unexpected pleasure."

"Hello, *Zio* Antonio!"

He stood and kissed her on the cheek. "Why didn't you tell me you were coming?"

"I wanted to surprise you!" she laughed, hugging him.

There was something familiar about the woman. Where had Dottie seen her before?

Simone stepped back. "It is over four years since I last saw you, and you don't look a day older."

As Simone patted her uncle on the cheek, Dottie saw the scar on the back of her hand. Dottie's heart skipped a beat. Surely, she must be mistaken! She looked closely at the delicate face and bobbed brown hair. It was the woman who had been sitting in the café with Hans.

"Are you all right, Dottie?" Mabel whispered, her face full of concern. "You look as though you've just seen a ghost."

Dottie picked up her wineglass and drained it. "I'm tired, that's all."

Mabel leaned across the table. Lowering her voice, she said, "Yolanda has hardly eaten anything, and she loves Italian food. I'm worried about her."

As Dottie turned to look, Yolanda keeled over, just missing the bowl of gnocchi. "She's fainted!"

Someone gasped; conversations stopped; a fork clattered onto a plate. Gradually, people began to speak in low voices, but the only words Dottie understood were *il medico*.

As she and Mabel hurried to Yolanda, Simone joined them. "I'm a midwife," she explained. She lifted Yolanda's wrist and took her pulse. "Is she a friend of yours?"

"She's my niece. Her name's Yolanda," Mabel said. "Can I do anything to help?"

"Yes, soak that napkin in a water glass and put it around her neck until she comes around."

Mabel followed the instructions. Dottie and Simone held on to Yolanda to prevent her from falling off the chair. After a short time, Yolanda opened her eyes and sat up. "What happened?"

"You passed out, Yolanda," Simone said. "You need to lie down for a while."

"Who are you?"

"I'm Antonio Morelli's niece. I'm also a midwife."

Yolanda looked at Dottie. "Has Arnold arrived yet?"

"No."

"I'm not waiting any longer." Yolanda proclaimed. "I'm calling the police."

"You stay put. I'll phone them," Dottie said. She told Simone about Arnold.

"We should take Yolanda back to the pool house," Mabel offered. "That way, she'll be there when Arnold shows up."

"I'm going to examine her and make sure she's all right," Simone replied. "At this stage of pregnancy, it's too risky to take chances. I'd rather she stay here in the villa so I can keep an eye on her. There's a sitting room just across the hallway." She turned to Yolanda. "Do you feel well enough to walk?"

"Of course!" As Yolanda stood, she swayed a little. Two male guests rushed over. With a hand under each arm, they guided her out of the dining room.

After the examination, Yolanda lay down on the couch, covered in a soft blanket. "Everything seems normal," Simone said to Dottie and Mabel as they headed to the dining room. "What she needs now is rest. Don't worry; I'll check her every few minutes."

"I'm going to make that phone call," Dottie said. After giving the police all the details, with the villa's phone number, Dottie returned to the sitting room to tell Yolanda, but she'd fallen asleep.

Dottie returned to the dining room, just as Antonio rose to speak. "My niece has informed me that Madame Gateshead is fine and is resting comfortably." he announced to his guests, smiling at Simone. "So, now, my dear friends, please relax and enjoy yourselves." Antonio sat again. Soon, the guests began to chat, and the atmosphere gradually returned to normal.

The main course, a choice of lamb with roasted red peppers or grilled tuna fish, was served. Dottie chose the tuna. Despite everything, she felt hungry.

Simone, seated in the empty chair beside Mabel, put down her wineglass as Dottie returned to her seat. "Did the police have anything to report?" she asked Dottie, her face full of concern.

"No," Dottie replied. "I gave them the villa's phone number, just in case."

"Remember the old saying," Mabel said. "'No news is good news.'"

They ate in silence, each lost in their thoughts. "That was excellent lamb," Simone said, placing her knife and fork together on the plate.

"Yes," Mabel agreed. "I feel very full. I don't know how I'll manage dessert."

"I always think that, but it never seems to stop me," Simone smiled. "Anyway, I'm glad we're sitting together. I wanted to get to know you a little." Dottie winced. The last thing she wanted was a cozy chat with Simone. "Yvette speaks very highly of you both. She said you met in Provence."

"That's right," Mabel said. "In fact, it was through Yvette and Pierre that we ended up staying here."

"Didn't you have a place booked?"

"We did. Yvette pointed out that the road leading to the farm where we had arranged to stay was very steep and narrow and quite dangerous in parts," Mabel said. "She insisted on contacting Antonio to see if the pool house was available. So, here we are."

Dottie concentrated on the tuna. She ate very slowly, avoiding eye contact with Simone.

Fortunately, Mabel liked to talk. "How did you manage to keep your visit a surprise? You must live nearby."

"No, I live in Rome." Simone stared into the distance. When she spoke again, her voice was muted. "But I have been staying in Lucca for the past week."

"I heard you say it's been three years since you saw your uncle. No wonder he's so pleased to see you,"

"Three years is a long time." Tears sprang in Yvette's eyes. She rooted in her purse and pulled out a tissue. "Excuse me," she sniffed, dabbing her eyes.

"Are you all right?" Mabel asked.

"Yes, thank you." Simone took a mouthful of wine.

Mabel cleared her throat. "Yvette told us that you organized the birthday cake."

"Yes, I expect you heard from Yvette about the near disaster this morning."

"We did. It turned out all right in the end, I gather."

"Oh, yes, the cake looks perfect, thanks to Maria." Simone's mouth curved into a smile. "I asked her to seat me close to Uncle Antonio," she confided. "I had hoped to get here early, but there was a pedestrian accident in Lucca that caused a big traffic hold-up."

Dottie tensed. "Was it a serious accident?"

"I don't know. The ambulance came, of course, and the police."

Dottie prayed the pedestrian wasn't Arnold.

Chapter 30

By the time guests gathered around the pool for champagne and dessert, the sun had given way to evening shadows. Miniature white lights had been woven into the nearby shrubs, creating a festive atmosphere. A long table draped in a white tablecloth and set with silver napkins and candles had been placed at the poolside. Crystal flutes sparkled like diamonds in the flickering candlelight. Another table was heaped with birthday presents. Mabel had made sure that their gift was among the assortment of packages, wrapped with bows and ribbons.

After Maria and her staff had served prosecco, Pierre proposed a toast to Antonio. Urged on by his guests, Antonio blew out the seventy-five candles while everyone sang 'Happy Birthday,' first in Italian, then English. Dottie looked around and realized that Fabian and his girlfriend were absent.

While the birthday cake was being served, Dottie wondered if the police had any news about Arnold. Feeling restless, she walked to the other side of the pool, plate and fork in hand. She cut a piece of cake and popped it in her mouth.

Yvette, also holding a plate with birthday cake, joined her. "I 'ave been sitting too long!" she pronounced.

"Me too," said Dottie, trying to lick icing off her lips.

"You 'ave icing on your nose, Dottie!" Yvette laughed.

Dottie spotted Pierre standing by the pool house, champagne flute in hand. Glancing around, he checked his watch several times. "Pierre looks edgy. Is he all right?"

"'e is tired. 'e will be 'appy when the party is over."

Across the lawn, the dog started to bark. "That dog, 'e is noisy. I think Fabian teases him."

The barking grew louder. Dottie saw a large dog leaping across the lawn toward the pool. She realized, too late, that the animal, its jaws wide open and tongue hanging out, was heading straight toward her. Terrified, she backed away

"*Attention!*" Yvette shouted.

Her warning came too late. Dottie fell backward into the pool and sank. She struggled to the surface and flapped about in a panic. "Help!" she yelled.

"Hold on, Dottie!" Mabel jumped in, creating a huge splash. "I'll get you to the shallow end." Someone threw a ring in the pool. "Grab this," Mabel ordered. "I'll pull you in."

Guests gathered close to the pool's edge as Dottie and Mabel climbed out of the pool. Maria appeared with two large towels. "From pool house," she said. "Here, you wrap."

Mabel smiled. "Thanks, Maria."

"Now, you take shower," Maria ordered. "I go to take care of other guests."

Dottie rubbed her face and hair with the towel before wrapping it around her. "That darned dog! He scared the life out of me!" She paused. "Thanks for rescuing me, Mabel. I'm going to take swimming lessons again when we get home. This time, I'll persevere until I can swim properly."

"Good for you."

Antonio and Yvette joined them. "I try to stop you, but it is too late!" Yvette cried. "How brave you are, Mabel, to jump in and save Dottie."

"Are you all right, Dottie?" Antonio asked.

"I'm fine, thanks to Mabel."

"I have spoken with my grandson," Antonio's voice grew stern. "He is on his way over right now."

Antonio and Yvette excused themselves and left. From the corner of her eye, Dottie noticed some guests were watching as Fabian joined her, the dog at his side. He held the Great Dane on a tight leash. "I'm really sorry about what happened," he blushed. "Nero is a wonderful dog. He makes a lot of noise, but he wouldn't hurt a flea." As though he knew he was being praised, Nero wagged his tail. "He has a kennel and a big enclosed area to run in, but I let him out because I wanted to show him to my girlfriend Lucy. We were playing with a Frisbee, and he behaved really well at first." Fabian hung his head. "Are you all right, *Signora* Flowers?"

"Yes, I'm sure Nero is harmless, but I'm afraid of dogs."

Fabian bit his lip. "I will return him to his run immediately. Come on, Nero."

Dottie and Mabel watched Fabian and Nero as they crossed the lawn. "It's a wonder Fabian's arm isn't dislocated," Mabel remarked as the dog strained on the leash.

"Let's go take a shower and change," Dottie said. "Then, we can enjoy the rest of the party."

As they were about to go into the pool house, two cars drew up by the side gate. Nero began to bark furiously. The gate opened, and four men in military-style uniforms, white belts across their shoulders, ran across the lawn. Looking shocked, people backed away as the men headed to the pool area, brandishing guns.

"*il Carabinieri!*" someone shouted.

"What did you tell the police when you phoned them about Arnold, Dottie? You must have really alarmed them."

"This has nothing to do with my phone call. I think it's a planned raid."

For a few moments, Antonio stood as though in a daze. As the *Carabinieri* drew closer, he turned and fled, his champagne flute shattering as he dropped it on the stone patio. He ran to the wooded area at the far side of the lawn, pursued by two policemen. The three disappeared into the woods.

The other two policemen tried to arrest Yvette. She hit one with her purse, and he backed off. After a brief struggle, the second policeman handcuffed her. Dottie couldn't understand the policemen's rapid-fire Italian but assumed they were telling Yvette why she'd been arrested. She shouted in French, then English. "I know nothing about drugs and guns! You 'ave made a big mistake! Pierre, 'e will tell you the truth!"

She was hustled into a van parked beside the police car. The guests stared after her in silence.

Mabel muttered. "It's like watching one of those TV cop programs."

"Unfortunately, this isn't TV,"

"Surely, Yvette doesn't think the police will believe her story," Mabel said. "How could she not know what was going on? Yvette and Pierre live together, for goodness' sake." She glanced around. "Speaking of Pierre, where is he?"

"I think he's escaped."

"Escaped? How?"

"Through a gap or hole in the fence, most likely." Dottie paused. " I'm pretty sure he knew about the raid."

"Just before I fell in the pool, I noticed him checking his watch and looking around. I'm sure he was expecting something or someone."

"How could he have known?"

"Someone on the inside I expect. Think about it. Why was Pierre so keen to have the champagne and cake served outside?"

"So he could get away quickly."

"Exactly."

Mabel pointed across the lawn. "They've caught Antonio."

Thanks to the extra lighting provided for the birthday celebrations, Dottie could see Antonio, in handcuffs, escorted by the two policemen. Fabian ran to his grandfather, followed by Simone. Shouting, Fabian confronted the policemen, his arms flailing. Antonio must have said something because the young man backed away. Simone started to cry.

A few minutes later, Dottie glimpsed Antonio's drawn face as he was led away to the van. His back bent, he looked much older than his seventy-five years.

As they watched Antonio hustled into the van, two figures loomed out of the darkness and headed over to them. Dottie's breath caught in her throat when she saw the familiar jet-black hair and goatee beard. "It's Lieutenant Piaf!"

"Goodness, you're right," Mabel replied. "What's he doing in Italy?"

"Who knows? I'm sure we'll find out soon enough."

"Look behind the lieutenant. That's Arnold!"

Tears stung Dottie's eyes as she rushed to her friend. "Thank God, you're safe!"

He sighed wearily. "Hello, Dottie. What an adventure I've had." He looked around. "Where's Yolanda?"

"She's sleeping at the villa."

Dottie Flowers and the European Caper

"At the villa?"

"She was feeling a bit faint. One of the guests is a midwife; she suggested it would be wise for Yolanda to rest. Don't worry, everything's fine."

"That's a relief. She's not supposed to be stressed. I worried about her all the time I was stuck in that warehouse." Arnold looked at Dottie and Mabel's wet clothes and hair and the towels draped around their shoulders. "What happened to you two? You look as though you've been for a swim."

"Well, in a manner of speaking, we have," Mabel said.

"A dog came after me; I stepped back and fell in the pool. Mabel saved me," Dottie explained, feeling cold suddenly. "Never mind about us. What's this about being stuck in a warehouse?"

Arnold looked a bit stunned. "Look, I'll tell you everything, but first, I have to see my wife."

Dottie took hold of Arnold's arm. "We'll take you to her."

As Maria answered the villa door, a loud moan pierced the air. They found Yolanda in the sitting room pacing the floor. When Arnold put his arms around her, she burst into tears. "Oh, Arnold, I thought you were dead! I was sure I wouldn't see you again." She winced with pain. "The baby's on its way. You'll have to get me to the nearest hospital as quickly as possible."

All color drained from Arnold's face. "Can you phone for an ambulance, Dottie?"

Dottie knew the best person to deal with this emergency. "Mabel, can you get Simone? Tell her what's happening. She'll know what to do. Cornelius is coming earlier than expected."

Chapter 31

Yolanda refused to be carried out of the villa on a stretcher. "I'm perfectly capable of walking!" she pronounced between contractions.

Once the ambulance arrived, paramedics helped her into the back, and Arnold climbed in after her. Dottie and Mabel were about to follow in their car, but they were stopped by a policeman. "No! No!" he ordered, holding up his hands.

Simone was allowed to accompany Yolanda to the hospital. "She'll be well taken care of," she assured the two women. "You should get changed. You'll get a chill if you don't get out of those wet clothes soon."

Dottie looked down at her soggy orange dress. She was glad she'd remembered to bring her sweats.

"I'll phone as soon as the baby is born," Arnold called out as a paramedic closed the ambulance doors.

Dottie and Mabel followed the policeman to the pool house. "The police will want to question everyone," Dottie said. "It could take hours."

"Simone's right. I'm already feeling shivery," Mabel said. "Thank goodness, I brought that fleece jacket."

***

Once they'd showered and changed, Dottie and Mabel joined the other guests in the small living room. Some were lucky enough to find seats, while the rest either stood or sat on the floor. At that moment, one guest emerged from the kitchen. Dottie remembered being introduced to him earlier that evening. He smiled at the two women. "I do not think you need to worry. The *polizia* do not ask many questions."

If only he knew, thought Dottie.

It took an average of five minutes for each person to be questioned. Two hours later, everyone had been interviewed, except Dottie and Mabel.

Mabel sighed. "With all the information we have, we could be here for quite a while longer."

A policeman opened the door. Using hand gestures, he indicated that they follow him into the kitchen.

The table, littered with papers, had been moved to the center of the room. Lieutenant Piaf sat studying one document, glasses perched on the end of his nose. He looked up as they walked in. "*Bonjour, mesdames.*" He glanced at the policeman. "This is Sergeant Lanza of the *Polizia di Stato.*"

The sergeant gestured toward two chairs in front of the table and handed each a form. He pointed to the top half of it. "*Riempire, per favore.*"

They sat down. Lieutenant Piaf peered at them over his glasses. His eyes settled on Dottie. "Thank you for your phone messages, Madame Flowers. I could not risk to phone you at the villa."

"I understand,"

"You must complete the top of the forms, mesdames," he said in a clipped voice. "Please include your home phone numbers."

As they filled in the required information, Sergeant Lanza settled his bulky frame into the chair next to the lieutenant. "I am here because Sergeant Lanza has asked me to help," Lieutenant Piaf explained. "He does not know the English well. I have explained to him that you were involved in this case when you lived in St. Siffret and that before you make formal statements, I must ask you questions of a general nature. Under the circumstances, he has agreed to allow this.

Either of you may answer the questions. I will take notes. So, we begin." He took out his pen and placed a writing pad in front of him. "*Mesdames*, how did you live at the villa of Antonio Morelli?"

Dottie was about to ask him to repeat the question, until she realized what he meant. "Through Yvette and Pierre."

"Yvette Gagnon and Pierre Tremblay?"

"Yes. When they found out we planned to stay on a farm in Tuscany, they were worried about the roads."

"Why?"

"They know the area. The roads are steep and narrow, and there are very few barriers."

The lieutenant looked puzzled. "Barriers?"

"Let me try," Mabel said. Her demonstration of a car plunging over a cliff was so effective it made Dottie shudder.

"Ah, *oui!*" the lieutenant nodded. "The roads, they are *dangereux*. So, it was arranged that you stay with Antonio Morelli?"

"Yes," Dottie replied.

The lieutenant stroked his goatee. "Did you observe anything *bizarre* at this villa?"

Dottie explained about the late-night visits and about seeing Carlos's van in the driveway.

"So now, you must tell me what happened when Yvette Gagnon and Pierre Tremblay came to the villa."

She told him about the dinner party. "There was tension between Antonio Morelli and Pierre."

"Do you know why?"

"We certainly do!" Mabel chimed in. "Antonio was upset with Pierre because Pierre couldn't find the drugs when he broke into the pool house."

The lieutenant's eyes narrowed. "Why would he search your pool house for drugs?"

Dottie told him about the wine jug. "Before we left St. Siffret, Pierre—or someone working for him—must have exchanged my jug with one filled with drugs."

"Please explain."

"I'd put the jug in my suitcase which I kept under the bed. One night, someone broke into the house."

"How do you know this?"

"I noticed my bedroom light was on when we came home that evening. Later, I discovered my jewelry bag was missing."

The lieutenant nodded. "So, you believe that the intruder found your jug and replaced it with one that contained illegal drugs. Is that correct, *madame*?"

"Yes." The lieutenant paused to make a few notes. "So, there we were," Mabel said, "carting contraband in the trunk of our car through France and Italy!" Her voice rose to a crescendo. "We could have been arrested for smuggling!"

"You are too excited, *madame*," the lieutenant declared. "This is a fagment of your imagination."

"Figment," Dottie breathed.

Lieutenant Piaf spoke with Sergeant Lanza for a few minutes. Dottie was impressed that the lieutenant seemed almost as much at ease speaking Italian as he did his native French. Finally, he turned to Dottie. "Where is this wine jug you speak of?"

"In my bedroom," she replied.

"But it's empty," Mabel added.

The lieutenant jumped up and began to pace around the tiny kitchen. "You tell me that drugs were placed in this jug. Now, you tell me it is empty." Red splotches had appeared on his face. "Again, you are playing the games with me, *mesdames*!"

"Please sit down, Lieutenant," Dottie urged. "I'll explain everything."

With an exasperated sigh, he perched on the edge of his chair. "Madame Flowers, I am running away from my patience!"

Dottie spoke in a soothing voice. "I promise it will all make sense once you hear what happened."

She explained that Mabel had wanted to use the wine jug for a special dinner. "Because there is very little space in the pool house, I'd left it in the trunk of the car. When I unpacked it, I noticed that the jug's design was different. It was not the one I'd purchased. I shook it. I could hear something inside. We found it had a false bottom. When we unscrewed the bottom, we found plastic bags filled with white powder.

"Pierre obviously bought what he believed was an identical jug, filled it with drugs, and replaced mine with this one," Dottie continued. "I guess he figured that when he got here a week later, all he'd have to do was retrieve the bags from the jug."

"When we discovered someone had broken into the pool house, we suspected it was Pierre, trying to find the wine jug," Mabel said, "so we set a trap for him."

"What is this trap?"

"We removed the plastic bags from the bottom of the jug," Dottie explained. "Then, we replaced them with new ones filled with icing sugar."

"Ah!"

"We made sure that Yvette and Pierre knew we'd be away for a few hours. When we returned, the bags were gone." She paused. "I realize this all sounds very far-fetched, but it's the truth."

The lieutenant didn't answer right away. He removed his glasses and rubbed his eyes. "Pierre Tremblay is the leader of a drug and gun smuggling ring everywhere in Europe. We need the strong evidence. Otherwise, he will again escape justice."

"I'll get the flour canister," Mabel declared.

"Flour canster? What is this flour canster?"

"You'll see." Mabel bustled to a cupboard, removed the canister, and carried it over. She signaled to Sergeant Lanza to clear a space on the table. Looking puzzled, he gathered all the forms and placed them in his briefcase.

Mabel removed the canister lid and plunged her hands in the flour. She pulled out three plastic bags and placed them in front of the lieutenant. "These are the bags that were inside the wine jug," she said with a flourish. In her excitement, Mabel knocked over the canister. Flour flew in all directions, but most of it landed on Lieutenant Piaf. His face and goatee turned white. His angry eyes flashed from the floury mask.

"Oh, dear! I'm so sorry, Lieutenant! Let me get you a tea towel."

Lieutenant Piaf grabbed the towel and mopped his face. Sergeant Lanza's lips twitched with amusement.

Dottie struggled not to laugh. "I'll get the jug," she said, rushing away.

The lieutenant's irritation gave way to curiosity as he watched Dottie remove the false bottom of the jug. "*Ingenieux!*"

He opened one plastic bag and dipped in his index finger. After tasting the powder, he confirmed that it was heroin. He struck his palms on the table, releasing another flour cloud. "Now, we 'ave the drugs, and we 'ave the false bottom. This is the proof we must need to send Pierre Tremblay to a long time in prison." Dottie suppressed a smile.

Sergeant Lanza spoke. "*Mi scusi.*" He and the lieutenant spoke briefly. Picking up his briefcase, the sergeant nodded to the two women and left the room.

Lieutenant Piaf checked his watch. "It is late. You will need to make formal statements. I will see you here at 10 in the morning."

"Lieutenant," Dottie said, "may I ask you a question?" He nodded. "Why did you come to Italy?"

Lieutenant Piaf sat back in the chair, a weary expression on his face. "After I received your message that Carlos Mancini and Nico Volpe were in Lucca, I decided to travel here myself. I got in touch with the local police. They told me they had a plan to capture Mancini and Volpe when a packet of drugs is put in their hands." He glanced at Dottie, a hint of a smile in his eyes. "This is called red-handed, *n'est-ce pas?*"

Dottie nodded, pleased he'd remembered.

"My greatest desire is to see Pierre Tremblay sent to prison for a long time, Madame Flowers." The lieutenant paused for a moment. "That man is responsible for the murder of my colleague and friend, Francois Bouchard."

Dottie swallowed hard. "He's a murderer?"

"He is ruthless. Nothing stops him. He does not perform the grisly job himself, of course." The lieutenant paused. "Have you heard of Marcel Ricci?"

"That's Tom Snead's next-door neighbor in St. Siffret," Mabel said. "Tom mentioned him in the note he left us."

"Marcel Ricci works for Pierre Tremblay. Yesterday, he confessed to the execution of Francois Bouchard." For a few moments, no one spoke.

"What about the man killed in the side street next to our house in St. Siffret?" Dottie asked

"He was one of Tremblay's mules," the lieutenant said. "He brought drugs from the UK often. He had become careless and could no longer be trusted to carry out his assigned tasks."

"So, Pierre Tremblay arranged for Marcel Ricci to kill him." Dottie shuddered. The whole time she and Mabel had stayed in St. Siffret, they'd been living next door to a murderer.

"How did this 'mule' manage to smuggle drugs on a regular basis without being caught?" Dottie asked. "Even though he used a suitcase with a false bottom, I'm surprised he hadn't been searched."

"Certain customs officials were part of the smuggling trade. When this man came through customs, they turned an eye that could not see."

"They turned a blind eye," Dottie said.

"The blind eye. That is it."

"Not only was Marcel Ricci a murderer, he also had keys to our house," Mabel said. "He could have walked in at any time of the day. Or night."

"I expect he was responsible for switching the jugs as well." Dottie sighed. "So much has happened. We need time to take it all in."

Lieutenant Piaf stood. "Now, I must bid you goodnight, *mesdames*. I will see you in the morning."

After the lieutenant had left, Dottie stood and stretched. "I'm going to bed. This has been a very long day."

Mabel nodded. "Me too." As she opened the kitchen door, she turned to Dottie. "I wonder if Yolanda has had the baby. I hope everything's all right."

"Don't worry. Arnold will be on that phone as soon as the baby's born."

***

The following morning, a loud rap on the door woke Dottie out of a deep sleep. When she opened the door, she found Maria waiting on the doorstep.

"Piaf, he phone," Maria announced. "Come with me."

Dottie tightened the belt of her dressing gown, slipped on her flats, and walked with Maria to the villa. She wondered what Maria thought about her boss being arrested. As though reading her mind, Maria spoke. "Mr. Morelli, he go to prison for a long time I think."

"What will you do?"

Maria shrugged. "I find another job, no problem. I do good work."

"I'm glad."

"Gino, my husband, he said Mr. Morelli should be in prison. He did not trust him. He say Mr. Morelli bad. He find out things about him."

Dottie felt a cold shiver skitter down her spine. "What happened to Gino?"

Maria did a fast sign of the cross. "He die. Over there." She pointed to the fountain.

"How did he die?"

"He fell on edge of fountain." Maria turned to Dottie, her face flushed with anger. "My Gino, he is strong. He not fall by himself. He is pushed." She opened the villa door. Her voice softened when she spoke. "Sometimes, when the moon shines at night, I see him walking in the garden."

So that's what Maria had meant on the night Mabel twisted her ankle. She'd thought they'd seen Gino's ghost.

"Why did you stay on after Gino died?"

"I wait until the man who is responsible for my Gino's murder is arrested. Now, that is done I leave." Maria's eyes glistened with tears as she looked at Dottie. "Do you understand this?"

A lump formed in Dottie's throat. "Yes. I do."

Dottie's head spun as she followed Maria into the villa. She walked to the hall table and picked up the receiver. "Lieutenant Piaf?"

"Ah, Madame Flowers! I apologize for calling so early in the morning."

"Is anything wrong?"

"No, I have some excellent news. Pierre Tremblay has been captured."

A wave of relief came over her. When did it happen?"

"Just after I returned to the police station last night."

"Where did they find him?"

"I do not think I will disclose this information to you," he replied in an officious voice. "It is the police business."

"I understand." Dottie paused. "It is too bad that you weren't there to see him caught."

"*Au contraire, madame*! The *carabinieri*, they insist I accompany them to the house where Pierre Tremblay was hiding."

"And so they should. After all, you've been a great help to them."

He cleared his throat. "That is so. In fact, I was responsible for his capture."

"You were?"

"Yes. Pierre Tremblay had taken the owner of the house hostage. He held the gun to her head. I told him that the plastic bags did not contain the heroin. He did not believe me. I challenged him to taste the powder." The lieutenant spoke rapidly as his excitement grew. "When he tasted the icing sugar, he became very angry. He was upset that two old bogs had deceived him."

"Old bags."

"I think that is an insult, *n'est-ce pas?*"

"It is. So, what happened next?"

"While he was distracted, two of the *carabinieri* grabbed him from the back and put the handcuffs on him."

"You must be very relieved, Lieutenant."

"Yes. With the strong evidence, I believe Pierre Tremblay will be in prison for many years." He cleared his throat again. "I must now go. I will see you in a few hours."

***

Dottie began to put the breakfast dishes away.

"Why don't we sit around the pool while we wait for Lieutenant Piaf?"

"I'm not sure I'm in the mood to sit. I keep thinking about Yolanda."

"Haven't you got a good book to read?"

"I have a Danielle Steele novel. That'll probably keep me occupied."

Dottie brought a jug of water and two glasses from the kitchen, and they settled on recliners. "The lieutenant's very pleased with himself. He played a major role in Pierre Tremblay's capture." Dottie repeated the story to Mabel.

"Good for him." Mabel poured water in her glass and took several sips. "It won't bring poor Monsieur Bouchard back, but at least, the lieutenant has the satisfaction of capturing the person responsible for his friend's death."

Footsteps clicked on the footpath. Dottie turned around. It was Maria, her face wreathed in smiles. "Mr. Gateshead, he phoned from hospital with message for you."

Mabel and Dottie sat up quickly. "What did he say?" Mabel demanded.

Maria did a sign of the cross. "Mrs. Gateshead, she has baby boy! Everything is well!"

Dottie smiled. "That's wonderful news! Arnold will be delighted."

"I'm a great aunt!" Mabel enthused.

"So, Cornelius is here at last," Dottie mused. "I wonder who he looks like."

"No, no," Maria shook her head. "The baby—his name is not Cornelius."

"Oh? What is it?"

"Mr. Gateshead say they do not have name. He hang up phone in a big hurry."

"I wonder what that's about." Mabel said, as Maria departed. "Yolanda was adamant about the name Cornelius."

"Knowing Yolanda, she's come up with another highfalutin name that Arnold doesn't like."

"I'm afraid my niece can be very stubborn at times."

"So can Arnold," Dottie added.

"Let's go visit them tomorrow," Mabel suggested. "The flight isn't until 8 p.m. so we'll have time."

"With a bit of luck, we'll get the chance to ask Arnold what happened to him yesterday," Dottie said. " All we know is that he got stuck in a warehouse and was rescued by the police."

"He'll have lots to tell us." Mabel smiled. "I can't wait to see the baby!"

And I can't wait to hear what name Yolanda has come up with, Dottie thought. *This could be very interesting!*

Chapter 32

Dottie and Mabel packed their suitcases right after breakfast. When they'd finished, they headed back to the living room.

"I'm glad that's over," Dottie sighed.

"Me too," Mabel replied. "I don't know about you, Dottie, but I'm thirsty. I'll make us a pot of Earl Grey." She disappeared into the kitchen.

Dottie heard a sharp rap at the door. She found Yvette standing on the doorstep, looking waif-like with dark rings under her eyes. "Can I come in?" Her voice was barely audible.

"Of course," Dottie said, ushering Yvette into the living room.

"I cannot stay long," Yvette said. Her face had taken on a gray pallor.

Mabel bustled into the living room, carrying a tray. "I thought I heard voices. Hello, Yvette. This is a surprise!" She put the tray on the coffee table.

"The police, they 'ave charged me with being an access..."

"Accessory."

"Yes. That is it. I want to go to Paris, but I 'ave to stay. I go to live in Lucca with some friends for a while. I cannot bear to live in the 'ouse that Pierre and I shared." Yvette's voice trembled a little. "I want to see you before you leave to tell you 'ow sorry I am for everything that 'as 'appened."

"Why don't you sit down?" Mabel suggested. "We're about to have some tea. I'll fetch another mug."

Once they were all seated, Yvette spoke. "Pierre and me—we meet in Nice two years ago. 'E is charming and attentive. We live together soon after we meet. We are very 'appy." She drew in a deep breath. "One day, 'e tell me about the cigarettes 'e is smuggling. I tell 'im this is wrong, and we 'ave a big fight. 'E convince me it is easy money. What an *imbecile* I am!"

"That day you come to dinner with the Roys, Pierre ask Marcel to take away the cigarettes from your 'ouse while you were 'ere for dinner. That's why I 'ad the 'eadache. Marcel, 'e signal to me when I was on the balcony 'e 'ad done the job. Now I know it was not the cigarettes. It was the guns!" She burst into tears.

Dottie spoke up. "Yvette, why are you telling us this?"

Yvette dabbed her eyes with a tissue. "Because you are my friends. I think you will not trust me anymore."

"Rubbish!" Mabel said. "You didn't know until yesterday that Pierre was into gun and drug smuggling."

Yvette's voice dropped. "I 'ear 'im on the phone one day. 'E talked about guns. I feel sick…" She rubbed her stomach. "I tell Pierre. 'E tell me that I make a mistake. 'E was very attentive and take me for dinner." She looked at Mabel. "I wanted to believe him."

"I can understand that."

"But 'e was a murderer! 'e arrange for poor Monsieur Bouchard to be killed!" A sob caught in her throat.

"You're not the first woman who's fallen for the wrong man," Mabel said. "Don't be so hard on yourself."

"I cannot 'elp it," Yvette blew out a long sigh and drank her tea in silence. "The tea, it is very good. Now, I must leave." Placing the mug on the coffee table, she stood. "Thank you for listening to me," she said, giving each of them a hug. She rooted in her purse and handed Mabel a piece of paper. "'ere is my e-mail address. I 'ope that you both write to me."

"I don't have a computer yet," Mabel said. "You'll have to e-mail your postal address to Dottie. She'll pass it on to me,"

"I will." Yvette looked back as she reached the door. "*Au revoir, mes amies.*"

They listened until the clatter of heels on the concrete pathway faded away.

Mabel sighed. "I feel sorry for Yvette. Imagine finding out the man of your dreams is a drug smuggler and a murderer."

"She'll survive."

Mabel glared. "How can you be so offhanded?"

Dottie shrugged.

"You've never really taken to her, have you?"

"No." Dottie picked up the mugs. "I wouldn't be surprised if she turns up on your doorstep one day."

***

Armed with a potted plant and a card, Mabel followed Dottie into the hospital elevator. "I hope this card is all right," she said. "The saleswoman kept nodding and smiling when I asked her if it was for a boy."

"She probably didn't understand English."

When the elevator doors opened, Dottie spotted Arnold down the corridor and waved. Returning the wave, he rushed over. "So pleased to see you both," he beamed. "Yolanda and the baby are sleeping at the moment. He was restless most of the night. Why don't we go to the visitors' lounge to give Yolanda a chance to get some rest? It's next door to their room, so we'll hear the baby when he wakes."

Dottie noticed that Arnold hadn't mentioned the baby's name.

They sat down in the visitors' lounge.

"Arnold, why don't you tell us what happened to you in Lucca?" Mabel asked.

"It was quite an adventure." He settled back in his chair. "After I'd bought a pendant for Yolanda, I was curious about that warehouse she'd talked about. I decided to take a look." He looked at each of them. "You know what they say about curiosity. Well, it almost got me killed.

The warehouse door was open. There didn't seem to be anyone around, so I wandered in. The only light came from the open door. Boxes were piled high with a narrow walkway between the rows. Then I heard men's voices coming from outside the warehouse. Heavy feet tramped toward it and the door rattled closed." Arnold leaned forward, his face flushed. "It was pitch black in there. I tried to get out, but the door was locked. Fortunately, I have one of those key rings with a flashlight attached. Reckoning I'd be in there for quite a while, I decided to look around to see if I could find anything suspicious."

"Like drugs," Dottie said.

"Precisely! The warehouse was packed with boxes. Everything seemed to be aboveboard. Then, I noticed a padlocked door almost hidden at the back of the building. I hoped it was a way out. Or, if it turned out to be a room of some kind, maybe there'd be somewhere I could hide. I found a piece of metal on the ground and hammered away at the lock. It took quite a while, but eventually, it broke. I opened the door." His eyes gleamed. "You wouldn't believe what I found."

"Go on," Mabel urged.

"Shelves of plastic bags filled with white powder, which I discovered later was heroin. And boxes of guns. Now, I was scared. When whoever owned the warehouse found me, they'd most certainly kill me. All I could think of was Yolanda and the baby. She'd have to bring him up by herself. So, I vowed to fight back. I armed myself with that piece of metal I'd used to break the lock. Not having any idea how long I'd be there, I sat behind a box next to the door and waited.

Hours went by. I tried to stay awake, but I must have nodded off. I woke with a start when I heard voices. Suddenly, the door opened, and the lights went on. Within seconds, I was surrounded by three men."

Dottie drew in a sharp breath. "How frightening!"

"It was terrifying." Arnold ran his hands through his hair. "Then, I realized that two men were in police uniforms."

"It's a good job you didn't hit one with that piece of metal," Mabel commented.

"To tell you the truth, when I heard the door opening, I froze," Arnold confessed.

"The police must have been very pleased when you showed them where the drugs and guns were hidden," Dottie said.

"Yes. They said this was the break they'd been waiting for."

"You understood what they were saying?" Dottie remarked. "I didn't know you spoke Italian."

"I don't. It was the other man, Lieutenant Piaf, who translated for me. While the police were clearing the contraband out of the storage area, the lieutenant and I had a chat. It seems that after you'd told him you'd seen the two drug smugglers in Lucca, he decided to come to Italy. He had holiday time owed to him, so it was a good opportunity to do some sleuthing. He was determined to find out who was responsible for his friend's murder."

Mabel sighed. "Monsieur Bouchard."

"Yes, an informant had told the police there was to be a drug delivery that evening, so Lieutenant Piaf joined the stakeout. Carlos arrived shortly after 10 in a white van. About half an hour later, a man rode up on a Vespa and handed Carlos a package. The police managed to grab Carlos, but the Vespa driver got away."

"Did Carlos try to lie his way out of it, or did he confess?" Dottie asked.

"A bit of both. He told the police he was picking up the package for Antonio Morelli. The police had been after Morelli for quite a while. Carlos claimed he had no idea what was in it. They didn't believe him, of course. They made him hand over the warehouse key. One policeman hauled Carlos off to the police station in the van."

"And when they got inside the warehouse, they found you."

Arnold nodded. "I told the lieutenant about Antonio Morelli's birthday party. He already knew about it. The police were planning a surprise raid to capture Morelli, Yvette, and Pierre. We drove straight to the villa. On the way, they phoned for backup. By the time we arrived, the extra police were waiting for us. The rest you know."

Dottie was puzzled. "If the police van was used to take Carlos to the station, how did you get to the villa?"

"In a squad car." A baby began to whimper. Arnold grinned. "That's our son. Come on, it's time you met him!"

They walked in the room and found Yolanda sitting at the side of the bed, putting on her tartan dressing gown. Mabel hugged her niece and gave her the plant.

"A red amaryllis! Thank you," Yolanda said. "Arnold, would you mind putting this on the windowsill?"

Dottie Flowers and the European Caper

While Arnold carried out his wife's request, Yolanda opened the card. "A very nice card," Yolanda said, "for a grandchild."

"A grandchild?" Mabel exclaimed. "It's that sales assistant's fault. She obviously didn't understand English."

"Never mind," Arnold soothed. "It's the thought that counts."

The whimpers turned into lusty cries. Arnold lifted the baby out of the *lettino*. "Come say hello," he said to the women, his face full of pride.

Mabel took a turn holding the baby. "He's very handsome," she gushed. "He's got your forehead, Arnold, but he's more like Yolanda around the mouth."

How could anyone compare a baby's features to an adult's, Dottie wondered. He looked healthy enough, but he was a baby, for heaven's sake.

Mabel handed the wailing baby to Dottie. She rocked him back and forth. The soothing motion had the desired effect and he stopped crying. When one of his tiny hands curled around her finger, Dottie felt a wave of emotion. "He's perfect," she murmured. "When are you going to give him a name? You were going to call him Cornelius."

"Yolanda's changed her mind," Arnold declared, a touch of irritation in his voice.

"I want him to be called Benito, after the doctor who delivered him," Yolanda explained. "Then, Umberto, because it means bright warrior, and Maximilian, after my father, God rest his soul."

"Benito, Umberto, Maximilian. That's a mouthful," Mabel commented.

"Precisely!" Arnold retorted.

"So, what does that matter?" Yolanda persisted. "It has a certain charm."

Dottie cleared her throat. "You might want to rethink your choice of names."

Yolanda frowned. "Why?"

"If you call him Benito Umberto Maximilian, his initials would be B.U.M." "Oh, dear," Mabel said, "imagine having those initials engraved on his briefcase."

Yolanda opened her mouth as though to reply but closed it again. A smile played on Arnold's lips. "Well, dear, it seems we'll have to start over with names."

"How about Horatio Maximilian?" Yolanda asked.

"Horatio Maximilian? Good grief, Yolanda, imagine the poor boy being saddled with names like that."

"Horatio was your father's name."

"Yes, but…"

"You know," Yolanda interrupted. "The more I think about it, the more I like it."

"Let's leave them to it," Dottie whispered to Mabel. "We have to get to the airport, so we have a good excuse."

After one last look at the baby, they turned to go. Arnold accompanied them to the elevator. "Keep working on the names," Dottie said. "Remember K.I.S.S."

Arnold looked puzzled. "K.I.S.S.?"

"Keep it simple, stupid. You don't want him to be teased when he goes to school."

"Right. Good advice. We'll get it sorted out. Can't see what's wrong with Michael or David myself. Thanks for coming. Have a good journey home. We'll see you when we return to Canada next week."

Chapter 33

After a final check through the pool house, Dottie and Mabel piled their luggage into the car. "Now, all we have to do is give our present to Maria and say goodbye," Mabel said.

Dottie took a last look around the villa grounds. Satana, Maria's handsome black cat, crouched in a flowerbed, his eyes glued on a small rabbit that hopped dangerously close. Birds splashed in the birdbath, and the sweet smell of fresh cut grass filled the air. Dottie wondered what would happen to the property now that Antonio Morelli had been arrested.

When Maria answered the door, Mabel handed the gift to her. "Thank you for everything."

To Dottie's amazement, Maria burst into tears. She thrust the gift back into Mabel's arms. "I cannot take it. My nephew. He steal parcel from your car!"

Things began to slip into place. Dottie caught Maria's eye. "You're talking about the parcel that went missing, aren't you?"

Maria rooted a handkerchief from her apron pocket and blew her nose. "Yes, my sister is sick, and he come here to stay with me. He help me serve at dinner sometimes."

Dottie remembered the nervous young man who'd poured the wine at Morelli's dinner parties.

"I find parcel in his bedroom in villa." Maria paused. "He is not a bad boy. He did not have any money. He wanted to give his mother a gift. Now, he work for me, he make some money and buy a box of chocolates and flowers for his mother."

"When we were out the other day, you slipped into the pool house and put it on the dining room table."

Maria nodded.

"You did the right thing," Dottie assured her. "We were pleased to get it back."

"And we'd be happy if you'd accept our present," Mabel added.

Maria hesitated, and then took the gift wrapped in red paper and decorated with gold bows. After tearing off the paper, she opened the box and peered inside.

Her face wreathed in smiles, she lifted the floral silk scarf. "*Bellissima*!" She wrapped it around her neck and twirled around, laughing. "*Grazie tanto*! Thank you.

***

Dottie and Mabel arrived at Pisa Airport well before the flight and returned their rental car. After checking their luggage, they settled in a corner of the busy departure area. Dottie tried to concentrate on a magazine article, but her mind kept wandering. She'd been too busy over the past few days to dwell on what had happened with Hans, but now, as she waited for the flight, she found it impossible not to think about him. During their time together, she had the impression that Hans was interested in her—until she'd seen him with Simone.

What would have happened if Simone hadn't turned up? She sighed. Now, she'd never know. Feeling tired suddenly, Dottie closed her eyes.

"Dottie, wake up!" Mabel shook her arm. "Look over there, by the window."

Stifling a yawn, Dottie turned her head. At first, all she saw were two little boys fighting over a toy. Then, she noticed a man sitting in the end seat. A lock of white hair fell over his forehead as he bent down to fasten a shoelace. Dottie's heart skipped a beat. It was Hans.

The last thing she wanted was some kind of confrontation. "Mabel, I'm going to find another seat. If he happens to glance over here, he might see us."

"Don't you think it would be better if you spoke with him, Dottie? It might clear the air."

Dottie bristled. "What do you mean?"

"You need to know what the situation is between him and Simone, for a start."

Dottie bit her lip. Mabel was right, of course. She had all kinds of questions she'd like to ask. "I'm not sure I'm ready to hear what he has to say."

They found two empty seats, well away from Hans. Dottie put on her sunglasses and opened a magazine, lifting it so it covered part of her face.

"Dottie, what are you doing?"

"What does it look like?" she snapped. "I'm trying to hide in case Hans walks by."

Mabel laughed. "If he does, I'm sure he'll recognize you. You're hard to miss."

Dottie put the magazine down on her knees and glared at Mabel. "What do you mean, I'm hard to miss?"

"Well, for a start, those oversized sunglasses."

"What's wrong with them? Lots of people wear this style."

"They wear them outdoors, not inside an airport."

Dottie sighed. "You're right. I'm overreacting." She took the glasses off and slipped them in her purse. Glancing around for any sign of Hans, she stood. "Watch my bag for me while I go to the washroom, would you, Mabel? I won't be long."

"There's no need to rush."

As Dottie turned to walk away, she collided with a man pulling a carry-on bag. "Sorry, I wasn't…" She froze. The man she'd almost knocked over was Hans.

For a few moments, they stared at each other.

Finally, Hans spoke. "This is a surprise, Dottie. I had not realized you were leaving today." He averted his eyes for a few moments. Then, he looked at her. "Have you got time for coffee?"

"Our flight isn't for another two hours," Mabel piped up. "Why don't you go ahead? I'll look after the carry-on luggage."

Before Dottie had a chance to respond, Hans took her by the arm. "There is a small café around the corner."

"Why are you here?" Realizing what a dumb question that was, she added, "I suppose you're off to the Netherlands."

"Yes. My flight leaves in an hour."

They found an empty table. Dottie sat while Hans bought two coffees. "Here you are, Dottie. Black, no sugar, right?" He handed the cup to Dottie. She busied herself with removing the lid.

Hans settled in the chair opposite Dottie. He opened a packet of sugar, poured it in his cup, and stirred slowly. After blowing on the hot liquid, he took several sips. Dottie tapped her foot on the tiled floor, wishing he'd get on with it.

Finally, he put down his cup and looked at her. He spoke in a low voice. "I have been meaning to call you. The thing is that someone has come back into my life quite unexpectedly. You met her at the party the other night. Her name is Simone. She is Antonio Morelli's niece."

Dottie sipped her coffee too quickly and burned her tongue. "Simone was very helpful when Mabel's niece Yolanda fainted."

Hans nodded.

"How long have you known her?"

His words tumbled over one other. "We met in Lucca three years ago. I was working on a documentary. She was staying at her uncle's villa. He was away on business so she had the place to herself." He paused for a few moments. "A few weeks later, I moved into the villa, and we spent the summer together."

Dottie's mind raced. "That's why you didn't want to accept Antonio Morelli's dinner invitation. It would have brought back too many memories."

"That was only part of it." He paused. "I could not accept a dinner invitation from a man I did not trust. Simone introduced me to her uncle when he returned from his business trip. Antonio Morelli was charming and friendly toward me, yet my instincts told me something was not right. It was not until last year that I heard rumors about his involvement in drug and gun smuggling." Hans sipped his coffee, lost in thought.

"What happened after the summer was over?"

"Simone returned to Rome to take up a nursing post. We kept in close touch at first. As time went on, I became more involved in my work. In addition to her full-time job, Simone decided to take midwifery courses. We saw each other less and less. Eventually, we barely communicated at all, apart from the occasional e-mail."

"Until she returned to Lucca for her uncle's 75th birthday."

"Yes. I did not know she was here. She was standing among a group of onlookers as we filmed the façade of a restaurant featured in the documentary." He fiddled with his coffee stirrer. "Our eyes met…"

"How touching!"

He shifted uneasily in his seat. "I should have called you."

"Why?" she laughed. "We hardly knew each other."

"I did not see it that way, Dottie," Hans sighed. "In fact, if things had turned out differently…"

"You mean, if Simone hadn't turned up!" Dottie snapped and immediately regretted it.

Hans looked deflated. "You are special, Dottie."

Dottie felt her chest tighten and forced herself to stay calm. "I really must go."

"Wait. You must give me your phone number."

"What for?"

Smiling, he leaned forward in his chair. "I am coming to Toronto in the fall. We can meet for lunch. Maybe dinner."

Dottie felt the heat rise in her face. "And how would Simone feel about that!"

"What harm is there in having a meal together?" Hans replied, his voice full of petulance

"You don't get it, do you?" She stood and pushed back the chair. "Goodbye, Hans."

She could feel his eyes following her as she walked away. Fighting back tears, she was glad he couldn't see her face.

***

Over a glass of wine with their airline meal, Dottie told Mabel about the conversation with Hans. "You were right, Mabel. In spite of what`s happened, it would have been worse if we hadn't talked."

"You would've been left hanging, not knowing what was going on."

"Yes." Dottie stared straight ahead. "I'm beginning to see things a lot more clearly. He had the gall to ask me for my phone number so he could contact me when he comes to Toronto." Dottie sighed. "It was flattering to have a sophisticated, attractive man like Hans pay attention to me and take me to dinner. But even if Simone hadn't come back into his life, I couldn't see it working out between us. He's got quite an ego, and I'm too independent."

I thought we had something special. Hans's words flashed across her mind. *So did I*, Dottie thought. She blew out a long sigh. "*C'est la vie.*" Turning to her paperback, she adjusted the light, put on her glasses, and began to read.

***

Dottie's neighbor Margaret brought Muggins back shortly after she arrived home. As soon as Dottie opened the door, the cat wriggled out of Margaret's arms and spent the next few minutes rubbing himself against Dottie's legs, purring. Afterward, he took a walk around the bungalow and inspected each item of furniture. Still purring, he settled on the window ledge in the living room to watch the birds.

Dottie wished she felt like Muggins, glad to be home and ready to settle back in a routine. She fought the temptation to feel sorry for herself. Even though things hadn't worked with Hans, she had a thriving business, was in excellent health (except for her blood pressure, which was now under control), and had four grandchildren she could visit more or less when she felt like it.

She prepared coffee in her Bodum French press, poured herself a mug of coffee, and sat to look through the mail. Margaret had sorted it into bills, magazines and flyers, and personal items, which made the task much easier. Dottie decided to tackle the personal stuff first, as there wasn't much of it. Besides, it would be more interesting than bills and advertising material.

The first letter she opened was from the seniors' photography club, informing her she'd won first prize in the annual photography contest. Suddenly, she wished Fred were here. He'd get a kick out of this. She didn't have his Brazilian phone number. Too bad.

Under a letter from her elderly aunt in Montreal, she found a postcard from Savannah. Whom did she know in Savannah? She turned over the card. Her spirits rose when she recognized Fred's bold handwriting. What was he doing in Savannah when he was supposed to be in Brazil?

It read, *Dear Dottie: Arrived two days ago, but Rick not here. Hope he shows up soon as I fly back to Rio in a few days' time. Fred. PS He'd left the back door unlocked so at least I have somewhere to sleep!* There didn't seem to be a date on the card. Or was it hidden under the airmail sticker? After boiling some water in the kettle, she held the card over the steam and removed the large stamp. Underneath was the date, June 14. That was more than a month ago, shortly after she and Mabel had flown to Provence. In addition to the date was a phone number, which presumably was Rick's number.

Frowning, Dottie put down the card. Fred's younger brother tended to get himself embroiled in questionable business deals, and Fred had bailed him out on several occasions. She bit her lip. Had Rick shown up? She would phone the Savannah number on the post card. With a bit of luck, Rick would answer, and she could ask him about Fred. If that didn't work, she would call Arnold as soon as he returned from Italy. He'd helped Fred get the job in the Rio de Janeiro law firm, so he would have the phone number or, at the very least, the name of the firm.

The doorbell rang. It was Mabel. "I've had a call from Arnold in Italy," she announced as she bustled in. "They've finally come up with the baby's names."

"Oh, good. I've got some sparkling wine. We can toast the grand occasion."

Mabel followed Dottie into the kitchen and sat at the table. "Arnold chose the first two, Yolanda the second two."

"The baby's got four names?" Dottie took the wine out of the fridge and unscsrewed the top. She poured two glasses and handed one to Mabel.

"Yes, Arnold chose Stanley (that's Arnold's second name, evidently) and Thomas (his grandfather's name)."

Dottie sipped her wine. "Stanley Thomas. Sounds good. What did Yolanda choose?"

"I've got it written down. Just a minute." Mabel rooted in her purse. "Here we go. Uzoma. It's a Nigerian name. It means, 'born during a journey.'"

"And what's the other one?"

"Donald. That means, 'ruler of the world.'"

Dottie started to laugh. "I don't believe it! Neither is thinking straight."

"What's so funny?"

"The initials."

"I see what you mean! First, the baby is a B.U.M. Now, he`s a S.T.U.D."

"I'll e-mail Arnold right away," Dottie said. "I have a feeling he`ll put his foot down this time and give the poor child a simpler name."

Even as she said it, Dottie didn't really believe it. Knowing Yolanda, she'd never be satisfied with a straightforward John or Michael.

The phone rang. "Dottie! Is that you?" There was no mistaking the gravelly voice of Tom Snead.

"Tom! Where are you?"

"Just got back to Montreal. I've listened to your message. You must have wondered why I didn't call you back, but my phone went missing. I'd been visiting some friends in Wales. They have a three-year-old kid who's fascinated with cell phones." He laughed. "His parents found it in his toy box and mailed it to me." He paused. "I want to hear all about your vacation, but you said you had something important to tell me."

"You might be sorry you asked," Dottie replied. "You'd better sit down."

Tom hesitated. "OK." She could hear a chair scraping on the floor. "What's the problem?"

When she eventually hung up the phone, Dottie turned to Mabel, rolling her eyes.

"What's that about?"

"I told Tom about his house in Provence being used to store illegal weapons and drugs and that his next-door neighbor, Marcel, is a murderer. You'll never guess what he said."

"Tell me."

"'How would you like to spend a few weeks in Wales next summer, all expenses paid.'"

"Whatever for?"

"He muttered something about making up for the stress we've been through."

"That's what he said last time," Mabel said. "I suppose you said no."

"Darned right, I did! It seems he and a group of speculators bought a castle that's been converted into a hotel and spa. It's quite luxurious, according to Tom."

"I have two nephews and a cousin who live in Wales," Mabel sighed. "I haven't seen them for ages."

"If you have any crazy idea about staying in Tom's castle, forget it! We took his offer to stay in his house in Provence. And look what happened."

Undaunted, Mabel lifted her wineglass. ""Let's drink a toast to Wales!" she cried. "*Yaki da!*"

Sheila Gale

About the Author

Originally from North Wales, Sheila Gale immigrated to Canada where she worked as a college professor teaching communications courses. Now pursuing a writing career, she has published several short stories, one of which, *Vintage Vampire,* is based on a prize-winning speech she gave at a Toastmasters Club. She is currently working on the third novel of the Dottie Flowers series.

Did you like this book?

If you enjoyed this book, you will find more interesting books at
www.CrystalDreamsPublishing.com

Please take the time to let us know how you liked this book. Even short reviews of 2-3 sentences can be helpful and may be used in our marketing materials.

If you take the time to post a review for this book on Amazon.com, let us know when the review is posted and you will receive a free audiobook or ebook from our catalog. Simply email the link to the review once it is live on Amazon.com, your name, and your mailing address -- send the email to orders@mmpubs.com with the subject line "Book Review Posted on Amazon."

If you have questions about this book, our customer loyalty program, or our review rewards program, please contact us at info@mmpubs.com.

a division of Multi-Media Publications Inc.

Dottie Flowers and the Skinner Gang

by Sheila Gale

Dottie Flowers is a glamorous divorcee in her early sixties who runs a successful real estate business, wears designer clothes, and lusts after Harley-Davidson motor bikes. Her friend, Mabel Scattergood, is a rich widow who drives too fast, shops at discount clothing stores, and eats junk food. Even though they're total opposites, they have one thing common: getting into trouble with the law.

In this series debut, bells ring and lights flash as Dottie wins the jackpot at a local casino. In the confusion that follows, George Fernandes, a sleaze she'd known in high school, is stabbed to death next to her machine. After being questioned by the police, Dottie and Mabel find themselves on a roller coaster adventure when they're chased by two of George's associates on a motor bike. They discover why they're being followed when Dottie finds emerald jewelry in her coat pocket. It's not only the pursuers who are after the emeralds: after Dottie's beloved cat is kidnapped by the Skinner Gang in an attempt to force Dottie to hand over the emeralds, she decides to take action.

Romance enters the scene when Dottie meets a handsome jewelry appraiser who offers to help her by getting the emeralds copied. Despite his charms, Dottie has doubts about his motive. Are her instincts right? Will Enrique double cross her?

Get ready for adventure, thrills, and romance in Dottie Flowers and the Skinner Gang.

ISBN-10:   1591463629   (Paperback)

Reunion With a Killer
By Rod Summitt and Richard Edgerton

Lee Bishop, a hardware sales rep, decides to make his last cross-country sales trip by car instead of flying. One of his main reasons was to stop in the town in Iowa where he went to school, both to see the school again and to visit with his old college roommate who is now the president of the local bank with whom Lee has been corresponding through yearly Christmas cards.

When he arrives in town, he tries to hook up with his old friend, Carl Kyle, but is told by his friend that he must leave town on business and that they won't be able to meet. Lee decides to drop in at the bank anyway for a quick hello, and when directed to Kyle's office sees a man who is a complete stranger.

Lee learns that while the man at the bank is obviously not his old friend, he is accepted by the townsfolk as the man who was once Lee's roommate at the local college. About ready to continue his trip and leave the perplexing puzzle behind him, Lee discovers that the editor of the local newspaper is Pete Riley, another old friend from college and enlists his help in solving the mystery of just who is the bank president and what has happened to Carl Kyle.

ISBN-13:   9781591460985   (Paperback)

Available from Amazon.com or your nearest book retailer. Or, order direct at www.CrystalDreamsPublishing.com.

Identity Theft

by Connie Slocum

Patricia Farmer headed off to college with a car full of friends and a trunk full of dreams. Like all freshman, she was just beginning to learn who she was. Unaware of the forks in the road of life that lurked just ahead, she had no idea that her forks would have more than the usual set of prongs. There was studying, forensic lab, friends and the normal chaos of college life.

Plus, she had two very different men in her life. Cameron was as clean cut as they came, and Tony, his complete opposite, the mysterious bad boy. Tony was the type females can't keep away from, the one she thought her friend Tina was in love with. Her attraction to both of them was overwhelming. Still, she juggled it all without faltering until her best friend Sunny was arrested for murder.

She vows to clear her friend's name. The problem escalates when she has to be on all of the roads at once, crossing paths with a serial killer. But which fork is the right one? And who is the murderer?

Find out by reading this new novel by author Connie Slocum: Identity Theft - It's Murder!

ISBN-13:   9781591463771   (Paperback)

Available from Amazon.com or your nearest book retailer. Or, order direct at www.CrystalDreamsPublishing.com.

LIVE Ringer
by Lynda Fitzgerald

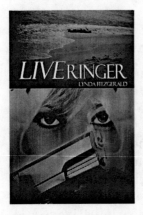

When Allie Grainger inherits her aunt's Cape Canaveral beach house, she wants time to mourn her aunt's death and her own failed marriage, but she hasn't been back in town twenty-four hours before she stumbles on the body of a woman floating in the water at the Canaveral jetty. At first, it seems that the only thing that links the victim to Allie is her appearance.

But when her police friends begin to connect the murder with a string of similar crimes up and down the coast of Florida, other similarities begin to emerge. They all were about the same age, blonde, and divorced. And they all looked like Allie.

Three men enter Allie's life: one is a childhood friend all grown up and turned cop; another, the editor of the local paper; and the third is a stranger who shows up on the beach the day the body is found. Allie is pretty sure one of them is the killer, and she begins to suspect she might be his next target. Summoning up courage that surprises even her, Allie begins trying to discover the truth.

But when the bullets start flying, Allie doesn't know which way to turn.

ISBN-13:   9781591463276   (Paperback)

Available from Amazon.com or your nearest book retailer. Or, order direct at www.CrystalDreamsPublishing.com.

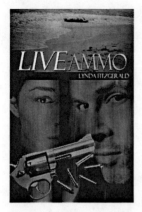

LIVE Ammo

by Lynda Fitzgerald

Sheriff Cord Arbutten's wife is dead — an apparent suicide — but his grown son claims she was murdered by the Sheriff. Rand Arbutten, an attorney who hates his father, vows he's going to prove it. When it comes to light that she was killed with the Sheriff's old service revolver right in the middle of a nasty divorce, the Governor suggests that Cord think about stepping down. Suddenly, the Sheriff is faced with losing everything, including his freedom.

Investigative reporter Allie Grainger gets involved when her best friend Sheryl, a Sheriff's Deputy, begs her to help. Allie barely knows the Sheriff, but she knows that Sheryl greatly respects him and that her deceased aunt, who worked for him for over twenty years, believed he was an honorable man.

Sidney Finch, a Sheriff's Deputy who idolizes the Sheriff, doesn't use charm to impede her investigation. He uses naked threats. Allie has to ask herself who he's trying to protect — the Sheriff or himself? She isn't sure how far Sidney will go to stop her, but since he has a hair-trigger temper and carries a gun, she absolutely doesn't want to find out.

This is the second book in this series. Check out LIVE Ringer for more Allie Grainger adventures.

ISBN-13:   9781591462637   (Paperback)

Available from Amazon.com or your nearest book retailer. Or, order direct at www.CrystalDreamsPublishing.com.

CPSIA information can be obtained at www.ICGtesting.com
Printed in the USA
LVOW130845160613

338678LV00001B/25/P